THE PRINCESS PAWN

The Princess Pawn

by

MAGGIE L. WOOD

SUMACH
PRESS

NATIONAL LIBRARY OF CANADA CATALOGUING IN PUBLICATION DATA

Wood, Maggie L.
The princess pawn/Maggie L. Wood.

ISBN 1-894549-29-5

I. Title.

PS8595.O6364P74 2003   jC813'.6   C2003-903807-6

Second printing October 2004

Edited by Rhea Tregebov
Copy-edited by Lindsay Humphreys
Cover illustration by Kasia Charko
Design by Elizabeth Martin

*Sumach Press acknowledges the support of the Canada Council
for the Arts and the Ontario Arts Council for our publishing program.
We acknowledge the Government of Canada through the Book Publishing
Industry Development Program (BPIDP) for our publishing activities.*

ONTARIO ARTS COUNCIL
CONSEIL DES ARTS DE L'ONTARIO

Printed and bound in Canada

Published by

SUMACH PRESS
1415 Bathurst Street #202
Toronto Canada
M5R 3H8
sumachpress@on.aibn.com
www.sumachpress.com

To Scot,
my very own knight in shining armour.

Acknowledgements

Special thanks to my writers' group. To Barbara
Haworth-Attard for teaching me about character development and for never letting me give up.
To Kim Kofmel for teaching me the craft of writing. And to
Norah Anderson for teaching me the importance of humour.
Without your criticism and praise (and the fact that you
made me rewrite everything over and over again), I never
would have developed the thick skin and stick-to-it-ness that
writers need
in order to keep sending those manuscripts out in the face of
rejection.

Also, very special thanks to Sumach Press for taking a chance
on an unknown and for giving me a dream editor like Rhea
Tregebov. Thank you.
Thank you. Thank you.

Cast of Characters

THE KELDORIANS:

Morwenna Somerell: Queen of Keldoran
Tarrant Somerell: King of Keldoran
Diantha Somerell Farrandale: Heir to the throne of
Keldoran and daughter to King Tarrant and
Queen Morwenna; wife to Prince Alaric
Sir Lachlan Montrose: Mage knight to Queen Morwenna
Lord Garnock of Grisselwait: Commander in
King Tarrant's army

THE CLARIONITES:

Cyrraena: Elf Queen of Timorell and
guardian to Mistolear
Nezeral: Elf Prince of Clarion,
from the House of Jarlath

PROLOGUE

THE ELF QUEEN AND TWO GLUM HUMANS stood facing each other. The ancient room they had chosen for the sending was dank and cold. Candlelight flickered weakly against its dark stone walls, while the low cobwebbed edges of the rough ceiling seemed to press down on them with a treacherous weight.

Cyrraena, the elf queen of Timorell, stared at the bright little head that poked up through the swaddling blanket. The Game spell had given the soft tufts of red hair a glow like dandelion fluff in crimson sunlight. She let one hand caress the sweet, springy curls, careful to keep her features even. The humans, one a king, the other a nursemaid, were eyeing her speculatively. She could not let them see her indecision or heavy heart. Especially now, when Mistolear's only hope rested in the small bundle she held in her arms.

A lump stuck in her throat. She looked away from the sleeping infant and scanned the gloomy faces watching her. *Be strong,* she told herself. *You must be strong for the humans.*

King Ulor's dull gaze troubled her, though. She glanced at his sad face. He'd lost so much. His wife. His son. The child's mother. And now Willow, the child herself — his only granddaughter. What if the grief proved too much for him? What if he wasn't able to hold back the opposing forces till Willow's aging process completed itself?

Cyrraena held the baby out to Nurse Beryl. The time for second-guessing had passed. Nurse Beryl's practised hands expertly cradled the child. She'd been nursemaid to the royal family for most of her life and had fought vehemently to be the one to accompany the tiny princess. Again Cyrraena felt the unease shift inside her. Nurse Beryl was indeed competent but had just passed into her sixtieth year. The fourteen-year span in the Earth realm would age her well into her seventies. If something should happen to her ...

But no. Cyrraena clenched her jaw, studying the hard-eyed nursemaid. The little woman was glaring at her. This impertinence, though, did not upset Cyrraena. It calmed her instead. She knew the nursemaid would let no harm befall the infant princess. That she would safeguard her with every ounce of her brave-hearted soul.

Cyrraena motioned to her attendant, who stepped forward, placing the gift into her outstretched hand. The pendant, a fragment of smooth white enamel fashioned in the shape of a swan, had been given to the princess Willow at her christening. As the child's nethermother, it was Cyrraena's right to bestow on her a magical virtue. She had chosen wisdom. It was an attribute, she knew, notoriously iffy for its time frame structures. But it was one, nonetheless, necessary if they were ever to succeed in the battle ahead.

She sighed, closing her fingers around the gift. Would fourteen years be enough? That was the chanciest thing about all this. Technically, the wisdom virtue didn't reach its full potential till adulthood. But if they waited the extra weeks, anything could happen. She placed the pendant around the child's soft neck, blessing her with a touch to each shoulder. *Faith,* she told herself, *you must have faith.*

A leather-gloved hand gently brushed her arm. "Your Majesty?"

Cyrraena looked into the concerned face of King Ulor. She smiled, hoping to take some of the grimness out of his features. "The crystal, then," she said. "Is it ready?" The king nodded, his eyes just as grim as before. Cyrraena gestured for him to begin the process.

He ceremoniously handed a crystal globe cradled in a gold-wire stand to Nurse Beryl. "Everything has been made ready for you," he advised, tilting her hand a bit to the left. "When the portal closes, you should find yourself directly inside the lodging house." He pressed the child closer against the nurse's chest, his hand lingering a moment on the babe's soft nest of red curls, then he stepped away.

"You may touch it now," he said, nodding to the bright crystal.

Nurse Beryl hesitated. Her forehead furrowed in consternation, then smoothed as she bowed it to touch the glowing crystal.

Instantly, the old nursemaid and the infant princess disappeared.

Cyrraena closed her eyes. "Please," she prayed to the Light. "Please keep them safe."

CHAPTER 1

WILLOW STOOD JUST OUTSIDE the cafeteria doorway, unaware of the kids surging past her or of the lingering, ever-present smells of french fries and hamburgers. The cafeteria was her place of attack. Her battleground. She surveyed its rows of tables and lengths of grey floor tiles like a general, mapping out her strategy. She imagined the room as if it were a big chessboard. In the left-hand ranks, around the pop machine, there was danger. Three or four neanderthals from the football team — or the Black knights, as she had dubbed them — were hanging around it, talking loudly and swilling back Cokes. If they noticed her alone and vulnerable, they'd move in for the kill. She tucked her long red hair into the back of her sweater and hunched her shoulders, trying to minimize her 5'91/2" height. The blend-in-with-the-wall defence was a tried-and-true dodge tactic.

Aim for the right-side ranks, she told herself, *and think invisibility.* The last thing she wanted was the DUH!-boys yelling out their stupid "Willow Flatlands" jokes or asking her to double for their field posts.

The back rank, where she needed to manoeuvre herself to, was, at present, occupied by the Black queen, cheerleader-captain and most-popular-girl-at-school, Melissa Morrison. Her head rook and bishop, Brianna Taylor and Megan

Jamieson, were on either side of her, holding a crowd of hangers-on pawns at bay. Willow walked slowly toward them, head down, pretending she was absorbed in her history notes. Hiding your true intentions, she had also learned, was a big part of winning at chess.

"Hey, Will! Sit with us!"

Willow looked around, her eyes blinking in fake surprise. In front of her, her white Chicklet teeth gleaming, was Melissa Morrison, waving Willow over to her table. *Yes!* thought Willow. *Operation Halloween Party was underway!* She nodded and tried to look natural, as if being asked to sit with the in-crowd was an everyday occurrence. She walked slow and calm toward the table, feeling like a beauty pageant winner. Everyone was watching, whispering and wondering why she, Willow Kingswell — skinny Ninth Grade Nobody — was being flagged down by Melissa Morrison.

The table loomed menacingly. She stopped and waited as two pawns slid aside to make a spot for her. Melissa was smiling, saying something nice about Willow's creamy wool sweater. The other girls, as if on cue, were nodding and agreeing with her.

Willow sat down, careful to keep her focus moving and not pinned to Melissa's incredible blue eyes or perfect sun-streaked hair. Not letting your opponent intimidate you was another important chess strategy.

She rested her gaze on a safe spot near her homework and practised breathing. The Shakespeare essay that she'd written for Melissa — her ticket to popularity — was all nice and neat, right on top of her history book. It was due today, which was why she'd just ditched her library study date with Abby to come here instead. She knew that Melissa would want to see it, and maybe — just possibly — show her appreciation in the way of a certain party invitation.

"I can't believe Mrs. Fraser won't do anything about that moustache." Melissa suddenly leaned forward, stage-whispering to all her attentive listeners. "I mean, God, I can hardly look at her when she's talking to me! And that mole she has. I swear, I thought I was going to gag when I saw the hairs sprouting out of it!"

Willow laughed mechanically with the rest of the girls. She had spent most of last weekend with Melissa and she knew how the conversation dynamics worked. Melissa said something. You agreed.

It'd been cool, though, being at her house. Melissa lived in the subdivision that backed onto the golf course, in a house so big that Willow's little brick bungalow could easily have fit inside with room to spare. And Melissa's bedroom, with its own balcony and fireplace, had been like something out of a magazine. Melissa's constant complaints, though, were that her sister's room was way better, that she needed a new TV and CD player and that her father was too cheap to get her her own cell phone. Willow had personally thought that the cell phone thing was a big mistake on Melissa's father's part, as the phone had rung about every thirty seconds, and it was always for Melissa.

In fact, the whole time Willow had been there, Melissa had either been on the phone or had been downstairs entertaining friends who'd just *happened* to drop by. The essay topic, Willow's entire reason for being there in the first place, hadn't even come up. But after just that one weekend, she had suddenly found herself semi-popular.

All Melissa's friends said hi to her now when they passed

her in the hallways. People wanted to sit beside her in classes. And even Dean Jarrett, whom she'd secretly had a crush on since seventh grade, had spoken to her. He'd only asked for her math homework answers, but at least it showed that he knew her name.

An image of Dean, with his crinkly blue-jean eyes and spiked hair, popped into her head. She had this long-running fantasy of him as her chain-mailed white knight, saving her from certain death and carrying her off to his castle on his great white charger. A fantasy, she smiled to herself, always guaranteed to trim down those really boring political science and algebra classes.

She sneaked a quick glance at Melissa. Yes, she was still bathing Willow in her tractor-beam smile of popularity. Willow blinked, suddenly struck by the absurd fact that all this was happening just because old Mr. Rosen, their English teacher, had made such a big deal over Willow's perfect score on his Shakespeare test. And that Melissa, who'd needed at least a C+ in English to go to Mexico on her Christmas break, had failed it.

"So, Will, is that my essay?"

Willow snapped out of her thoughts. Melissa was talking to her. Asking her a question. "Huh?" she said, blinking stupidly.

"I *said*," replied Melissa, obviously ticked to be repeating herself, "is that my essay?" Her look of annoyance shifted to one of calculation as she pointed to the red folder on top of Willow's books. Willow smiled in sudden comprehension and handed it across to her.

Melissa fanned through the pages with burgundy-painted nails. "So ..." she asked with a bored smirk, "what topic did I pick?"

Snorts erupted from her girlfriends, which prompted some eyelash batting from Melissa. "*What?*" she asked innocently, which, of course, caused a whole new round of snorts.

Willow stared at them with something close to nausea. She'd known all along that this part — when she actually gave her work to Melissa — would bother her. She just hadn't expected it to feel this dirty. Like she'd given over state secrets to enemy spies or something. A smile forced its way onto her face. *Think about the party,* she told herself. *Just keep thinking about the party.*

Melissa was blinking at her with eyebrows raised, waiting for her to describe the topic.

She could do this. Willow forced herself to meet Melissa's blue gaze. Mr. Rosen had assigned *A Midsummer Night's Dream,* and she had tried to pick a topic that Melissa would understand. "It's about the struggle between men and women," she finally blurted out. They were all silent now, watching her expectantly. "You try to show how Oberon's attempted domination over Titania is the same as Lysander's and Demetrius's over Hermia and Helena. And then you tie it all up into the universal theme of how males wish to dominate and subdue females."

"You didn't use words like 'dominate' and 'subdue' in the essay, did you? If you did, Rosen will know I didn't write it."

Willow shook her head. After reading a previous sample of Melissa's essay writing, she knew enough not to use big words.

"Good," said Melissa, chucking the folder on top of her books. "And thanks. You don't know how important this is to me." She twisted a blonde curl around her finger and gave Willow a grateful smile.

That's it!? Willow's eyes flitted to the folder and back to Melissa again. She'd just spent the last three nights by *herself* working on it, and Melissa wasn't even going to *read* it!

"So, Will, I know this is short notice and everything, but do you have plans Friday?"

"I — I," Willow stammered, taken by surprise. Ohmigod! *Check and mate!* This was it! Her big invitation to the party. But before she could say anything, Dean Jarrett swooped down on Melissa, covering her eyes with his hands and bending close to her ear. "Hey gorgeous," he whispered. "Guess who?"

Melissa leaned back into his leg, wriggling her head and shoulders. "Umm-mm," she purred. "Matt Damon, right? No wait, it's Brad Pitt." Dean's hands dropped from her eyes and down to her shoulders. "Nope. Even better," he said. His hands slipped into her open shirt front, massaging bare skin and jutting collarbone.

Willow's face burned. Any time Dean was around, her breathing stuck in neutral and the trademark bright red flush inched up her face and into the roots of her red hair. *No-no-no-no!* her mind shrieked. *Don't let it happen! Concentrate! Breathe!* She dug her fingernails into her thighs until she was wincing in pain. The flush cooled off to light pink.

Dean shook the table as he avalanched into the space Melissa and Megan had created for him. "So, what's up with the party?" he asked, grinning. "Anybody wearing one of those skimpy little French maid outfits?" He glanced hopefully around the table. His gaze settled on Willow. "Hey," he drawled, "with your long legs ..." He let the sentence dangle.

Willow felt her face go way past red.

"*Dean!*" Melissa slapped his arm playfully. "God, you're

such a pervert! Leave Will alone. I was just going to invite her, and now you'll scare her away." She turned her full-force smile onto Willow. "So, you'll come, right? It's Friday night at my house. If you need a ride, Megs can pick you up. Okay, Megs?"

Megan Jamieson nodded. "Oh yeah, sure," she said, smiling. "You live on Meadow Brook, right?"

"Right," Willow answered, mouth curled sardonically. *As if she didn't know.* Megan Jamieson had lived two blocks away from her for ten years. She knew exactly where Willow lived and just how to avoid it.

"Anyway," interrupted Dean, leaning toward Willow, "about that French maid's costume ... " Both Melissa and Megan elbowed him in the side. "*Ow!*" he bellowed. "Jeez, I was only asking."

Willow knew she was lit up like the red lights on a Christmas tree, but she didn't care. Melissa Morrison had just invited her to a party, and Dean Jarrett had flirted with her. She was locked in a daze, savouring the moment. By the time she'd noticed Dean's gaze and his scornful sneer, it was too late.

"Hey guys," he hissed, "look who's coming our way. It's Abi-whale Addams." His feet started making loud stomping sounds as if some elephant were approaching.

The flush drained from Willow's face. *No,* she thought. *Not now, Abby. Don't come over now.*

But Abigail Addams wasn't the sort of person to be intimidated by Melissa or Dean. If she wanted to talk to you, she'd talk to you. Willow hunched over her books, hoping Abby hadn't noticed her. Not that she didn't like Abby. But Abby was ... well, Abby.

She was what polite people would term an individual. Which meant, in other words, that she wasn't like everybody else. She said what she wanted to say. She wore what she wanted to wear. And, despite the fact that she was the fattest girl in the school, she didn't take any guff from anyone.

Willow had met her last September after her purse had gotten stuck in her front bike forks and she'd done a complete flip-over in the school parking lot. While everyone else was pointing and laughing, Abby had been the one to help her to the nurse's office. She'd even waited for the nurse to bandage up Willow's cut hands and scraped cheek, and then had walked her home, balancing her bike between them. Willow had been fascinated by Abby. By how she had such confidence and never let the other kids' taunts get to her.

They had one biology class and an art class together. Willow had picked her for her bio lab partner, and right now they were working on a worm reproduction project. She knew that that was why Abigail wanted her. To discuss Walter and Fred's impending parenthood.

Dean's feet stopped their pounding and his face lit up with a crooked grin. "Hey, Liss," he said loudly, leaning toward Melissa, "you should invite Abby to your party. Looks like she's already got her costume!" Smirks and suppressed giggles erupted all around the table.

Willow flinched. She waited for Abby's comeback. Abby, she knew, would demolish Dean. But there was only silence and a light tap on Willow's shoulder. Willow turned to see Abby wearing her usual uniform of black jeans, black leather jacket and bright, neon-coloured, "Save-the-Whales" T-shirt. Abby knew the joke about her name. The T-shirt, she said, was a "poetic statement against their cruelty." She and Willow had even laughed about it. But now all Willow could see was how big the shirt made Abby look. How like a huge orange target.

Willow cringed in embarrassment as she lowered her gaze to Abby's pointed, shiny black cowboy boots. *Oh Abby,* she thought, sighing inwardly, *not boots. Nobody wears* cowboy boots!

"Hey, Will." Abby's voice was tight and uncomfortable, her deep grey eyes taking in the situation with a narrow glance. "Thought we were meeting in the library."

Willow peered at her watch, pretending to be surprised at the time. She'd tried to catch Abby before math class to cancel, but hadn't been able to find her. "Sorry," she said, smiling sheepishly. "I guess I ... I just forgot."

Willow grimaced. That had definitely sounded lame. She heard tittering laughter behind her. She mentally directed Abigail to the end of the cafeteria and out through the doorway.

"We still have some time. Do you want to go now?" Abby's cool gaze swept over Willow. She hadn't bought the "I forgot" excuse, and now she was testing Willow. *Come with me,* her hard eyes were saying, *and I'll forgive you. But stay with these pinheads and, that's it, I'm outta here!*

"Sorry, Abby," interrupted Melissa. "But Will promised to help me with my English. Right, Will?"

It was an escape! A way out. Willow looked back and forth between Abby and Melissa, trying to think of a reply that wouldn't offend either of them. Abby's hard eyes were beginning to change, brimming with an unfamiliar shine. She looked like ... Willow felt a sour lump stick in her throat ... like she was about to cry.

Abigail blinked, smiling tightly. "Don't worry about it," she said, starting to back away. "It's no big deal."

Willow watched as Abby left, Dean's stomping sounds accompanying her heavy heel-clicking walk toward the cafeteria doors. A sick feeling bubbled up inside Willow. She flung an arm over her books, ready to scoop them up and go after Abby. But Abby's stiff black-leathered back had just exited into the hallway and Melissa was asking Willow if she had a costume for the party. Willow's hand fell from her books. She couldn't talk to Abby. At least not now, with Melissa and the others watching.

"I have a ... a Guinevere costume," she finally answered, flicking her eyes away from Dean and keeping them on a nice neutral spot on Melissa's forehead. The sick feeling was still in the pit of her stomach, but she shrugged it off. She'd just wait to talk to Abby, maybe meet up with her next study period or something. The thought made her feel in control again, and she started to describe her green velvet Guinevere gown to Melissa. Abby would understand, she told herself confidently, once she explained things to her.

❧

Willow caught up with Abby after school. Abby was alone, walking along Hewitt Street with a sleek black clarinet case bouncing vigorously up and down against her leg. "Hey, Abby, wait a minute," Willow said as she coasted her bicycle to a stop. "Can I talk to you for a sec?" The other girl gave her a stony glance and kept right on walking, knocking Willow's bike with a disinterested hip check.

Willow gaped for a surprised moment then pedalled after her. "Abby, listen. I can explain about this morning. If you'd just ... "

"You know what, Will?" Abby stopped mid-stride and turned to face Willow, her thin, wind-whipped hair blowing around her angry face. "I don't care about your explanation. Because *nothing*," she snapped, "could excuse what you did today."

"What are you talking about?" As far as Willow knew, she hadn't done anything! "I mean, I *am* sorry about not meeting you at the library. But come on! You don't have to make a federal case out of it."

"I'm not talking about the library."

Just then a school bus rumbled past Willow and Abby, the groan of its shifting gears filling their tense silence. Voices shot out at them. "Hey Abi-whale!" someone yelled. "You should be wearing a sign!" "Yeah!" someone else shouted. "Danger: *Wide Load!*" Laughter drifted over Hewitt Street then disappeared into the whine of its steady traffic.

Some of the anger seeped out of Abigail, leaving her sad and defeated-looking. "At the cafeteria you didn't say anything," she said quietly. "You just sat there while those morons made fun of me." Her clear grey eyes misted into shadows. "I thought you were different," she whispered.

Oh man! Willow felt her face redden. Abigail had always been able to take care of herself. Had always had her own insults and comeback lines. It never occurred to Willow that Abby would need or even welcome her help. But now that she thought about it, everything made sense. Abby hadn't demolished Dean in the cafeteria because she'd been waiting for *Willow* to do it!

"Abby, I ... " Willow began, but Abigail turned away from her and started marching down Hewitt Street toward the apartment building where she and her mom and little sister lived. Willow started to coast after her then braked, dragging her feet on the sidewalk. What was she doing? She couldn't stay friends with Abigail. Not if she wanted Melissa to like her. She watched the other girl's heavy stride for a moment, feeling mean and guilty. Abby had been a good friend to her, and she definitely didn't want to hurt her, but ...

"Hey, Will!"

Willow turned to see Dean Jarrett sticking his head out the window of Rick Burke's red Camaro and grinning at her. "Forget Guinevere!" he yelled. "Think French maid!" Then both he and Rick made hooting noises and Rick gunned the Camaro.

A hot blush swept over Willow. She waved at Dean, who'd swivelled his spiky blond head around to watch her. Oh man, he was *so* cute! She couldn't miss that party. She just couldn't!

All the way home she rationalized the situation, trying to convince herself that she was doing the right thing. Maybe Abby was just being too sensitive. After all, Dean Jarrett teased everybody. He didn't mean anything by it. It was just the way he was. Maybe if they had a chance alone together, she could ask him to go easy on Abigail.

A shiver of excitement ran through her. Being alone with Dean Jarrett was actually a possibility! She imagined his look of lovestruck awe when he saw her in her gorgeous Guinevere costume. No, he wouldn't be able to see her legs in it, but Dean wouldn't care when he saw how beautiful it made her look. He'd ask her to dance, of course. And it'd be a slow song, so he could hold her close. Willow's eyelids lowered dreamily, oblivious both to the cold northerly wind and to the fact that she couldn't dance.

Leaves pelted her, raining down from the oak trees that lined both sides of Meadow Brook Street. Willow ploughed through the leaves, eager to get home and try her costume on again. She could already see herself practising what she'd say to Dean at the party. Imagining them alone, stealing a moment together out on Melissa's big wrap-around front porch.

As she coasted into her driveway, she visualized Dean tilting her chin up and kissing her. No, she'd have to change that last part. He wasn't tall enough to have to tilt her chin up. It'd be more like he'd lean over and then kiss her.

She propped her bike against the faded red bricks of her tiny bungalow, not noticing at first that every window in the house was tightly curtained and the front light was on. As she walked toward the doorstep, though, the living room blinds started to do a nervous little flutter-dance. And then, a few seconds later, the light flicked off and on, off and on, as if it was sending out coded messages.

Panicking, Willow dropped her bookbag and raced up the front doorstep. Nana must have had a relapse. She jabbed her house key into the lock, praying that everything would be okay.

Suddenly, the key flew out of her hand.

"Princess, you've returned!" Her grandmother pulled open the front door and grabbed Willow's wrist. "Make haste!" she said, glancing about. "We haven't a moment to spare."

"Nana, what ... ?" was all Willow managed to get out before the old lady yanked her inside the house.

CHAPTER 2

"THE SUMMONING!" Nana whispered breathlessly. "'Tis come, Your Highness. 'Tis finally come!" She whipped around to look into the living room, her eyes dark and feverish, her hair swinging in stringy white strands around her head.

Willow stared at her grandmother, a long-ago memory seeping into her mind. *Witch-girl! Witch-girl! Willow is a witch-girl!* The neighbourhood kids had called her "witch-girl" because of Nana. Because of Nana's long black dresses, her queer way of talking and all her crazy mismatched furniture. A chill ran up Willow's spine. For a second, she could see what they had seen. She saw the witch.

Nana turned and began pulling at Willow's arm again. "Must ready ourselves. Must ready ourselves. So much to do. So much."

It was then that Willow really took in her grandmother's appearance. The frazzled hairdo. The too-bright eyes. And the dirty blouse with the top buttons popped off. Her eyes trailed down to Nana's long black skirt. It was on backwards with the zipper gaping wide open.

Warning bells tripped off inside Willow. She'd been right. Nana *was* having another relapse.

"Na-na." Willow made her voice soft and musical as if she were speaking to a child. "Slow down," she said, putting her arm around the little woman and gently rubbing her shoulders. "Why don't we sit for a minute? Besides, I don't even know what a summoning is. Aren't you going to tell me about it first?" Silently, Willow prayed the voice trick would work. She had to get Nana to calm down.

Her grandmother stepped back and stood blinking at her, clearly startled that Willow wouldn't know what a summoning was.

Willow squeezed Nana's shoulders again. "Listen," she continued soothingly, "you sit right down here, okay?" She led her over to the couch by the fireplace.

Nana sat down and Willow wrapped her in a multi-coloured knitted afghan. "There," she said, smiling, "feel better now?" She brushed hair from the old lady's eyes, looking anxiously into her face. She seemed a bit better. Her breathing was deeper, and she didn't look so agitated.

"Like a fire?" asked Willow. That would do the trick. Her grandmother loved fires. Nana nodded and Willow grabbed a matchbook from the mantel and knelt down by the fireplace. She lit a match and held it to the packaging of her store-bought fire log, watching as orange flames swept across the top edge and then slowly consumed all the dark paper underneath.

Last year had been the start of Nana's dizzy spells and memory lapses. At first, she'd only forgotten small things, like her doctor's name or his office's street number. Then it started to get worse. She'd forget they had a fridge, and put food out in the snow to keep cold. Or she'd think the remote control was a telephone and try to make calls on it. The full-scale delusions didn't start till late in the spring. Willow took her to see her doctor who did all kinds of tests, but nothing came back positive. All he could say was that Nana was probably in the early stages of Alzheimer's.

Willow sighed. She'd just begun to hope that the doctor had been wrong. For a full month now, her grandmother had been acting normal. She'd been cooking and cleaning and playing chess again, just like her old self. There'd been no dizzy spells. No blackouts. And most of all, no weird delusions about living in a castle and being a nursemaid to some medieval princess.

Twisting around, Willow grabbed the poker and jabbed the fake log with its sharp point. Right now, her grandmother probably thought she was the fireplace servant or something. When Nana was in her castle-fantasy mode, she had a lot of servants: a cook, a maid, a gardener, a whole squadron of armed guards and a kitchen boy named Gwaine. Did kitchen boys light fires?

She sighed again and gave the log another jab with the poker, trying to push aside her fears. What if Nana had to go to a hospital or a nursing home this time? What would Willow do? Nana was her only family. She'd probably be stuck in a foster home or something.

"Gwaine," said a voice behind Willow's back, "the fire looks fine now. I need you to go and fetch the princess. And no dallying in the kitchens, either."

Willow rolled her eyes. So, she'd been right. Kitchen boys did light fires. She stood up and walked out of the living room, waited a second, and then walked back in. When Nana was like this, it was better to humour her. If you tried to explain reality, she'd just stare blankly, her eyes glazing over like tinted windows. Couldn't see in. Couldn't see out.

Nana leaned over to a low table beside the couch and

reached for her favourite ornament, a delicate gem-cut crystal. "Princess, look," she said, reverently displaying the crystal on its golden stand. "The crystal has begun the summoning spell. We must prepare. I don't know how much time we have before the spell reaches its peak again."

Summoning spell. Why did that sound so familiar?

Willow sat down on the couch, suddenly realizing where her grandmother's "memories" were coming from. "Where does the spell take us?" she asked.

"Why, to Mistolear, of course, Your Highness." Nana smiled as if they'd just shared a joke.

Mistolear! So that was it. Nana's mind wasn't trapped in the past. It was trapped in the fantasy world of her own games and stories.

Willow stared at the old brown couch that had been her pretend princess carriage and the chair that had been her magic horse, Moonbeam. Nana had been inventing Mistolear for her ever since Willow could remember. Making up thrilling adventures about knights and princesses and elves and magic. Heck, for the first six years of her life, Willow had actually believed she *was* a princess trapped in an alternate dimension by an evil elf lord. But crabby Mrs. Letton, her grade one teacher, had soon squashed that idea.

Nana held the crystal out to Willow. "Look after it, Princess. I'm too old to keep watch."

"What, uh ... should I do with it?" asked Willow, taking the crystal and holding it up to the light. It seemed ordinary enough; same faceted globe as always. She shifted it around in her hand. The way the light reflected colours into it was pretty, but there was definitely no glow. She wondered if maybe Nana needed to see an eye doctor too.

"Keep it with you, Princess," said Nana, stroking Willow's hands. "That's all. Just keep it with you. And when it glows, we'll touch it together and ... and go back home." She smiled vaguely and lay back against the couch cushions, her eyelids falling closed.

Willow tucked the afghan up around her grandmother's chin. "Don't worry," she whispered. "You rest. I'll take care of it."

She bent down to kiss the wrinkled cheek. "I'll take care of everything."

Willow set the last pot to dry in the dish rack and peeled off her rubber gloves. She was really worried about Nana. After dinner, her grandmother had asked "the maids" to pack their belongings, and then she'd gone to her room and gone right back to sleep again. That wasn't like her at all. She was usually a night owl, prowling around the house till long after Willow had gone to bed.

Maybe she should call Dr. Pembleton. Back in the spring when Nana's dizzy spells and weird memories had been at their worst, Dr. Pembleton had asked Willow to document Nana's behaviour and keep him informed of any new developments. But Nana had been doing so well lately that Willow hadn't spoken with him in a couple months.

She fingered Dr. Pembleton's doodled-on, dirt-smeared phone number which was taped to the wall beneath the telephone. Nah, there was no sense in calling him now. He wouldn't be there at night, and she'd just have to listen to his answering service telling her that he'd get back to her in the morning.

Willow sighed and sat on one of the wobbly kitchen chairs. She leaned an elbow on the table and stared at the crystal sitting on top of her school books. She'd been about seven when she and Nana had started playing that summoning spell game. Touch the crystal. That's all you had to do, and you'd be magically whisked away to another world.

Another world. She reached out and ran her fingertips over its curves. It'd be nice to be someplace else. Someplace where there were no problems and nobody ever got sick.

The stack of unpaid bills on the edge of the table caught Willow's eye. Despair swept over her. Nana had always been vague about finances, but they'd always managed, as long as they'd been careful. But lately Nana had been letting things slip, and Willow couldn't help but notice the envelopes marked "Second Notice."

She fingered the pile of bills. What if Nana wasn't paying the bills because she didn't actually have any money? The thought stunned Willow. No money meant no way of looking after themselves. And what if Nana eventually had to go into a nursing home? Who would pay for that?

Just then the clock over the sink chimed 10:00 p.m. Willow shook off her gloom. She still had math homework and a writing assignment to do. Cheery thoughts of nursing homes and illness would have to wait till later. She scooped up her books and carried them, along with the crystal, into her bedroom. Across the hallway, she could hear Nana's chainsaw snoring. She grinned, closing her door against the rattling, staccato sounds. Her tiny grandmother could saw logs with the best of them.

Willow's homework desk was cluttered with teetering books, discarded computer printouts and her new, slightly used Toshiba computer — a spiffy laptop she'd worked all summer babysitting to buy. She tossed the printouts — rejects from Melissa's essay — into the makeshift recycling box beneath her desk, setting the crystal and her homework in the newly cleared spot. Algebra, she decided, placing the heavy math book on the floor, could wait. She popped open her laptop and pressed the On button. Mr. Rosen's writing assignment *had* to be more interesting than solving quadratic equations.

Willow settled into her desk chair and typed *A Ghost Story by Willow Kingswell* on the laptop's glowing white screen. She stared at the working title that Mr. Rosen had requested they use. Her plan was to do something weird with it. Like write about ghosts that haunted nail polish remover or purple shoelaces. Bizarre things that nobody would expect.

She started writing. *Once there was a ghost,* she typed. Then she stopped, peered at her first sentence and backspaced it away. *A ghost once lived in a,* she tried again. But no, that wasn't right, either. She mouse-zapped the words this time, watching as the highlighted text disappeared with a quick flick to the Delete key. Blank space filled the screen, simulating her blank mind.

Willow played with the mouse, circling it around and around the empty page, till it hovered over the Start button at the bottom of the screen.

Why not? She might as well get in a quick game, because she obviously wasn't going to be finishing any homework. She left-clicked the Start button, went straight to Programs, then clicked on Expert Software, pulling up her CD-ROM chess game. The screen filled with an ancient-looking chessboard topped with three-dimensional animated playing pieces, still set in the same positions from her last saved game.

Willow frowned at the screen. Things were not looking too good for her White guys. Her king was in check from a Black knight and soon to be in double check from Black's sneaky, marauding queen. She looked around at her players. There were still a few moves open. She mouse-dragged her bishop over to E4, watching as the bishop's magical staff raised high in the air and nuked the Black knight with a lightning bolt. The knight's armour made clanking sounds as he fell to his square, disappearing.

White's move popped up in a box at the bottom right-hand corner of the computer screen. Willow blinked and squinted at the words. It was still disconcerting how fast the computer made its moves. When she and Nana played, moves were pondered in minutes, not in instantaneous seconds. She clicked the Redo button for a replay of Black's last manoeuvre. A pawn had stepped forward a space, opening up an attack route for Black's bishop.

Willow stared at the screen, her mind as empty of strategy as it had been of story ideas. She rubbed soothing circles into her temples. Her head was too plugged up with worry — that was the problem. Worry about Nana, worry about herself and worry about the future.

Her fingers slid from her temples down into her hair, curling around a thick red strand. Memories she'd been trying to suppress suddenly washed over her. Smoke. Flames. Carpet blazing, the fire edging dangerously close to the curtains. The last time Nana had been stuck in castle-fantasy mode, she'd almost burned the house down trying to cook food in the fireplace.

Tears sprang into Willow's eyes. Maybe it was her fault, Nana being sick again. For being selfish. And deceitful. She'd lied to Nana. Told her she was going to Melissa's party when she really hadn't been invited yet. And so poor Nana had spent hours hunched over the sewing machine making Willow the Guinevere costume. It must've been too much for her.

She gave her moist eyes a quick backhand and swivelled around in her chair. The green velvet gown hung from a hook on the wall beside her bed. Nana had been so excited about making it for her, as if Melissa's party had been some sort of royal ball or something.

Willow stood up and pulled off her jeans and sweater. She took the costume from the hanger and slipped it on, shivering as the cool silk lining pressed against her warm skin. When she had the buttons done up, she walked over to the full-length mirror across from her desk and stared at herself in its dusty glass. The costume clung like skin, giving faint curves to her lean body. She slid her fingertips over the soft folds of emerald velvet. The colour suited her, deepening her hair to a shiny copper and her brown eyes to a lustrous chocolate. She felt beautiful in it. Like a real princess.

It needed something, though. Willow turned from the mirror to her bureau, where an old metal jewellery box sat beside her three chess trophies. She opened the dented lid and took out a necklace. Light flickered along the thick gold chain and the delicate white-enamel swan that dangled from it. Carefully she clasped it around her neck. The swan, Nana had said, was an heirloom. It had belonged to Willow's mother's family and been given to each eldest daughter for over a hundred years. Willow's mother had been its last owner.

Willow drifted over to the mirror to stare at the swan, studying its smooth enamel feather bumps and the delicacy of its gold-sculpted bill and feet. There was a tiny crown around its neck that attached it to a thick gold chain. She traced a fingertip along the sharp edges of the crown, trying to imagine her mother wearing it.

Nana had told her about the house fire that had killed both her parents when she was a baby. There were no photographs, no bits of clothing, no special ornaments, nothing that had survived the fire. Nothing except her, Nana, Nana's crystal, and the swan in its battered jewellery box. Sometimes, though, when she wore the necklace, Willow imagined she could feel her mother. Could actually talk to her.

But right now she didn't want to think about the faceless woman that she'd never met. She wanted to think about Dean. She closed her eyes, holding a clear image of her beautiful princess look. The fantasy she was aiming for was her favourite one, the one with the smooth stride of a white charger and Dean/Lancelot's strong arms wrapped around her.

After a few seconds, a ragged sigh escaped her lips. It wasn't going to work tonight. There were no knights on white chargers coming to her rescue.

Or, for that matter, falling in love with her at Halloween parties.

She turned abruptly from the mirror and plopped back into her desk chair. She had to forget about Dean and the party. Nana would need her. Tomorrow they'd make an appointment with Dr. Pembleton. Whatever it took to keep Nana out of a nursing home, they were going to do it.

Yawning, Willow turned off her computer and flipped down its screen. She might as well get to bed early. Couldn't risk Nana waking up first and trying to cook pancakes or muffins in the fireplace. She rubbed at her neck and yawned again. A light suddenly wavered in front of her. Willow blinked at it, then shielded her eyes as it flared to blinding white.

Heat seemed to explode in her face. "Jeez!" she yelped, twisting her head. She moved away from the desk, squinting back at the glare. Dazzling light sparked and flickered, then became a steady white glow.

Willow slowly raised her eyes, opening them wide at the light's unexpected source. *Nana's crystal.* The light was coming from Nana's freakin' crystal! *But it couldn't be,* she thought, wheeling her chair back to the desk. She stuck her nose close to the stone. This couldn't be real! Nana was whacko. She hadn't really seen the thing glowing. It'd all been part of her dementia.

So then why are you seeing it, too? a small voice inside Willow said.

Willow reached out and gingerly touched the stand. It was burning hot. She snatched her hand back, gnawing on the corner of her lip. What had Nana said before? Something about touching the crystal. They both had to touch it together. She pulled her fingers into her velvet sleeve and carefully picked up the stand. *What if it were true? What if Mistolear really existed?*

God! Willow snorted. Now she was sounding as whacko as Nana.

But what if it does? persisted the small voice. *You have to show her.*

Willow glanced at her alarm clock. It was past eleven. Probably time for a Nana-check anyway. She stood up and carried the crystal across her bedroom and into the hallway outside Nana's closed doorway. Hesitating, she studied its brightly lit facets. Could something scientific explain this? And what if she showed it to Nana and it got her all upset again?

Willow turned to go back to her bedroom. She couldn't risk upsetting Nana. But as she stepped inside her room, a feeling of unease came over her. She couldn't quite put her finger on it, but she knew something was wrong. Something not quite right. Then it hit her. It was too quiet. Where was Nana's chainsaw snoring?

Blood drained from Willow's face as she bolted for her grandmother's bedroom. She opened the door, holding the stone out like a flashlight. The room was dark and eerily silent.

"Nana?"

No answer. Willow darted over to the bed, setting the crystal on the nightstand. Her grandmother was lying on her side, looking comfortably asleep.

"Nana?" Willow whispered. She gently shook an exposed shoulder. "Nana? Are you awake?" No movement. Not an eyelash flutter, a sigh or even a breath. A new and terrible thought took hold of Willow. She flung back the blankets and felt Nana's thin chest for a heartbeat. Nothing.

"*No!*" she cried out. She raced to the phone, dialing 911 as quickly as her trembling fingers could push the buttons. "Hello! Hello! I need an ambulance! *I need an ambulance!*" The lady on the phone tried to calm her. "Okay, Miss," she said, "take a deep breath and tell me what the problem is."

"My grandma's ... my grandma's not — not *breathing*."

"What's your address?"

"10 — 1012 M-Meadow Brook Street." Willow's voice sounded thin and childlike, her breath coming in ragged shudders.

"It's okay," soothed the dispatcher. "You just sit tight. An ambulance will be there in just a few minutes. What's your name?"

"Willow."

"Okay, Willow. You're doing real well here. Do you know what happened to your grandmother? Did she fall or anything like that?

"No. I — I just went in to — to check on her. I thought ... I thought she was a-asleep."

"Are your parents there?"

Willow hesitated. Would they take her to a foster home right now — *tonight* — if she told them the truth? "They — they're out."

"Do you have their number? Do you want us to contact them?"

"No. No, it's okay. I'll — I'll do it." Before the woman could ask any more questions, Willow hung up the phone, her chest heaving. Oh God! Oh God! Nana had to be okay. She just *had* to be!

A tight ache gripped Willow's heart and a harsh, accusing voice pounded in her head. *This is your fault*, the voice kept saying. *You should have called the hospital. Called Dr. Pembleton.* The phone suddenly began ringing. Willow didn't answer it. She stumbled back into the room and clung to Nana, rocking her back and forth. "I'm sorry!" she sobbed. "I'm so sorry!"

It felt like a long time had passed before Willow tenderly laid Nana back down. Where was the ambulance? Why hadn't they come? Willow shivered when her fingers grazed Nana's cool skin. More tears spilled down her cheeks. She wiped at them and pulled herself to her feet. She knew it didn't matter anymore. It was too late.

In the dim light, she could see the crystal's soft, burning-ember glow. Anger suddenly exploded inside her. *That stupid crystal! That's what did this! Made Nana so upset that she started having delusions again.*

Willow reached for the crystal, ready to fling it into the garbage. But her hand curled into a fist instead and slammed against the wall. Everything — her fear, her worry, the months of dealing with Nana's illness on her own, came crashing down on her. "Okay, Nana," she hissed. "If you're going to leave me, then I'm going to leave, too!"

It was a crazy, straightjacket kind of idea, but it reeled inside her head. She stormed across the hallway into her bedroom. Nothing but a mess. *Everything* was a mess. She whipped her head around to look at the clutter. Her chess trophies were special. She'd take them. She clanged them together and scooped them up into her arms. Her clothes and her stuffed animals and her books — they didn't matter. Her gaze fell on the almost-new laptop. No way was she leaving that behind. She dropped the trophies onto her bed, exchanging them for the unplugged laptop.

She sat hugging the computer to her chest and staring at her image in the mirror. *There. I have the three things that matter the most: my costume, my necklace and my computer.*

She trudged back into Nana's room, the silk rustle of her gown sounding suddenly loud in the peaceful quiet. Nana still lay on the bed as if she were asleep. Willow scowled. Nana was *gone.* Had left her here all alone. She turned to look at the crystal. She could hear a siren wailing down the street. But she didn't care. She didn't care about anything anymore. Her fingers flinched as they grazed the crystal's hot surface. "Okay, Mistolear," she spat, "ready or not, here I come!"

CHAPTER 3

"WELL, HERE SHE IS. How was the portal, Highness? Not too bumpy, I would hope."

Words. Willow could hear words. Someone was speaking to her. She tried to focus but everything around her was spinning. She stumbled forward.

"Hold off, Lady Merritt. The poor girl's not yet got her sea legs."

Strong hands grasped at Willow, saving her from a face-first sprawl. Her cheek pressed up against smooth leather, and she felt herself being lifted and set on a chair. The room spun and careened like a Tilt-A-Whirl ride. Willow clutched at her laptop, trying to anchor herself down.

"Is she hurt?"

"No, no. Just a bit dizzy. She'll be right as rain in a moment."

Those voices again. Willow squinted, struggling to see where they had come from. Dark shapes hovered around her. "Wh-who's there?" she asked.

"'Tis an odd thing that she's holding. What do you make of it, Sir Baldemar?"

"An object from Earthworld, no doubt."

A gentle hand lifted Willow's chin.

"Look at her, milord. She has the look of her mother."

One of the dark shapes was beginning to take form.

Willow could make out a young brown-haired woman all dressed in blue. She was patting Willow's arm and smiling at her.

"Are you alright now?" the woman asked. "Can you speak?"

Willow squeezed her eyes shut then opened them again. The strange woman was still there. She tried pinching herself next, but it didn't work, either. The dream was actually getting clearer.

"Sir Baldemar, what is she doing? Do you think mayhap she's cold?"

Willow heard a low chuckle. "No, milady. I uh — I believe the young lady is attempting to awaken herself."

"Wh-who are you people?" Willow finally managed. "Where am I?" Her eyes scanned rough stone walls that rose up past flickering torches to a high, curved ceiling. In front of her a gold and purple cloth covered most of the wall space. It was shaped like a shield, the large swan embroidered at its centre reminding her of a coat of arms she'd once seen in a book.

"Nurse did not tell you?" The brown-haired woman's eyes opened incredulously. "But how could you have ... Where *is* Nurse Beryl, anyway?"

Nurse Beryl? Willow didn't know any Nurse Beryl. And even if ... Wait a minute. Beryl. Beryl was Nana's first name. Beryl Kingswell. "You mean my — my nana?"

"Yes. Where is she? Why did she not come through the portal with you?"

The pain came rushing back. Willow refused to let it. She looked up at the ceiling, blinking away tears. "Nana's ... Nana's dead," she said flatly.

A heavy-set man with lank brown hair and wrinkled

robes suddenly appeared from the shadows. He moved slowly toward Willow, stooping so that he could grip her shoulders. "My dear Willow," his voice rasped, "you have our deepest sympathies." The flickering torchlight danced in his sad, wet eyes, making them gleam like blue icicles.

Willow squinted at him, ignoring the thin tear-stream that trickled down his cheek. For some strange reason he seemed to be glowing. A livid light was emanating out of him in a bright purple halo.

"'Twas not meant to happen this way," he muttered. "The elf queen made promises. She pledged me your safety."

This time, Willow stared straight into his face, his bleak, unfamiliar face. Alarm jerked inside her. "Who are you?" she asked suddenly, shrugging his purple-stained hands away. "And my name. How do you know my name?" She stood, still clutching the laptop, and looked wildly around the room. Things were beginning to spin again. "*Where am I?*"

The other man, the one named Baldemar, stepped forward. Willow gasped. He was glowing too, only his colour was a deep midnight blue. It made him look like a tall, wide-shouldered phantom. Ghosts and elves and portals — it was too much! Before she could scream, he pulled a gold medallion from his shirt front and held it up. "Be still," he said, the words rumbling from his chest like a loud cat purr. A weight seemed to press on Willow. She sank back down into the chair, weak and light-headed.

"Now, then." The tall man dropped the medallion beneath his shirtneck. "I think 'tis time some explanations were made." He bowed low to Willow. "Princess Willow," he continued, "you are now in Carrus, the capital city of Gallandra in the lower magical realm of Mistolear. This gentleman to my left is your grandfather, King Ulor Farrandale, high king of Gallandra." The stocky man with the sad, glowing face and blue icicle eyes nodded at her. "And this," Baldemar tilted his head slightly toward the young woman, "is Lady Merritt du Aubrey, lady-in-waiting to the queen. And I," he bowed low again, "am Sir Baldemar of Tamarvyn, your grandfather's humble mage knight."

Willow leaned back in the chair, rubbing her fingers across the top of her computer. What a great dream this was! Ladies-in-waiting. The king of Gallandra and his humble mage knight. They were perfect. Exactly how Nana had described them.

"Willow, do you understand what Baldemar is saying?" asked the King Ulor dream figure. "Do you understand that I am your grandfather?"

Willow smiled at him and decided to play along. After all, it was only a dream. She nodded.

"Do you know who you are? Do you know that you are Princess Willow Farrandale, heir to the throne of Gallandra?"

Princess Willow Farrandale, heir to the throne of Gallandra. Willow liked the sound of that. It had real snob appeal. She imagined Melissa Morrison and her friends bowing and scraping to her. *Yes, Your Highness. No, Your Highness. Can we kiss your butt, Your Highness?*

"Princess Willow, did you hear what the king said?"

Lady Merritt's voice cut into Willow's daydream. Or was it a night dream? She'd never had a dream inside her dream before.

"Princess? Princess? Sir Baldemar, I believe your calming spell has been too effective. Look at the child. She's practically in a stupor!"

"Well, perhaps 'twould be best if we let her rest for now," said the king. "She will need her strength for the morrow."

"Very well, Sire," said Lady Merritt, helping Willow to stand. "I'll escort Her Highness to the prince and princess's old chambers."

Willow, her laptop cord dangling against the skirt of her green velvet Guinevere gown, smiled and followed the woman, happy and obedient as a trained puppy.

❦

Flowers. Something smelled like flowery perfume. Willow sniffed at her sheets.

Whew! They reeked of it. Must be that new detergent Nana had used the other day. She turned over onto her back and rubbed her eyes. Jeez, what a night! She'd had the strangest dreams. Crazy stuff. Like Nana dying and then herself being beamed into Mistolear like some character in a Star Trek episode.

Oh well. She'd better get moving. She had to make the phone call to Dr. Pembleton today. Willow ran her fingers through her hair and sat up. That was weird. Her room was still dark.

She peered into the dim light. Wait a minute. This wasn't her room! Her mouth dropped open. She was buried under a bulky mound of blankets, totally naked, in the middle of an enormous four-poster bed with purple carpets hanging all around.

Willow quickly kicked the woolen covers away and grabbed at a linen sheet. Wrapping it around her shoulders, she crawled across the mattress and pulled back an inch of the heavy bed curtain. A brick wall and a narrow round-topped shuttered window appeared.

She stuck a bare foot onto the chilly stone floor and crept, shivering, over to the window. Hinges creaked as she drew back the shutters, and cold air rushed over her, turning her breath into frosty white puffs. There was no glass. Just a big open space.

Flip-flops churned queasily in her stomach as she glimpsed the high stone walls and cone-tipped towers that encircled an outdoor courtyard. Her eyes squeezed shut. If she just waited a minute, maybe things would go back to normal again. She counted seconds off inside her head, trying to ignore the ripe smells of churned soil and farm manure that were drifting in with the cold air. A dog yelped, and then she heard indignant pig squeals. Children's raucous laughter echoed up to her.

Willow covered her head with the sheet and plugged her ears. "Da, da, da, da," she hummed loudly. "I'm awake! I'm awake! I'm awake!" Finally, she lowered the blanket and blinked her eyes open. But nothing had changed. The dog being chased by the dirty kids, the scrawny chickens, goats and sheep, the weird hairy little pigs, and the six women in the white-veiled nun costumes stirring the huge vats of soapy, steaming water — they were all still out there.

Willow banged the shutters closed and backed away from the window, her heart thumping wildly against her chest. What was going on? It was like a twelfth century movie set out there! She gnawed at the inside of her cheek and slowly turned around. The shadowy room with its canopied bed came back into view. It was furnished with an elaborate chest, a desk and chair, tapestried wall hangings and a very large fireplace filled with glowing ashes.

Was this real? Had she actually travelled through time and popped into some alternate universe or another dimension or something?

Or ... she pinched her arm really hard to test her next theory ... had her daydreams finally gone psycho on her? A red thumbprint appeared on her forearm. The pinch definitely hurt. She had to be awake.

A light tap on the door made Willow jump. She turned to see a pretty brown-haired lady poking her head around the doorway.

"Princess Willow, you've awakened. I trust you slept well?" She breezed into the room wearing a bejewelled red and black dress that was, without a doubt, the most spectacular outfit Willow had ever seen in her life. A short, plump woman followed her, carrying some towels and a water basin.

Speechless, Willow stared at them and nodded.

"I am the lady Merritt," said the brown-haired woman, giving her an elegant curtsy. "We met last night, but I fear you'll have little memory of it. Sir Baldemar's spell was mayhap a little too strong. The king," she prattled on, ignoring Willow's bewilderment, "has sent me to help you ready yourself for breakfast." She unfurled a cream-coloured bundle: it was a long dress. "The seamstress used your garment for measurements and was able to alter some extra gowns for you. And these," she held out a pair of matching slippers, "should fit as well, as you seem to have taken after your grandmother in both height and hoof.

"Now," she continued, "we shall assist you in your dressing. And then we'll take you to the king."

Willow watched as the shorter woman bustled behind a tapestried dressing screen then reappeared a few seconds later minus the water basin and towels. "Will ye be needin' any help with yer bath, Princess?" the woman mumbled. Her eyes darted a quick peek at Willow then she glanced away uncomfortably.

"Uh ... no. No, that's alright," said Willow, finally snapping out of her daze. "I think ... I think I can manage." She ducked behind the dressing screen, anxiously clutching at the bedsheet dragging behind her. This was getting *way* too weird. Why were these women bowing and calling her Princess?

She plunged her hands into the water basin and splashed hot rose-scented water over her face. She had to pull herself together here. There *was* a logical explanation for all this, and she was certain it *didn't* include a magic crystal ride to Mistolear.

A thin white dress came flying overtop the screen. "Yer shift, Highness."

Willow pulled down the flimsy material and held it in front of her. What was this supposed to be? Underwear or something? It looked like a sleeveless nightie.

Reluctantly, she dropped her sheet and stepped into the shift. Since she didn't seem to have any regular clothes, and her feet were beginning to turn blue, now was not the time to rock the boat.

The woman, who seemed to be some sort of servant, came around the screen and quickly stuffed and laced her into Lady Merritt's cream-coloured dress, fitted pointy slippers on her feet, and then smoothed out her hair with a silver comb.

Willow raised voluminous, floor-touching sleeves and looked at herself in a gold wall mirror.

"I look ... I look ... " she started.

"Like a proper princess," finished Lady Merritt.

No, that wasn't what Willow had had in mind. She glanced at the servant woman and Lady Merritt and then back at herself in the mirror. Had it escaped everyone's notice that she was glowing? Willow squinted at the thick glass in confusion. Her hair looked like red neon in a Vegas casino sign and her face and neck were emanating a vampirish shade of pearly white.

"What's wrong with the mirror?" she asked, twisting her body to the left. The glowing twisted with her.

Lady Merritt ignored the question, coming up behind Willow and placing a light band around her head. "To complete your attire," she said, smiling. She gave Willow's shoulder a pat. "Your lady mother wore this. 'Twas a wedding gift. In fact," said Lady Merritt, swinging her arms out, "this room was your parents' bedchamber. Your nursery was through that door there."

Willow stared at the thin gold circlet, all concerns over her strangely glowing skin suddenly evaporating. Her fingertips explored the crown's sharp pearl-topped spikes. She couldn't breathe. Blood was pounding in her ears. Nana had always told her that her parents had been killed in a house fire. That there had been nothing left. Nothing but the swan necklace and Nana's crystal.

"Are you alright?" asked Lady Merritt. "You look a mite pale."

Willow shook her head. "It's just ... I thought ... I mean ... " She continued to gaze at the circlet, her fingers now following a trail of sparkling diamond bumps. "Is she ... is she alive?" The question popped out before she could stop it. She hadn't really meant to say it out loud.

"Well ... I — I ... " Lady Merritt's mouth opened and closed like a gasping fish. "N-no, dear," she finally stammered. "I — I thought you knew. She was Captured a few days after your birthing."

"Captured?" said Willow. "You mean, like, she's a ... a prisoner somewhere?"

Lady Merritt shook her head. "I'm sorry. I should not have spoken of it. Come now." She squeezed Willow's fingers and smiled kindly. "The king, your grandfather, awaits us. He will answer all your questions and concerns." She turned toward the servant woman, ordering her to tidy up the room, then led Willow down a long hallway.

Numb, Willow followed after her, still not willing to accept what was happening. There had to be a logical explanation. She was *not* a Mistolearian princess. She did *not* time travel. She ...

"This way," said Lady Merritt. She took Willow's arm and gently steered her down another hallway, then stopped in front of an imposing brass-handled door guarded by a thin sword-carrying boy. "We have arrived," she announced. She waved her hand at the boy in a curt, shoo-bug motion and waited as he opened the door for her.

As Willow passed him, she noticed that he gave her an odd look, as if she had a big green spinach wad stuck between her teeth or something.

"Lady Merritt," said a deep, raspy voice. The purple-glowing man from last night rose from a chair and came toward them. He seemed in good spirits, Willow noticed, and a little better groomed than what she remembered from the night before.

"I give thanks to you for tending to my granddaughter," he said. "She looks most lovely."

Lady Merritt nodded and gave a quick curtsy. "Thank you, Your Majesty. 'Twas not difficult. The princess has Your Majesty's good bones, of course. And all that marvellous height. Just like her grandmother." Sad grey eyes suddenly filled with tears. "Queen Aleria would have been so pleased to have met her."

King Ulor's face sagged at the mention of Queen Aleria. Willow frowned. If the king really was her grandfather, then Queen Aleria must be her ... her *grandmother?* The king managed a tight smile as he ushered Lady Merritt into the hallway.

Willow stared after him, taking in the gold crown, the floor-length purple robes and the ring with a ruby the size of a quarter on his hand. He was definitely a king; and yes, he had definitely introduced himself as her grandfather. But there was no way! It was all impossible. A *big* mistake!

"Well, my dear," said King Ulor, returning to the room and offering her his arm, "what say you to some food and a bit of wine to break your fast?"

"I think — I think there's been a — been a mistake," Willow stammered. She had to get this straightened out now, before things got too complicated. "I'm not your granddaughter. I — I can't be."

King Ulor dropped his arm. He gave Willow a long, sorrowful stare and then reached out to touch the curve of her cheek. "There has been no mistake, my dear," he said gravely. "You are, indeed, my granddaughter."

"But I can't be. Look, my parents died in a fire when I was

a baby," she tried to explain. "And I don't have any other relatives except my real grandmother and she's ... and she's ..." *What?* Sick with Alzheimer's. Dead in her bedroom. Willow blinked back a sudden rush of tears and turned away from the king.

"I want to go home," she whispered. "I *have* to go home."

CHAPTER 4

K ING ULOR PATTED Willow's shoulder. "I am truly sorry about Nurse Beryl. Was she ill? The chessboard gave us no indication of such a problem."

"She probably had Alzheimer's or something like that and ... and ... " Willow wiped at her eyes, getting her emotions under control again. She turned to the king. What was that he'd just said about a chessboard?

"I am not familiar with this ... Alt-hammers." King Ulor stroked the long brown hairs of his beard. "Is it similar to the head-hammering sickness?"

"Head-hammering sickness? Is that like a headache or something?"

"Yes, 'tis like a terrible ache in the head."

"Well, no, that's not Alzheimer's," she explained. "Alzheimer's damages your brain. It makes you forget things."

The king nodded as if he understood. "The memory sickness. Yes, we have such things here as well."

"Umm ... Your — Your Majesty?" No, that didn't sound right. Too formal. "Uh ... sir?" she tried again. "You said something — something about a chessboard."

King Ulor drew in a deep breath. "Ah, yes, the chessboard," he sighed. "I was hoping to eat first. But I can see that you will need to view it — *if* I am ever to persuade you to call me Grandfather." His eyebrows arched slightly.

Willow felt her face redden. "Sorry; I didn't mean ... "

King Ulor shook his head and waved aside her apology. "No, no. 'Tis quite alright. There's no shame in caution, my dear. No shame at all. And, if the truth be told, in your place, I am sure I would find myself thinking the same way." He moved away from Willow and strode over to the fireplace mantel to stand before a large three-footed brass candlestick. Wrapping his hands around its midsection, he blew out the thick dripping candle, then slowly tilted the candlestick backwards.

Willow watched bug-eyed as a section of stone slid to the side. Her heart pounded loudly in her ears. She knew what was in there. The candlestick. The hidden tunnel. Standing in the king's bedchamber. It was all the same. Exactly like Nana's Gallandrian story. The one about the king's secret room where he kept the magic chess set.

King Ulor relit the candle and wriggled it from the stand, then turned back to Willow. "Well, come on, then," he said, smiling resignedly. "Best to get it over with."

The passageway twisted into a dark, narrow corridor that smelled like musty basements and damp earth. Willow lifted her skirts with one hand and palmed the other along the rough stone walls. She stopped for a moment, shocked once again to see her skin glowing with a pearly light.

Up ahead, King Ulor was rounding a corner, taking his candlelight and purple glow with him. Willow dropped her hand and hurried after him. Her own glow problems would have to wait till later.

King Ulor stopped in front of a low wooden door. He held out the dripping candle to Willow, then reached for a key that hung from a chain beneath his robes. Unlocking the door, he gestured for Willow to go ahead of him.

Carefully shielding the candle with her hand, Willow ducked through the doorway into a large dark room. King Ulor took back the candle and walked along the wall, lighting lamps with it. Willow stared after him, as section by section the room lit up to show an enormous circular chamber with a vaulted ceiling. She blinked when her gaze fell to the middle of the room. It was right there. Exactly as Nana had described it. A huge chess set sitting on top of an elaborate white marble pedestal.

Willow's scalp prickled as she moved slowly over to the pedestal. She felt light and airy, her thoughts spinning off in all directions. She reached out to touch one of the pieces, a tall, slim bishop, turning it to look for the carved face. It was there — a tiny man-face sculpted onto the surface of the heavy stone chess piece.

"Do you play?" asked King Ulor, startling her with his low, raspy voice.

Willow nodded and set the piece back on its black square. There were no words in her mind, only images. Images of Nana's ancient wooden chess set and endless hours of learning and playing. She'd learned chess the way others learned ballet or to play the piano. Practise. Practise. Practise.

The king stared at her face a moment, then glanced down at the board. "Ah, I see the change now," he said, lifting a white pawn. "Nurse's piece has become the blacksmith's son." He set the pawn down again, a troubled frown creasing his brow as he continued to study the chessboard. Lamplight flickered behind him, casting shadows, blackening his purple glow to a bruised plum. Willow squinted at him. Were those tears in his eyes? Finally, the king turned back to her. "And how would you move," he asked quietly, "if you were playing White?"

Willow's thoughts came into focus again, edging out confusing new questions and old memories. Chess was solid. Logical. Something she could hold onto and understand. She studied the board, testing possible moves, deciding almost instantly that White was in deep trouble.

His queen and half of his pieces were gone. And what was left of his army was hopelessly bunched in the right-hand corner.

Both these guys must be idiots, she thought. Neither one had castled his king and Black was wasting his queen in a useless back rank position, when he could've used her to finish the game a long time ago.

Willow fingered the back of White's far-right pawn. It was the only pawn with a clear file. "I'd either try to queen this pawn and checkmate the Black king, or, I'd sacrifice it and use the rook to checkmate."

She dropped her hand and looked to see if the king was buying her line of reasoning. She knew neither ploy could really work. Black was still too strong. He had all his pieces, except for his far-end pawns. And his bishops and knights were just too well-placed. White would need a bona fide miracle to win.

King Ulor was silent. He rested his thumb and forefinger on top of the White king as if he were planning his next move, then he lifted it away from the board and held it out to Willow.

Time seemed to stop as Willow watched him turn the king around. It was like one of those moments in a horror movie when you see someone from the back and you just know that when he turns around he's going to have blood-dripping fangs or no eyeballs.

She gasped. It was King Ulor's face that was carved on the chess piece. *This isn't happening. This can't be happening!* King Ulor handed her the piece. She clenched her fist around it.

"Look at it," he urged. "You must look at it."

Willow's fingers slowly uncurled from around the king. She held it closer, touching the curve of rounded forehead, the long straight nose and the pointed beard. It was him, alright. Even the small eyes and lips were his, all carved with that same incredible precision.

"Did Nurse not tell you about the Game? Did she not tell you *anything* at all about who you are?"

Willow shook her head no, but at the same time she knew that Nana *had* told her. Not in a direct way. Nana had known she could never do that. But in other ways. Ways that wouldn't make Willow look like some kind of mental case.

That was what the stories and role-playing games were all about. The costumes. The chess. Even her summer riding lessons, which had seemed so extravagant. Everything had been Nana's way of preparing her for Mistolear.

She saw Nana teaching her chess, weaving the game into an elaborate story. Two kingdoms turned into chess pieces by an evil elf prince. One kingdom in need of a new queen. Her pulse throbbed in her temple like a finger flicking under her skin.

"The image is mine, Willow," said King Ulor. "And this one," he picked up the far-right pawn, the one with the clear file, "is yours."

Willow stared at the tiny perfect face carved into the stone chess piece. Her own tiny perfect face.

"We've been placed under a Game spell," he continued. "A very powerful one, which, I am afraid, we are in grave danger of losing."

Willow felt as if her insides had been turned into mush. Dimension travel must take a lot out of you. She blinked at King Ulor. He looked concerned. She started to speak, to say something about Nana's lessons, but her legs trembled and swayed, suddenly crumpling under her like a buckled rag doll's.

CHAPTER 5

WILLOW OPENED HER EYES. Everything was black around the edges. Her lids slid shut, fluttered, then opened again. Lady Merritt's face floated over her, a small frown puckering her mouth. She dabbed a wet cloth to Willow's forehead. "There, there, dear. Don't try to rise yet. I fear you've had a bit of a tumble."

King Ulor, his face also creased with worry, appeared behind Lady Merritt. "Is she alright?"

Ignoring Lady Merritt's protests, Willow pushed away the wet cloth and sat up, gingerly massaging a sore spot beneath her circlet. "I'm okay, I just fainted. I feel fine now." Not exactly the truth. But it got them to stop hovering.

"Here, drink this," ordered a gruff voice. The man that Willow had mistaken for a ghost the night before was now standing in front of her, holding out a red-jewelled goblet.

Willow accepted the drink, trying to look past the blue glow to his rugged face. Her opinion didn't change much. He still looked like he could scare the heck out of little kids on a dark night. She took a big gulp from the goblet and immediately began to cough and sputter, the clear liquid burning its way inside her.

Lady Merritt leaned her forward and began whacking at her back. "No, no, dear," she said between whacks. "Illysian wine." *Whack!* "Has to be sipped." *Whack!* "Never gulped."

Whack!

Willow sat up, trying to smother her last coughs. For such a fragile-looking woman, Lady Merritt could deliver some pretty solid back whacks. "Thanks. I think ... *cough* ... I'm okay now." She took a delicate sip from the goblet and wiped at her damp lap.

Lady Merritt stood up from the couch and smoothed out her skirts. "Shall I tell Cook to bring up your breakfast now?" she asked the king.

King Ulor nodded. "Yes, thank you. That is just what the princess needs. Some sustenance."

Lady Merritt curtsied and began to leave the room but then turned back before reaching the door. "And would Your Majesty like minstrels this morning?"

Willow choked back an irreverent giggle. For a second, she'd thought Lady Merritt had sounded like a fast-food cashier. *And-would-you-like-fries-with-that-Sire?*

King Ulor gave Willow another concerned glance and waved Lady Merritt out. "No, no, not today. Too many important matters to discuss."

Important matters! Now *there* was an understatement if she'd ever heard one. Willow took another mouthful of wine and realized that the stuff wasn't half bad. Sort of had a fruity taste. Like Kool-Aid with a kick.

"Best not to drink any more on an empty stomach," warned the blue-glowing man. "'Twill muddle your head."

"Yes, 'tis true," agreed King Ulor. "Especially if you are unaccustomed to it. Come now," he said, taking Willow's hand and giving it a grandfatherly pat, "and sit by the fire with me."

Willow flushed and clung to his arm, letting him guide

her to a large leather-backed chair. She sank onto it and ran her hand under her circlet again. She was suddenly very hot.

"Perhaps some water would be more to your liking," said King Ulor, noticing her discomfort. The man with the blue glow lifted a dark ceramic jug, pouring water into a cup as King Ulor helped her into her chair.

Willow thanked them and sipped at the cold water. The chess room was starting to come back to her. The magic game. The girl-faced chess piece. Somehow, whether she wanted to believe it or not, she was a part of all this. And whatever the reason they had sent her away, they now wanted her back.

There was a short rap at the door and the guard entered, ushering in three servants who placed bread and butter on the table, refilled the wine goblets and served plates of bacon and bowls of cheese and fruit.

Willow thanked the slack-jawed wine server, who was staring at her dumbstruck, and reached for her water again.

"Okay," she said after the servants had left. "*What* is going on? Why does everyone keep looking at me like that?" She held out her hands. "Is it because I'm glowing like a light bulb?"

King Ulor picked up a bread loaf and tore it in two. He passed half the loaf to her and slathered a small mountain of butter onto his own. "No, 'tis not the glow. Everyone who is a chess piece in the Game has it, so they're quite used to that. I'm afraid 'tis more your appearance. You were, after all, but a babe when last they saw you. And now here you are, scarce more than three months later, a full-grown young woman."

Willow sat blinking at him. *Three months?*

"What did you say? Did you say ... three months?"

The king, his goblet halfway to his lips, froze, his hand

tightening around the thick stem. Slowly, he sat the wine goblet back on the table and held her stare. "Yes," he said, "'tis right. Fourteen weeks, to be exact."

Fourteen weeks! Willow could feel her head starting to spin again. But how could that be? She'd lived with Nana for as long as she could remember. Fourteen *years*. Not fourteen weeks!

"Are you ... " she paused, finding it hard to get the words out, "are you saying ... I've only been gone for fourteen *weeks?*"

The king blinked at her, confused, then looked to the blue-glowing man for help.

"Yes," said the blue man matter-of-factly. "You were born a bit over three months ago. Your mother, the princess Diantha, was Captured two weeks after your birth. Your father, Prince Alaric, and grandmother, Queen Aleria, were Captured three days after that. And you were sent to Earthworld with your nurse to dimension age. You see, the elf queen cast a spell on you so that for every year you have spent on Earth, only a week has passed in our Mistolearian realm."

King Ulor's hand reached out to touch hers. "We had no choice. You are Queen Cyrraena's netherchild and the only one who can stop this Game."

Fourteen weeks.

Willow still couldn't get past the fourteen week thing. It was just too bizarre. Too insane! *No,* she reassured herself. *It couldn't be true.* Fourteen weeks was just over three months, and in three months it'd be the New Year ... and Nana and she were going to have a party and ... and ...

She felt a feathery touch cross her knuckles and then a squeeze. King Ulor was still holding her hand, pulling her back to him.

"At present," he said, "we are under siege from King Tarrant's army." He paused and looked uncomfortably at his purple-stained hands. "I had better explain things more fully. You see, Tarrant Somerell, king of Keldoran, is your mother's father. Your maternal grandfather. His capital city of Tulaan is the back rank of the Black team, as my capital city of Carrus is the back rank for White." He stared directly into Willow's eyes. "The Keldorians attack us because they somehow believe we have Captured your mother, the princess Diantha."

There was that word again. *Captured.* Everyone kept saying it, but no one would explain what it meant. Willow withdrew her hand from King Ulor's and focused on his face. "What exactly does that mean? Being *captured.*"

The king pointed to a desk where Willow could see a normal chess set sitting on top of some books. "The game — would you bring it here, please, Sir Baldemar?" he asked the blue-glowing man, who rose from the table to obey. Sir Baldemar set the game between Willow and King Ulor, then sat back down again.

"In an ordinary game of chess, capturing is done like so." King Ulor moved the White queen down a clear file and knocked her into a pawn. Willow nodded. She knew how to play chess. "Well," continued the king, "Capturing in our magical Game is somewhat similar. If a Player on the opposing team kills or 'Captures' one of us, we are also removed from the Game." He picked up the Black pawn and placed it along the sidelines of the chessboard.

Willow nodded again. The way the king had explained it had made her think of Nana. Nana had taught her chess that way, by making believe that the pieces were real people. "So then, the players that are captured, are they ... are they dead?"

King Ulor didn't answer right away. He looked forlornly at the chessboard. "We think so," he finally said. "When we're Captured, we change into one of these." He held up the side-lined pawn. "The rules were never made very clear, and we've only just started to play, but ... " He took a deep breath. "The one time Queen Aleria, your grandmother, saw your mother as a chess piece, she did not see a life force."

"No life force?" What did he mean? That her mother was truly dead? Willow's heart hammered. The seed of hope that had suddenly sprouted there withered. She trembled. Jeez, what was wrong with her? She'd believed her mother was dead for fourteen years now. So why did it hurt so much to think that it was actually true?

"I am sorry, dear." King Ulor patted her shoulder. "I wish I could give you more hope. But it is, I believe, better to be prepared for the worst."

"But how ... how could Queen Aleria know? I mean, what if the captured players just went ... someplace else?" Willow figured anything was possible in this crazy place.

King Ulor sighed. "'Tis possible. But not probable." He replaced the pawn on the chessboard and picked up the White queen. "The Game spell is just like real chess. The Queens have all the power."

A shiver prickled Willow's neck. *The Queens have all the power.* She remembered Nana saying those exact words.

"Queen Aleria has all the magic of Gallandra inside her. She can heal. She can conjure." King Ulor placed the queen piece gently back on her white space. "*And* she can see auras and life forces. So, you are correct. If Aleria did not see your mother's life force, then your mother is either dead or she is not in the playing piece."

Another spark of hope flared in Willow. She squashed it down. This was ridiculous. Her mother was dead and had been for years.

Composed now, she buttered a slice of bread and looked from King Ulor's purple glow to Baldemar's blue one. "Okay, so let me see if I have this straight, then. You're saying that you guys, my father's family, and the Keldorians, my mother's family, have been put under some kind of spell that makes us have to play chess. Only *we're* the chess pieces, right?"

Both King Ulor and Baldemar nodded.

"So right now, you guys, the White side, are losing." She remembered what King Ulor had said about being under siege from King Tarrant. But it didn't make sense. Hadn't she seen kids and animals playing in the courtyard this morning? How come they weren't cowering inside or fighting? "Where is this Keldorian army, anyway? I thought you said your castle was under siege."

"Well," admitted King Ulor, "they did breach Carrus's gates about four days ago. But the castle walls are a different matter. They're twice the thickness. And with no magic in their siege machines, we have at least another fortnight to put your plan into action."

Willow blinked at him. "My plan?" She didn't remember making any plans.

"To queen the Pawn and checkmate the Black King."

"What! You can't be serious," Willow snorted. That's what she'd said to him in his magic chess room. But she'd only said it as a joke. She didn't really think it could work.

"You see," said King Ulor, lifting a white pawn and moving it down to Black's back rank, "if you, as a Pawn, can get *here*, you will become a Queen, just like in an ordinary game of chess. But queening in this Game means more than just extra movement ability. You will have immense magical powers that will allow you to stop King Tarrant from winning." He smiled at Willow and squeezed her fingers. "It's your challenge, my dear. We're all counting on you."

Willow's eyes widened. What was he saying? Did he actually want her to try and *capture* her own grandfather?

"But we, of course, would not want you to harm the Keldorians," King Ulor added quickly. "We only want you to prevent them from attacking us." He took a long sip from his wine goblet. "Your other grandfather," he sighed, "is, I'm afraid, a bit of a hothead. He believes that we were the ones who killed his only daughter — who was a Black Pawn in the Game — to keep her from being queened. Utter nonsense. We all loved Diantha dearly. No one here would have harmed a hair on her head."

"However," interrupted Baldemar, "she was, nevertheless, Captured." He gave Willow an assessing stare. "We suspect enemy spies from the south may have tricked one of our Players into harming her in some way, then planting a bloody knife as evidence. Or ... " a hard glint appeared in his dark eyes, "we may have our own traitor here in the palace."

"In either case," continued King Ulor, "we must get you to Keldoran so you can put a stop to King Tarrant's war, and then we can all decide what to do about Nezeral."

Click. Click. Click. The pieces fell into place. Willow's stomach sank like a rock. Nana's faerie tales, she realized, never *were* faerie tales. They were, each and every one of them, absolutely *true*. The one about Nezeral came flooding back to her in an overwhelming wave.

Nezeral had come to Mistolear from another realm. He

was not like a mortal man. Nana had called him a *fey*, saying that his blood was of the ancients and that, unlike humans, he could live forever.

"He came here, didn't he," she said, "because of King Tarrant?" She needed to be sure she wasn't just making things up.

Both King Ulor and Sir Baldemar nodded. "You know of the summoning then?" asked King Ulor.

Willow rubbed at a throbbing temple. "I think so. King Tarrant was dying, right? I think he had a lung fever. And didn't one of his mages break some kind of ... magic law?"

"Yes, 'tis all true," sighed King Ulor. "Nezeral is an elf prince from Clarion, which is in another dimension from ours, just as is Earthworld. However, Clarion is an upper realm, and both Mistolear and Earthworld are lower realms."

"And you're not supposed to be together, right?" added Willow, remembering one of the laws of summoning. "Beings from the upper realmworlds are not allowed to mingle with beings from the lower." Nana had never said exactly why this was so, but if Nezeral's little *game* was any indicator, Willow could now see why that particular rule was in place.

"The clause to that law, of course," continued King Ulor, "is that if an upper-realm being is summoned or invited to a lower realm, he may choose to come. The great difficulty is that he also may or may *not* choose to leave."

And from Nana's story, Willow knew that Nezeral had definitely chosen to stay. True, he had healed King Tarrant, but then he'd started making outrageous demands. He'd ordered Diantha to marry him, even though she was already engaged to Prince Alaric. And then he'd commanded the king to hand over all his lands and wealth. When King Tarrant refused, according to Nana, Nezeral had offered him a sporting chance. *Pick a game*, he'd said. *If I win, you cede to my demands. If you win, I return to Clarion.* King Tarrant, who was a brilliant chess player, picked chess, but there was no way he could win. It was all a trick. Nezeral never wanted Diantha or the king's wealth. He only wanted a way to make King Tarrant enter into a game. And once begun, King Tarrant was doomed to lose, as the Game itself was rigged by one of Nezeral's spells.

Once King Tarrant lost, Nezeral went back to his initial demands, but the king, backed by his wife, Queen Morwenna, refused. It was just the excuse Nezeral needed. With his awesome powers, he changed both the Keldorians and the Gallandrians into battling chess pieces. For the side that lost, the consequences would be terrible.

The rest of the story gripped Willow. She could hear Nana's lilting voice telling it to her as a bedtime tale:

At the moment the Game spell took effect, all magic was gone from the land, taken from mages and healers and placed into the Queens. But neither Queen Aleria nor Queen Morwenna would use their powers to attack the other. They refused to play the Game and, instead, continued on with their lives and allowed their two children to wed. All went well for the first year. The Queens learned to use their powers and went about their kingdoms helping the sick and needy, casting the crop spells and teaching the people the old ways of threshing and brewing and baking that didn't require magic.

At the birth of their granddaughter, the infant princess Willow, there was great joy in both kingdoms, with two days of feasting and celebrations. But on the fourth day, a terrible tragedy occurred. The princess Diantha was found in her chambers, her body turned into a Black Pawn, lying beside a bloody dagger. Rumours spread quickly, and before King Ulor could send word to Keldoran, King Tarrant had already been informed of his daughter's death. He was told that the Gallandrians had murdered her to assure themselves that she would never reach the back rank of the Game, never be queened. He immediately sent an army to attack Gallandra. Queen Morwenna, despite her grief, tried to argue against it, but it was no use. King Tarrant was like one bewitched.

Queen Aleria and the prince, on their way to explain to the Keldorians what had happened, met Tarrant's forces, were Captured and turned into chess pieces. King Tarrant ordered King Ulor to hand over the child or go to war. King Ulor tried to reason with him, but to no avail. In desperation, he was forced to send his tiny granddaughter and her nurse to another realmworld ...

So there you had it. Willow gulped back tears, fighting to hold onto her calm. She was a three-month-old infant princess from another dimension, trapped by a psychotic elf prince into being a player in a magic chess game, *and* apparently the only one, according to some elf queen, who could break the spell. Nope. Nothing crazy about that. No insanity there.

The king, who had been speaking about his plans for Nezeral, clasped one of Willow's hands, drawing her back to the conversation. He pointed to Sir Baldemar. "Baldemar here," he explained, "is a mage knight. Do you know what that is?"

Willow nodded. In Nana's stories, a mage knight was a very powerful man, skilled both in weaponry and magic.

"Well, then," continued King Ulor, "you would also know what a capable protector he is, so you will have no need to fear for your safety."

"My safety?"

King Ulor continued to squeeze her hand and smiled encouragingly. "The Keldorians," he explained, "are laying siege to the front of the castle, so most of their attention is directed on our north wall. There is, however, a secret postern gate that will allow you and Sir Baldemar to escape unnoticed.

"Varian has been notified by messenger bird ... Oh, dear me, I'm getting ahead of myself. You wouldn't know Varian. Varian is my younger brother, Prince Varian Farrandale. His lands are in Torinth, bordering Thorburn Wood. He will be meeting up with you with a contingent of knights and will accompany you and Sir Baldemar the rest of the way to Keldoran." King Ulor unclasped Willow's hand and leaned back heavily in his chair. "Of course, getting King Tarrant to treat with us will be the hard part. The man's part mule, you must know. But ... " he leaned forward again, a bright gleam in his eye, "do not worry about that, my dear. Once he catches sight of you, looking for all the world like your mother, I am sure he will see reason. Come now, then, enough of this serious talk. Shall I take you for a tour around my castle?"

Willow didn't answer right away. She was still trying to process all this new information. "Ah, you know," she finally replied, rubbing at her temple, "I have a bit of a headache. So if you don't mind, I'd kind of like to just lie down."

"Of course, of course," said King Ulor, helping Willow to her feet. "We'll call Lady Merritt to escort you back to your chamber. And dear, do not worry about the escape. Plenty of time for all that tomorrow."

A wry smile twitched onto Willow's face. *Right,* she thought, *plenty of time for all that tomorrow; that is, if I'm not too busy fighting pirates with Peter Pan or slaying witches with Dorothy.*

CHAPTER 6

THE HEAT FROM THE BLAZING FIRE was beginning to thaw the numb chill from Willow's fingers and toes. She edged to the far side of the mattress, her jaw clenching against the drifting food smells.

She didn't want to be warm. She didn't want to eat. She did *not* want to feel better.

Lady Merritt had just been in, giving her, yet again, the duty-of-a-Gallandrian-princess speech. And then the servant woman had come in with her eat-something-you'll-feel-better one. All afternoon the two of them had been clucking at her like a couple of wet hens, pleading with her to speak to King Ulor, to eat something or to at least try on the jewels and gowns that they'd been trying to bribe her with. It wasn't going to work. She couldn't be bought, or bullied, or shamed.

She took a deep breath and clenched her eyes shut again, whispering earnestly, "I am not in Gallandra. I am on Earth. I am only sleeping, and when I open my eyes, I will be awake and in my own bed." Then, slowly, she peeked out of one eye.

The bright purple and gold of Princess Diantha's bed canopy blared into view. *"Damn!"* she muttered, striking her fist against the mattress. "Damn! Damn! Damn!" Ever since her conversation with King Ulor and Sir Baldemar, a kind of desperate panic had set in. If this were all true, if it wasn't a dream, then Nana really was dead. Instead of letting the pain overwhelm her, she'd been trying to convince herself again that it *was* all only a dream — an incredibly vivid one, to be sure — but still just a product of her own overactive imagination.

She sat up, her mind skirting away from the pesky reality of cold toes and hungry belly. It was not real, she insisted stubbornly to herself. And the sooner she accepted that, the sooner she'd wake up.

Willow grimaced at the stiffness in her neck. She'd been lying in that one rigid position on top of the bed covers, trying to wake herself up, for hours. Her limbs felt like wood.

Another thing, she thought, yawning and stretching her long legs out over the bed, that shouldn't happen in a dream. But maybe trying to wake herself up wasn't the right thing to do. Maybe she needed to find something that couldn't be explained. Something that didn't jive with Nana's stories.

Her eyes flew to the wide-open window at the foot of her bed, shining with light from the white cloth strips that the servant woman had tied to it earlier. What was it Lady Merritt had said about glass? Something about it disappearing when the magic had disappeared, so that now they were forced to use wax-dipped fabrics instead. She went to the window, pressing a cloth corner between her fingers. Crumbly pieces of the colourless wax broke off and fell to the floor.

Willow stared at the cloth, gouging out another wax chunk. Well, that was the first thing that didn't make sense. No magic meant no way for her to be here.

A sudden draft blew cold fingers of air around her face and neck. She dropped the window cloth, turning back to the warmth of the room. Maybe what she needed was to get away from everything. If she could find someplace that seemed reasonably normal, *then* her mind might release itself from the dream. She'd wake up in her own room and Nana would be there and everything would be fine. She crept to the closed door, pressing her ear to the wood.

There was a guard outside her room. She'd heard his armour rattling every time he opened the door for the servant or Lady Merritt. He was still out there. Or someone was. She could hear feet scuffing against the floor. Willow suppressed the urge to scream and stomped back to the bed, angrily kicking over a stool in her path. Something white and gold soared through the air.

"What the ... " she started to say, but then remembered her swan necklace. She'd left it on the stool the last time Lady Merritt had been in. She also remembered the crazy elf queen story Lady Merritt had told her about it. About how she, Princess Willow, had been chosen as a "netherchild" and "gifted" with a powerful elf emblem.

Willow scooped the necklace from the floor, smiling sardonically. *Hey, maybe my elf godmother will help me. Wave her magic wand and send me back to Earth.* She flopped onto the edge of the bed, leaning back against the pillows.

According to Lady Merritt, this scenario hadn't been far from the truth. It had been Queen Cyrraena's idea to send Willow and Nana to Earth in the first place. She had cast the aging spell and she'd been the one to pick Willow as Mistolear's champion in battling Nezeral. Queen Cyrraena was supposed to be some kind of guardian of the place. But Willow didn't know what to think. To her, Queen Cyrraena sounded mental. After all, why would anyone in their right mind pick a baby to be a champion?

Dangling the swan at eye level, Willow frowned. So why hadn't Nana ever mentioned the elf queen or the gift stuff? Elf was just another word for faerie. And back home, Nana'd had shelves overflowing with books on faerie and Celtic legends. So it wasn't like she hadn't had the opportunity. Willow sat back up again. But maybe Nana hadn't known about the pendant, or maybe she'd forgotten because of her dementia. Willow sighed and dropped the chain over her head. She supposed she'd never find out now. She ...

A relaxing and pleasant heat suddenly warmed her skin. Her eyes drooped and a lazy feeling swept over her. Like soaking in a hot tub.

From a distance, she could hear voices outside her room and then the sounds of the guard clanking away down the hall. A soft knuckle-rap to the door broke through her trance, and she opened her eyes. Energy suddenly flooded through her. She felt incredibly alive! Incredibly focused!

The knock sounded again, louder this time. A soft voice spoke from behind the door. "Princess ... are you awake?"

Willow blinked again. *What the heck had just happened?* She pulled out the necklace and held it in her hand. The swan had done something to her. For a minute there, all of her problems had suddenly vanished.

"Princess ... ?"

"Umm. Yes. Yes, I'm awake. You can come in." She dropped the necklace back down her bodice and stood up.

A tall teenage boy hesitantly entered the room, giving her a curt bow.

Willow stared rudely. She couldn't help it. It was like seeing a ghost. And not because of his glowing red skin, either. But because of his short, tight-fitting chain mail, thigh-high leather boots and real sword. It was like he'd stepped out of her imagination. Granted, his hair was brown instead of blond and his boots sagged a bit at the knees, and even she could tell that his sword was way too long for him, but still, there he was, her Dean/Sir Lancelot, big as life. A Sir Lancelot that had just stooped to one knee with his dark, wavy hair falling romantically over his shoulders from his bowed head.

She pulled her eyes away from his long hair and gave her head a little shake. "Okay," she said, turning her attention back to his face. "What's the problem?" The black eyes blinked up at her, confusion written all over them. She was obviously breaching some form of princess etiquette.

"You — you may rise," she tried again, using what she hoped was a princess-sounding voice.

This time he didn't hesitate. He stood up, closed the door, and then came toward her, determination fixed grimly on his face.

Willow stepped backwards. She had just clued into the fact that she was alone with an armed stranger and apparently with no guard outside her room.

The guy went for his sword, suddenly whipping it out of its bright green scabbard and holding it high.

Willow gasped, but just before she could scream, he dropped to one knee again, the sword dropping with him, its sharp tip grating against the stone floor.

"I, Brand Lackwulf," he began loudly, "son of Cedric Lackwulf, lord of Rueggan, and squire to Prince Alaric, do solemnly swear to serve and protect thee, Princess Willow, heir to the throne of Gallandra and Keldoran, for all thy days." He paused for a moment, leaning forehead to sword pommel, and then said dramatically, "I pledge thee my loyalty, my sword, my life."

Willow gaped at the top of his bowed head, limp with relief. *I'm alive! He's not going to kill me.* She heard a creaking sound and saw a leather boot tip jiggling up and down. He was waiting for her to say something again, but this time he seemed totally annoyed.

You may rise, and *Arise, Sir Knight,* didn't have any effect, except to earn her a scathing glare. And, *Please get up. I don't know what to say,* got her a tight-lipped frown.

"Look, Brand or Cedric or whatever the heck your name is," she finally hissed, "tell me what I'm supposed to say and *I'll say it!*"

"*Arise Sir Brand. I accept thy oath of fealty,*" he snarled.

Willow repeated his words and tried not to look nervous when he stood back up and angrily plunked his sword back into the green scabbard. When he turned toward her, though, the sword tip swung out and knocked over a big candle holder at the foot of her bed. Willow bit her bottom lip to keep from smiling.

"You'd best be true in your ignorance, Princess," he warned, straightening his sword with furious dignity. "To mock a knight's fealty pledge is a grave matter."

Fealty pledge! Willow's temper flared. He had nerve. Bursting in here and scaring her half to death and then all but calling her a liar! She'd tell him what he could do with his *fealty pledge!*

Brand dropped his gaze and fiddled with his sword pommel. "I — I gave my squire's pledge to your father," he said quietly. "You are the first to have my knight's."

Willow's sharp retort died on her lips. She could see that this fealty thing was a big deal for him. And now that he was up close, she could also see that he was about sixteen, majorly cute and at least a whole two inches taller than she was. Her ears started to heat up and her stomach quivered.

"Well, I — I really wasn't making fun of you. Where I come from there aren't any knights or squires or kings or anything like that. Nobody makes ... fealty pledges."

He glanced at her, interest sparking his face. "Sir Baldemar told me of your Earthworld. That it has no magic. How might one live without magic?"

"I don't know," said Willow, smiling. "How *might* one live without TVs and telephones and video games?"

Brand looked blank. "Tee-vee?" he said slowly. He didn't try for telephones or video games. "What is tee-vee?"

"Never mind," said Willow, shaking her head. "It's not important." She shifted her gaze around and smoothed out her skirts. "Umm. You wanted to talk to me about something, though, didn't you?" She figured that the king had probably sent him to tempt her into coming down for dinner or that Lady Merritt was on a nag-break.

Brand surprised her by taking her hands in his. "Princess Willow, nobody knows of our meeting, and what I am about to say to you must be kept in the strictest confidence."

Willow stared down at his large rough hands, which were glowing a bright rosy pink. A commingling, she realized, of his red glow and her white one.

"Do you understand, Princess?"

Willow nodded. She didn't, really. But she was mesmerized by how small her long fingers looked against his and how it seemed to make her insides flutter and her cheeks feel red.

"I know the king has shown you the Game and told you of his plans to send Sir Baldemar to Keldoran with you. But did he tell you what position Sir Baldemar plays?"

Willow let her hands slide from Brand's. Just when the dream was getting good, he had to go and mention the dumb game. "No, I don't know his position." She felt anger begin to creep through her. Was that all anyone cared about — the stupid game?

"Sir Baldemar is the king's last Rook. His last Bishop lies abed with a fever. And I am the last Knight." Brand took a deep breath and sighed. "You saw the Game. You know what will happen if he sends his last Rook, don't you?"

In her mind's eye, Willow saw the pieces. The rook and bishop were all the king had left for protection. Use the most powerful one to guard a pawn and the game would be over in a few quick moves. "Yeah, so? He'll just lose the game sooner, that's all."

Brand stared at her in disbelief. "How can you say that? We have to play! We cannot just give up." His nostrils flared angrily and then his eyes suddenly narrowed. "You do not know what shall happen if we lose, do you?"

Willow flounced onto the bed. She couldn't believe this guy! A total, perfect stranger, and he thought he could just waltz in here and tell her how she should think!

"You do not know, *do you?*"

"To tell you the truth, I don't really care." Willow plopped back into her rigid position on top of the bed covers and said in her iciest voice, "You can go now."

Brand folded his arms and stood there eyeing her contemptuously. Finally, he shook his head. "What manner of princess are you? To allow your own kingdom to fall to ruin, when 'tis in your power to save it." He stomped over to the bed and hauled her to the floor by her arm. "Your father would be shamed by your cowardice. But I do not care, and you *will* hear my words!"

"*Ow-w!*" Willow punched at Brand's chest with her free hand. "Let go of me, you jerk! Who the heck do you think you are, anyway?"

Brand grabbed both her arms and pinned them to her sides. "No. Now listen to me. If the Game is lost, the losers become chess pieces. *Permanent* blocks of marble. Do you understand? *We cease to exist!*"

Cease to exist? This boy, and the man who kept telling her he was her grandfather? What if it were true? Their lives were somehow in *her* hands?

Willow twisted away from him. "Stop yelling at me!" Her voice cracked. *He thought she was just a coward.* She felt tears pricking at her eyes. No way! She bit the insides of her cheeks. There was no way she was going to cry in front of this jerk.

"Look, twenty-four hours ago, I didn't even know this place existed. I didn't know about the game. About being a princess. About my parents. Nothing." Brand looked surprised but didn't say anything. She sniffed and blinked back more tears.

"You people are total strangers to me. Yet you *all* expect me to just jump right in and save you. Well, maybe I can't. Or maybe I don't want to. All I really want to do is just leave here." She brushed past him, heading for the door. She'd had it with this place, and she was going to find the king and that Baldemar guy and *make* them send her home.

"Princess ... wait." Brand reached out and held onto her arm, gently this time. "I am sorry. Sir Baldemar said you were to have been trained. That — that you would be ready. But ... "

Willow stopped and turned, not sure if he was sincere or just trying to get her to stay.

"There *is* no way to leave," he said. "You *do* know that, do you not?"

Blood drained from Willow's face. Since she'd arrived here, the thought that, if she really wanted to, she could leave any time had helped somewhat to keep her sane. Her safety net, so to speak. Panic prickled down her spine. *Trapped. I'm really trapped in some crazy, schizoid world!*

"I mean, until Nezeral is defeated, there is no way you can return to Earthworld — or any other dimension, for that matter."

She began to breathe again. Maybe Brand was just trying to scare her. Make it so she'd think she had to follow whatever it was he'd planned. She eyed him suspiciously. "And why can't I?"

"You left the linking crystal in Earthworld," said Brand, sighing as though only a complete idiot would do such a thing. "And unless Queen Cyrraena sees fit to make us a new one, no one shall go anywhere."

It was true. The crystal had been sitting on the night table and, instead of picking it up by the stand and then touching it, she'd just touched it. She glared at Brand and crossed her arms. "And how do I know you're not lying? Just so I'll do what you want?"

Brand's eyes glittered and his voice lowered dangerously. "Very well. Come with me, then. We'll go down to the great hall, and *you* can ask the king and Sir Baldemar for yourself."

Willow didn't like his smug smile. People who knew they were right and you were wrong smiled like that. "Okay, so let's say I believe you. What am I supposed to do? You got a plan any better than King Ulor's?"

"Yes, I do." Brand dropped the smug-smile look. "'Tis why I am here. I will take you to Keldoran myself. If Sir Baldemar is here to protect the king, you and I shall have a much better chance of making it."

Actually, his plan *was* better, thought Willow. At least with a rook and a bishop — albeit a sick one — the king might have a slim hope. And maybe the other side would be so engrossed in trying to trap him, they wouldn't notice an advancing pawn.

"So, okay," she said, "let's say I go with you. What happens if I do get to Keldoran? I'm supposed to get some sort of powers, aren't I? What happens then? I hope you're not expecting me to use them to capture my mother's family?" The king hadn't expected her to, but who knew what dumb boys with swords would do.

"No; certainly not," he snapped. He ran nervous fingers through his hair and looked unsure of himself. "We are going to find Nezeral. It is *him* we want. He is not invincible, you know. He must have a weakness. We shall simply have to find it."

Willow snorted. Yeah, right! Find the weakness of an all-powerful elf. No problem. Piece of cake.

Brand's chin went up and his jaw clenched so that Willow could see deep dimple grooves along each side of his mouth. She knew she'd ticked him off again, but she didn't care. It was funny! She and this teenage wannabe hero were supposed to set off and destroy the evil elf prince. The whole darn thing was just so hilariously funny that she couldn't stop herself from laughing. And she did. She couldn't help it. Too much had happened. She started laughing and she couldn't stop.

Couldn't stop the gasping hiccups and streaming tears — or the big fat thud of her behind hitting the floor.

"Princess, are you well?" asked Brand worriedly. He hunkered down beside her, patting her shoulders, trying desperately to calm her. She supposed he'd never seen a princess sitting butt-first on a floor before, laughing like a fool. Especially about a minute after she'd been close to tears. *Butt-first!* The image only brought on more gales of laughter.

"Oh gods, I — I am sorry, Princess," he stammered. "I did not mean to — to ... Are you well?"

The laughter was beginning to peter out some. Willow slid her hands behind her and leaned back. Was she alright? She shouldn't be, but amazingly she felt surprisingly fine. Weak and light-headed — the way she'd feel after a really good cry.

Hazily, she turned her head toward Brand and saw him staring at her, fear written all over him. He thought he'd caused her freak-out. Willow smiled at him. "I'm okay," she croaked. "I think I just needed a good laugh."

Brand stood up, looking totally insulted. "Well, are you to come to Keldoran with me or not?"

Willow considered his question. It was either him or Sir Baldemar, and, since it seemed probable that she was going to be on Mistolear for awhile, she figured one secret trip to Keldoran was probably as good as another. And there was that tempting dream about riding off with a knight in shining armour to consider. She stared at Brand. No armour. But he did say he was a knight, and his chain mail T-shirt was definitely shiny. Maybe that's what she should do, then. Just go with the flow. Do what they wanted. And then, make them do what *she* wanted — which was to make another linking crystal and send her back home.

"Okay, I'll do it. I'll go with you."

CHAPTER 7

"*I* CAN'T BELIEVE YOU'D FORGET to bring a lantern. It's totally dark in here. We're lost aren't we? How do you know we're not lost?" Willow leaned forward in her saddle, straining her tired eyes. The moon had been close to full when they'd sneaked through the old postern gate. Definitely a bright enough night for seeing clay paths and cobblestone roads. But no, Brand, *Mr.-Know-It-All-Boy-Scout*, had to insist on travelling through a pitch-black forest. Even though for the twenty minutes that they'd been packing up their horses, they had seen neither hide nor hair of any enemy sentry guards.

Willow watched Brand now as he rode ahead of her, a stiff shadow, making clicking sounds to urge his horse forward. He didn't bother to dignify her questions with an answer.

"Princess, I can assure you that you can trust Brand," said an eager voice from behind her. "He knows Ashburn Wood as well as any forester."

Willow turned around in her saddle and smiled at the narrow outline of Malvin Weddellwynd, the mage apprentice, a tall, skinny boy Brand had chosen to take along with them to teach her magic. He wasn't part of the game, but he was so white-skinned that he still appeared to glow. Willow could see him squinting at her, his pale wispy hair illuminating his egg-shaped head.

"Thank you, Malvin. I guess if *you* trust him, then ... " she gave a sigh, "I'll have to, too."

A disgusted snort erupted up ahead.

Willow chuckled. Maybe this was going to be more fun than she'd thought. She wriggled her numb bottom around, trying to get her circulation flowing. But then again, maybe it wasn't any fun. Nothing was worth five straight hours in a hard leather saddle.

"Are you planning on stopping any time soon?" She stood in her stirrups and bounced up and down a few times. "My butt feels like a slab of meat. I need a break."

"We stop outside the forest," Brand replied without looking back.

Willow's lips tightened. "And when exactly will that be? Before or after my butt falls off?"

"See here, Princess," said Brand, gritting his teeth and spinning to face her. He had put some special powders on their faces to counteract the glowing, but even so, his face had a fiery sheen to it. "I am trying to get your *butt*, as you call it, to Keldoran in one piece. And to do that, we need to put at least a day's ride between us and Carrus. Now, *please* stop talking! Ashburn is full of wolves." And, as if on cue, a choir of mournful howls suddenly pulsed through the forest.

Brand grinned maliciously as Willow nervously scanned the forest, and then turned away, heel-kicking his horse to a trot.

Jerk! Pompous pig! she wanted to spit out, but Malvin's broad white forehead bobbed into view, effectively leashing her tongue. "Princess," he said softly, "I know 'tis a long way. If you need rest, give over the reins and lean against your horse. I shall guide you."

Willow smiled gratefully. At least *someone* knew how to be

nice. "Thanks, but I think I'm okay." She didn't mention that she'd rather walk barefoot through live coals than conk out before Brand did.

He still hadn't forgiven her for laughing at him, that much was obvious, and a couple of cracks about how slow and picky girls were had made it so she couldn't forgive him either.

She pulled her cloak edges tighter, snuggling the reins and her cold hands against the warmth of her swan pendant. It was still giving off heat, but it hadn't done the energy jolt thing since she'd last touched it. She peeled off damp leather gloves, alternating her grip between the swan and the reins. She'd sort of formed a crude theory about it: 1 elf-made gift + 1 elf god-mother = 1 princess with a magic necklace. Willow sighed. She wondered just how much help, if any, Queen Cyrraena and her necklace were going to be to them.

Malvin rode up beside her again, holding out a dark object. "A drink, Your Highness? I have mutton pasties, too, if you are hungry."

A ravenous gurgle bubbled up from Willow's empty stomach. She glanced to see if Brand was watching — he wasn't — then took the water skin and two mutton pasties, biting gustily into the greasy little pies. They were cold, but she didn't care. She hadn't eaten meat pie in ages.

Warm, flour-dusted memories and spicy meat smells suddenly flooded through her. Nana had been a magical cook, making everything from scratch with no cookbooks or recipe cards and with lots of secret ingredients. Willow's mouth watered at sugary tart and crusty pie images. And sauces. Nana's to-die-for sauces.

She bit deeply into the second pasty, blinking away tears.

It was weird how one minute she could be fine and then the next filled with so much grief. She drank from the water skin, trying to push thoughts of Nana to the back of her mind. There was no way she wanted to start bawling in front of Brand and Malvin.

The food helped to make her feel better. She handed the skin back to Malvin. "Thanks, you're a real lifesaver."

Even in the dark, Willow thought she could see Malvin's red face. She smiled to herself. At least she wasn't the only one with a blush problem.

They rode a few more hours until the darkness started to thin, spreading to a gloomy grey light. Brand announced the stop and Willow slid from her horse, saddle-stiff and bone-weary, without even the strength to walk the pins and needles out of her sore rump. She barely noticed Brand helping with her horse or Malvin setting up her blankets, just sank into dreamless oblivion.

❦

The next morning Willow awakened to a round of quick sneeze blasts, one after the other, like gun shots. She peered over her blankets at Malvin, sleeve-wiping his dripping nose. "Sorry, Princess. 'Tis my allergies. I didn't mean to awaken you."

"Doesn't matter," said a voice down by her legs. "She must rise now — if she wishes something to eat."

Willow pushed back her covers and leaned on an elbow. A few feet away, Brand was adding dirt to smother a dwindling fire and Malvin was seated on a fallen log, rubbing his hand over a glass ball. Bare-limbed trees formed a dark semicircle around them, with the thick forest on one side and clear open land on the other. The horses milled by the opening, munching on long field grasses.

Brand tossed her a chunk of bread and some cheese. "Here. We are breaking camp soon, so eat up."

Willow scowled at him. "Thanks a lot," she muttered, sitting up and picking dirt specks from the bread. She broke it in half, eating the soft middle part and leaving the crust. Brand rolled his eyes at her and strapped on his huge sword.

"Well, it appears that we have not yet been discovered missing," proclaimed Malvin. "Checked the king, Sir Baldemar, Lady Merritt and the servants. Not a soul knows we've left."

"Check the Black Knights, then," said Brand, "and the rest of King Tarrant's forces."

"No need to worry, Brand. There is no movement on the board, yet. Probably will not start till after we pass through Graffyn."

Willow stared at the round glimmering object in Malvin's hand. "What are you guys talking about? What is that thing?"

"You mean this, Highness?" Malvin held the ball toward her. "'Tis an image globe. It brings up any image you wish to see. Would you like to try?"

Willow nodded and Malvin sprang from the log to sit beside her, pale hair flying and blue eyes bright with enthusiasm, like an overeager science nerd trying to explain one of his lab projects. "You see, Princess, it works quite simply. Merely hold it in your hands like so." He cupped the ball between her two palms. "And imagine what it is you wish to see."

Willow stared into the glass, rubbing her thumbs over it. *My room at the castle,* she thought. *I want to see my room at the castle.* Instantly, colours began to swirl inside the globe, quickly solidifying into the purples and golds of her bed and the greys and orangey-yellows of firelight flickering over stone walls.

"Wow! This is really cool! It's just like watching TV." She held the ball closer, peering through a slit in the heavy bed curtains at the girl-shaped lump that she and Brand had placed under the covers. Didn't look as if anyone had noticed it wasn't her. Hair brush, circlet and food tray were still sitting on the bedside table, food tray still untouched. No, wait. There was something beside it.

"What's that?" Willow pointed at a spot on the ball. "That thing by the food tray?" She could make out a small wood-carved figure with little wings and a body.

"Oh that," said Malvin, squinting. "'Tis only a faerie trinket. Peasants use them for good luck. A servant must have put it there."

Someone had wished her well. Willow felt a small tug of pleasure.

"There's no real magic in them," Malvin went on. "Just superstition and old hags' tales."

Willow looked at the ball in her hands. The colours were beginning to fade, leaving the glass clear again. She frowned. *"This* is magic, though, isn't it?"

Malvin nodded and reached for the image globe, cradling it gently between his fingers. "Truth be told, there's little magic left in the entire kingdom. When the Finder Shadow came, it spell-sucked magic from every nook and cranny."

"The Finder Shadow?" asked Willow.

"'Tis the spell Nezeral used to steal everyone's magic. When it first came across the land, it was like a big black shadow, and every person and mechanism it passed over were sucked dry of magic. Till there was neither mage capable of casting a spell nor any charmed mechanism left in all the land."

"But what about your image globe — and what about the crystal that brought me here? And that — that medallion *thing* Sir Baldemar used when I first got here."

"'Tis a shame," said Malvin, "that you ... aah ... left the crystal in Earthworld."

"What about them?" Willow ignored the soft-pedalled criticism and let out an exasperated breath. "How did they stay magic? Like, how come castle windows disappeared but the linking crystal and your image globe didn't?"

"Oh, 'tis simple," said Malvin. "There're two types of magic. *Intrinsic* and *extrinsic*. This globe is intrinsic." He cupped the ball under Willow's nose. "Magic has become a part of it. Something separate from the mage. Do you see?"

He didn't wait for an answer but stood and began pacing, waving the globe around for emphasis. "Now windows, on the other hand," he paused to look at her. "No, actually, not all windows, but some, are extrinsic. You are doubtless thinking of the castle windows back in Carrus. They are unlike most. Sir Baldemar wrought them cunningly so that they draw heat in the winter and coolness in the summer. Most windows are just ordinary mage glass, but Sir Baldemar's were made with an extrinsic spell that he had to monitor continually. You see, Highness, in this type of magic, there is always a connection between the mage and the object. Anything happens to the mage, like an untimely death or a loss of power — *poof* — whatever was conjured disappears. Have I explained properly, Highness?"

Willow gave him a vague, math-class uh-huh. She understood now why Brand had brought him along. If someone was supposed to teach her magic, she supposed a guy who sounded like a walking textbook was the perfect candidate. But still ... he hadn't answered her question. "You said the Finder Shadow sucked the magic out of people *and* mechanisms." She pointed at the image globe. "So why didn't it suck the magic out of that?"

"Oh, I see what you are speaking of." Malvin nodded in sudden understanding. "When our most important Player, Queen Aleria, was Captured, the elf queen, Queen Cyrraena, realized that we were in grave danger of losing the Game altogether. She smuggled these few magic items to us so that we might survive until you returned. They are, I believe, the only magical mechanisms in either Gallandra or Keldoran."

"Enough now, Mal. End the magic lesson." Brand strode over and handed Malvin a padded sack. "We must reach Graffyn by nightfall."

Malvin nodded and carefully slid the image globe into the sack. "We can speak more of this at lunch time, Princess," he said, adding a shy, "if you like," at the end. Then he bowed and turned away, carrying his globe over to the horses.

Willow wolfed down the rest of her bread, pocketing the cheese remains for later, then yawned, stretched stiff leg muscles, and pulled up the edges of her new leather boots, admiring their soft brown sheen. At least she'd convinced Brand to get her boys' clothing. Camping and horseback riding in long dresses was definitely not her idea of a fun time. She stood up, brushing crumbs from her tunic. And no way was she even going to *attempt* to ride sidesaddle.

"Would Her Highness mind quickening up the pace a

little?" Brand sat atop his horse, glowering down at her. "It would be best to leave before winter sets in."

Willow stuck her tongue out. *Big jerk!* Why had she ever thought he was cute?

She walked toward him, nose held high, smugly aware of how long and trim her legs looked in the dark hose and leather boots. She tossed back her ponytail and pretended not to notice Brand's dark stare.

Ruby, her horse, was already packed and saddled. She neighed softly as Willow scratched her under the noseband of her bridle. "That-a-girl," crooned Willow. "Good girl." She patted the sleek chestnut neck and moved around to Ruby's side, digging in the roomy saddlebag for her gloves. She found them wedged between her laptop and an extra tunic. Impulsively, she lifted out her computer and turned to Malvin.

"Hey, wait a minute," she called out. "Don't put that globe thing away yet. I want to try something first."

Brand glared impatiently.

"Oh, c'mon Brand," she said, refusing to let him intimidate her. "It'll just take a sec."

Malvin pulled the image globe from its padded sack and trailed Willow over to the fallen log. She sat down, opening up her computer and setting it on top of her lap. Of course, there was no place to plug it in, but with a six-hour fully charged battery, she didn't think that would be a problem. Unless something had happened to it going through the portal thing.

Willow crossed her fingers, waiting for all her programs to load up. If her idea worked, maybe she'd find some interesting strategies they could use to end the game. The screen flickered, suddenly brightening into her blue-green Start Menu background. She ignored Malvin's shocked gasp and used her little built-in track-point mouse to open up her chess program.

"Make the globe show you King Ulor's chess set. And then tell me what position each piece is in." She brought up her program's chessboard editor, using it to make an exact duplicate of the magical game being played between King Ulor and King Tarrant. When Malvin finished dictating the positions to her, Willow saved the game and then adjusted it so that both opponents were played by the computer. She made them both average players and then pushed Start.

The three-dimensional pieces moved with amazing speed, making it hard to keep track of who moved where. But within thirty seconds the game was over, with Black winning easily. She opened up the game again, this time making White a pro and Black a beginner. The game took a little longer, about a minute, but the result was still the same — Black winning by a landslide.

Willow sighed. "It's no use. No matter what we do, Black will slaughter us."

"Is the mechanism moving the pieces?" asked Brand, who'd dismounted from his horse and was peering over Willow's shoulder. "Or are you?"

"The computer's doing it right now." Willow adjusted the skill level again, making White a grandmaster and keeping Black a beginner. This time the game lagged on and on as White took forever to make its moves.

Malvin's finger reached out hesitantly and brushed the top of her liquid crystal display screen, making it ripple like silver water. "Magic," he whispered in awe. "But Earthworld is a material realm. How is this possible?"

"It's not magic. It's just a computer. A machine. Right

now batteries are making it work."

"Bat-trees ... " repeated Malvin slowly. "Are bat-trees magic?"

Willow closed the game file and exited out of her chess program. "No," she said, shutting down the computer. "Batteries aren't magic either. They're just able to generate electricity, but only for a short time. So, I don't want to waste them."

"Can this mechanism help us to navigate the Game?" asked Brand. He had a spark of excitement in his eyes that hadn't been there before.

"Don't know," said Willow, shrugging. She couldn't stand his eagerness. Now they expected some kind of techno-magic from her. She clicked the top shut and stood back up. "It can play the game and show moves. Maybe if I keep fooling with the skill levels, it can come up with some new strategies. Ones that no one's thought of yet."

The light in Brand's eyes faded. "No," he said, "you were right the first time. Black is poised to slaughter us. Getting you to Keldoran and trying to stop the war is our only hope." He spun around and quickly mounted his horse. "Hurry. We've lost enough time this morning."

Willow packed up her computer. One minute she was some sort of hero and the next he was yelling at her. Ignoring her screaming muscles, she did a quick, graceful mount up, thankful for once for all those butt-breaking riding lessons she'd had to take every summer.

"Well, come on, then," she whispered, spurring Ruby forward. "Wouldn't want to keep *Sir* Brand waiting, now, would we?" She blinked back tears. Nana wouldn't want her to cry in front of *strangers*.

CHAPTER 8

$\mathcal{B}$RIGHT SUNSHINE. Crystal blue skies. No clouds. No rain. It had been an almost enjoyable day, thought Willow as she pulled her gloves back on. She took deep, earthy breaths. She loved late fall, especially those damp days that were indistinguishable from spring.

Behind her, Malvin was just finishing a twittering flute song that sounded like happy little sparrows singing. Willow turned to smile appreciatively. His flute songs had made for some really great wandering minstrel daydreams. Malvin blushed and smiled back at her. "I'm not very good yet," he mumbled shyly. "Still learning." He leaned down, slipping his flute into the saddlebag, and then checked for the round bulge at the bottom.

Willow sighed. She hoped he wasn't going to bring out the darn image globe again. Every time they stopped for a break, Brand and Malvin ignored her to do their endless boring globe checks.

Of course, the first few times hadn't been boring at all. Lady Merritt finding the empty bed and armoured knights squeezing through the postern gate had been pretty entertaining. And seeing Brand's goofy relief dance when Baldemar made his decision to stay in Carrus was worth a few laughs. But the last twenty times they'd checked, nothing had happened. Absolutely nothing. The globe had focused only on

King Ulor and his sad weary face, which, if Willow was honest with herself, was starting to give her a guilt complex.

Malvin straightened back up and pulled on his cloak hood. *Oh, thank you!* she mouthed, rolling her eyes. He'd left the globe in the bag. She copied him and pulled her own cloak hood low over her face. It was early evening now, and they were at the outskirts of Graffyn. Brand was covering up, too. Through the day he'd explained to Willow the dire situation around the areas that had been affected by Nezeral's game spell. Neighbouring cities like Graffyn that were stuck between the two kingdoms had had *their* magic taken away, too. And even though it had been less than four months since King Tarrant had actually started to play Nezeral's game, it had been over a year since the cities and villages that comprised Gallandra and Keldoran had had any magic.

Willow let her thoughts take her back to Earth. From what Brand and Malvin had said about how the Mistolearians used magic for everything from cooking and cleaning to running machinery, she figured it was probably similar to the way they used electricity back home. A prickle of foreboding went through her. She could well imagine the chaos in her world after a whole year without electricity. And from Brand's stories of sickness, pollution, poor harvests and roving gangs of thieves, she could see that the Mistolearians weren't in any better shape.

True, the queens had magic and had helped out as much as they could. But Brand had said there were dozens of cities and villages between the two kingdoms and thousands of people. The queens couldn't be everywhere at once. And now with the game started and Queen Aleria captured, Queen Morwenna was sticking to Keldoran, and the other

Mistolearians were trapped with no magic at all. Bands of peasants had started converging on the bigger cities, looking for food. Rioting had started. And a black market had sprung up, charging exorbitant prices for everything from boot leather and nails to clean water and food. Willow huddled deeper under her cloak hood. Castle nobles, especially game players, weren't exactly a popular sight.

They started riding again, past black fields and a brown, sluggish waterway, till Graffyn's main city gate appeared up ahead. Willow reined in her horse and stared. Enormous sand-coloured walls loomed ahead of her, spreading out as far as she could see, with roofs and chimneys and pointy spires rising above them.

"Whoa! They go *all* around the city like that?" Willow's hood fell back as she stretched up her arms to the high walls.

Malvin nodded.

"Yes, it intimidates the thieves," said Brand. "Just what the merchants would wish. Graffyn and Carrus are now the main fair cities on the trade routes."

Malvin lifted his head, peeking at Willow from beneath his hood. "They are both very old cities. Their walls were built centuries ago. Most of the newer cities use magic ones. But, of course, since there is no magic, now ... " he swept his hand toward Graffyn, "walled cities are definitely superior."

"Ssh! Enough talk," ordered Brand. "There's the gate-house." He turned to Willow. "How is my glow?" he asked, lifting his hood up to his forehead. "Is it dull enough?"

Willow peered at him. The thick sticky powder that he'd plastered over his face had definitely toned down his red shine, but it sort of made him look like a stage actor with a bad makeup job. She fingered her own cheek, wondering if she looked as waxy. "As long as no one gets too close, you might pass for normal."

Brand frowned and pulled his cowled hood over his eyes. "Keep your head low and covered. And do not say anything." Then he rode slowly toward the gatehouse.

"State yer business," said a gruff voice from high above them. Willow risked an upward glance. A ruddy, broad-faced man wearing an eye-covering helmet stuck his head and a jutting spear tip from the gatehouse opening.

"We're Kernish wool buyers," answered Brand. "Come for the start of the winter fairs." He looked up so the guard could see a small portion of his face. "Hear Graffyn's got the finest wool markets in the kingdom."

"Aye, 'tis true," said the guard. He peered further out the opening, taking in the fine cut of their cloaks and value of their horses. "Yer a bit early for the fairs, though, ain't ye? They don't start till the end o' the month."

Brand's stiff posture relaxed, a friendly smile crossing his face. "Ever been to Kern? Snow starts in early fall and is up to the cold god's armpits by winter."

The guard, who clearly was aware of Kern's arctic reputation, laughed, then turned to the inside of the guardhouse and roared, "Up with the gate, Rolf! We've got some cold Kerns down below."

A clinking, creaking sound accompanied the painstaking rise of an iron-barred gate under the arched gateway. When the bars were fully raised, Brand pranced Dusk, his black warcharger, over the dry moat drawbridge and through the wide passageway that opened onto the cobbled streets of Graffyn. Willow and Malvin followed, slower, and with a little less showiness, peering at thick iron doors and spiralling stone staircases.

They were in the oldest part of the city, where long narrow streets and high, squeezed-together houses choked out warmth and daylight. Willow gasped at the crowded buildings, astonished to see their upper stories leaning together like precarious bookends while their lower levels shouldered the streets like cliffsides.

They rode single file, with Willow in the middle, Brand leading and Malvin bringing up the rear. She glanced nervously from side to side. Garbage lined the streets, emanating an almost unbearable stench. She removed one of her gloves and discreetly inhaled from it, fighting back a queasy stomach knot.

The narrow street wove and twisted, then opened onto a local market square. Willow tentatively sniffed the air. More pleasant odours from cookshops and houses mingled with the putrid stench. She took the glove away, breathing in short shallow gasps.

Market merchants were just beginning to pack up their stalls for the night. Willow pulled back her hood to see their painted banners and bright circus colours. Some people continued to linger and barter, their archaic costumes making them look like rustic actors at a Renaissance fair.

Brand pressed through the crowds, weaving a path through the fruit and pie sellers who shouted their cut-rate prices at them. Fabric vendors caressed shimmering silk with ringed fingers, and black-robed spice merchants held up vials of cloves and cinnamon and gold-coloured saffron. All around them wagons, carts and wheelbarrows creaked along, siphoned with the crowds into narrow little street warrens.

Brand turned a sharp left and headed toward a wide, clean

street at the edge of the market. Other well dressed people, walking and riding horseback, moved in that direction, filing past a clump of destitute-looking peasants.

Willow watched as one by one the townspeople, heads straight, passed them by, ignoring the outstretched arms and wretched cries of, "Alms! Alms for the poor!" Her heart was wrenched at the sight of the thin, ragged children clutching at their mothers' skirts. Brand was riding by like the rest, not looking. Willow dug in her pockets, finding the cheese hunk that she'd stored for a snack. She tossed it to a spidery little girl with enormous eyes.

Three rough-looking men immediately came up to her, hands outstretched, demanding their share. Ruby reared over them and Willow screamed.

Brand and Malvin were at her side in a second, kicking and yelling and pushing the men back. One of the men caught hold of her cloak, almost pulling her from the saddle, but Brand shoved him aside and grabbed at her reins, yanking Ruby's front legs back to the ground.

Then total chaos broke loose.

Guards appeared with short clubs and spears and began beating all the beggars. Ruby reared again and bolted away from Brand. Willow clung to the saddle with one hand, trying desperately to reach her dragging reins with the other. Ruby veered right. Willow went left. Almost. Strong thigh muscles kept her in place until her fingers latched onto Ruby's mane. She hauled herself upright, seizing the saddle pommel like a vise clamp.

By the time Ruby calmed down enough for Willow to retrieve the reins, they found themselves in a dark deserted alleyway, far from the ruckus of the market square.

Willow took deep breaths and waited for her body to unclench. "Oh man," she whispered as she collapsed against Ruby's neck. Sweat trickled down her forehead. Her legs felt weak and slipped limply from the stirrups.

From where she rested, she could see stained walls and black windows with thin jagged bars overtop them. Debris cluttered the street. A plump mouse skittered by, hugging the wall's foundation. Willow popped back up again, scanning all around. *Oh God,* just where the heck was she, anyway? No, never mind that! Where the heck were Brand and Malvin?! Panic jolted through her. It was almost night! She couldn't be lost *here* at nighttime!

A scared moan escaped her lips. *No! Hold on. You're not going to lose it.* She turned Ruby around and backtracked to the end of the alleyway, peering determinedly at the maze of dreary streets.

Darn. They all looked the same. She didn't recognize a single thing that would clue her in as to which one led back to the market. She was either going to have to stay put or ask someone for help. Neither plan was very appealing. Already some more rough-looking men were leering and pointing at her. She chose the road that led away from them.

"Please," she wished, "let this be the right way." She pulled out her swan pendant and repeated the wish, hoping some magic might help her. Nothing happened. There had to be a trick to it. She tried making the wish again, this time closing her eyes. She didn't know what she expected to happen, shimmering lights maybe or a voice or something, but when she opened her eyes, nothing was different.

Ruby snorted impatiently. She was tired and hungry and it was clear she didn't like this dark street any more than

Willow did. Willow stroked her warm neck. "Sorry, girl. I'm tired, too. Don't worry, though. We'll find our way outta here."

Ruby's ears flattened. A dark shadow came rushing around the corner, scurrying and hugging the walls like the mouse had. Willow urged Ruby forward and called out, "Wait. Can you help me? I need to find the market square."

The figure began to run. "No, come back!" cried Willow. She raced Ruby down the street after it. "Please, wait!"

A banshee screech tore through the darkness. "Keep back, ye filthy vermin!" the creature yelled. "I've a sharp blade here, and the wits to use it!"

CHAPTER 9

WILLOW REINED IN HER HORSE as a stout, wild-eyed girl with a heaving chest and stringy blonde hair jumped out of the shadows waving a knife at her. "Stay back, I tell ye! Stay back!" she shouted.

"Hey, take it easy," said Willow. "I'm not going to hurt you. I'm lost. I — I just need directions."

The girl took some deep breaths and looked Willow over from head to toe. Then she lowered her knife, tucking it into an over-tight waistband. "Alright," she said finally, "where're ye headin'?"

"The market square. I got separated from my friends there."

"Well, I'm goin' that way myself. I'll guide ye, if ye like." The girl reached her hand up to Willow.

Willow stared at it — at the thin, almost delicate wrist and the plump, meaty palm — then at the two hundred odd pounds that went along with it. "I — I ... " she stammered. This girl didn't actually think Willow could lift her up onto Ruby?

The girl's hand dropped away, embarrassment staining her cheeks. "The reins," she said softly. "Loosen them, and I'll lead ye."

Willow turned a mortified red and tweezed nervously at a speck in Ruby's mane. *I'm a jerk! A total stupid jerk!* She lowered the reins, wanting to apologize, but a meek "Oh," was all that came out, with a phony, rubber-band smile stretched across it.

The girl chuckled good-naturedly and reached for the reins. "Thought I wanted ye to haul me up, didn't ye?"

Still red-faced, Willow nodded.

"Well, now, don't be feeling bad about it. I know ye didn't mean nothin' by it. Ye don't look strong enough to lift a goose, let alone the likes of me." The girl gave Willow another smile and started leading Ruby down the street.

Willow couldn't help staring at the bulk beneath the girl's coarse woolen cloak. How did people get like that? She glanced down at her own bony wrists and back to the girl again. What did they eat? She remembered the time Abby had tried to help her gain weight. She'd made her eat four huge meals a day with lots of chips and desserts for snacks. But they had given up after only three weeks, when all Willow had gained was a measly two pounds and a zit farm for a face.

"The name's Gemma," the girl spoke. "I'm maid-servant to Mistress Swinton, the wife of Pastry Cook Swinton."

Pastry, eh? thought Willow. That'd help.

"Are ye new to Graffyn, then?" asked Gemma.

"Ah, not exactly. My friends and I are just passing through."

"What's yer name? Ye don't sound like ye're from around here."

Willow hesitated. Was she supposed to say her real name? Brand and Malvin hadn't said anything about disguising it. She decided to stick with the truth. "Willow," she answered.

Gemma threw a skeptical glance over her shoulder. "Willow, is it? And next ye'll be tellin' me ye're a princess or an elf lass."

"What? How do ... What do you mean?"

Gemma rolled her eyes. "Come now, ye're not trying to tell me ye don't know the elvish names, are ye? A babe in a cradle knows that much."

"The elvish names ... ?"

"Aye, ye know — the twelve names." Gemma sang them off like a nursery rhyme. "Zinna and Caltha the lovely flowers, Vinna and Ivy the choking vines. Xylia and Felda are wood and field, Ulva and Fawna the creatures' delight. Willow and Laurel the trees of wisdom, Cynara and Acacia the thorns of pride."

Willow stared. Nana had never told her about any elvish names. Or that Willow was one of them.

"Our own wee princess was a netherchild," continued Gemma. "Named Willow, like yerself."

"*Was?* What do you mean was?"

Gemma threw Willow another disbelieving look. "Where ye been livin', girl? Are ye tellin' me, ye've not heard the rumours?"

"I — I don't know," said Willow. "I just thought she was still alive, that's all."

"Well, that's what King Ulor would have us believe," sniffed Gemma. She turned down another narrow street. "But she hasn't been seen in over two months now, and the Graffyn mages say she's dead. That the little mite wouldn't eat." She bowed her head. "Goddess quiet her sweet spirit," she whispered, touching a fingertip to her lips and kissing it.

"Well, what does the king say?" Willow hadn't counted on people thinking she was dead. It made her wonder about her grandparents in Keldoran, and whether or not they'd even actually believe she was their infant granddaughter.

"Oh, he's not made any proclamation. Keepin' real quiet about it, he is. There's another rumour, though. That's she's been sent to a different dimension. That King Ulor had dealings with the elf queen, Cyrraena."

Willow wanted to ask more about the rumours, but Gemma was already suspicious of her. Another dumb question and Gemma just might decide Willow was a spy or something. "Why do you think the king would hide the princess's death?" she asked instead.

"Wouldn't you, if your kingdom were crumblin'?" Gemma stopped for a second and reached up to pat Ruby's nose. "He's losin' the Game real bad. Lost the Queen and his son. If the people knew he lost his little granddaughter as well, there'd by riots. His only heir then would be his brother, Prince Varian. And believe you me, nobody wants to see that strutting peacock on the throne."

"But if people think she's dead, why aren't they rebelling then, like you said?"

Gemma snorted and started walking again. "They do," she laughed. "Just stay another few days and ye're likely to see one. We have one most every other fortnight. Last one was over flour shortages. The one before that, over leather prices. And now with the war and all, it's only a matter of time before they decide to have one over the king's heir."

"There she is!" roared a familiar voice.

Willow looked up to see Brand and Malvin racing down the street at her, their faces drawn into pale worried masks.

"What were you thinking?" Brand thundered. "Giving food to a beggar, and right in the market square!" A vein popped out on his forehead and a fist smacked the top of his thigh. His horse moved forward a little, nearly trampling Gemma.

"You there!" Gemma exclaimed. "Watch yer mount!"

"And who is *this?*" he asked, thrusting his hand at Gemma. "You know we cannot afford to be trusting strangers. We must ... "

"Brand."

"We must ... "

"Take. A. Downer." Jeez! He was acting like she'd ridden off on purpose or something. "You know, it's not my fault the horse took off!" she yelled back at him. "I couldn't reach the reins after you pulled them out of my hands."

Brand looked ready to spit nails. "And if you had not caused the riot in the first place, I might not have had to."

Willow choked in disbelief. He was blaming her! The only one who'd had the decency to try and do something!

"Umm ... pardon me," cut in Gemma. She stood uncomfortably between their skittish horses. "I'm not one to meddle in another's affairs, so if ye don't mind, I'll be on my way." She handed the reins back up to Willow. "It's been nice meetin' ye, lass. Take good care of yerself."

"No, wait," said Willow. "Can't we at least give you a ride or something?" She ignored Brand's malevolent glare. Gemma was the first person to help her who didn't want something in return. And besides, it served Brand right for trying to blame all their problems on her.

"It's a bit of a ways. And I don't want to trouble you any," said Gemma.

Willow turned imperious eyes to Brand, who frowned and clamped his teeth together, but finally rolled his eyes in mock defeat. "Very well, then," he sighed. "How far?"

"Do ye know Pastry Cook Swinton's shop? On Grand Street, over by the west market?"

Brand nodded and reached out his hand. "Come on, then," he grunted. "'Tis on our road."

The pastry shop sat dark and empty as they rode their horses up to its closed doors and shuttered display windows. The building was three storeys high, and, in the part above the shop, Willow could see a cloudy yellow light flickering behind the windows. Pie smells still clung to the air.

Gemma slid from Brand's horse and thumped to the ground. "Well, thank ye kindly," she said, brushing out her skirts and smiling cheerfully. "Didn't much fancy that walk, I tell you. Streets aren't safe anymore."

Willow dismounted, too, and held out her hand to Gemma.

Gemma gave it a hearty shake and stared up at her. "Good goddess. Ye're tall as a tree. Are ye part giant, girl?"

People said stuff about Willow's height all the time, but weren't usually that direct. Somehow, it didn't bother her. She laughed and clapped Gemma's shoulder. "Listen, thanks for helping me. I'd probably still be lost if you hadn't."

"Ye're welcome indeed, and thank ye for the ride, lass." She pulled away from Willow. "But I'd best be gettin' in now. Mistress Swinton's awaitin'."

Willow hopped back up on Ruby's saddle and waved goodbye.

Gemma waved back. She stood beneath a sign with a pie painted on it. "Now, if ye have time tomorrow, stop by for some pastry. I'll be mindin' the shop myself and mayhap can spare a pie or two." She winked and waved, making the pie sign rattle as she disappeared into the darkened pastry shop.

CHAPTER 10

THE STAFF AND DAGGER was a large inn about a quarter mile west of the pastry shop. Four storeys high and built with its own stables and courtyard, it sprawled along the wide, well-kept avenue bordering the west market and was, according to Brand, the best inn in the city.

Willow had her doubts. From where she stood, just inside the doorway, the place looked like a dive. She curled her nose at beer fumes and sweat stink, peering into the dim, smoky barroom. It was just a thug hangout with booze, loud voices and lots of leather. "What is this?" she whispered to Brand. "A medieval biker bar?"

He didn't answer. He had a stunned look on his face as if he had the wrong address or something. "I do not ... " he began, but before he could finish, a large tower of a man wearing an eye patch and red silk clothing suddenly swooped over him, giving him a hearty shoulder clap that rattled his chain mail.

Stepping back, Willow stared at the big man. Between the eye patch and the gaudy clothing, he looked like a pirate rock star.

"Squire Brand! 'Tis good to see you, lad. I've not seen hide nor hair of a castle swordsman for six months now." He pumped Brand's hand like a tire iron and gave him a gap-toothed grin.

"And how goes it with the king, lad? Does he still stand a chance against Tarrant? The rumours are not good, you know. Not good at all. *Ah*, but where are my manners! We need a drink first. You look near parched." He signalled to a harried-looking barmaid, then pulled Brand into the murky barroom.

Willow followed, sticking close beside Brand and Malvin, blinking as pungent lamp smoke filled her eyes. She slipped her hood back to see better.

"How goes it, lass?" someone yelled out. "Come by me and take a wee drink." A big hairy guy just to the right of her lifted his mug and made a gross smacking sound, puckering his lips like a fish.

She glared at him. *As if,* she thought, flipping him her finger. Only thing worse than a jerk was a ...

A hard arm suddenly shot out and knocked her back. Brand was in front of her, pulling out his sword, and Malvin was behind her, keeping her from falling. Pirate-Eye was blocking Brand, trying to prevent a brawl.

"Do not worry, lad," he said. "We are well prepared here. Your lady friend has nothing to fear." A finger snap and another hand signal produced three heavily armed men who hustled hairy-smacking-guy out the door.

Pirate-Eye smiled another gappy grin and then held back a doorway curtain for them. He led them down a hall and into a small private room decorated with furs and different types of wooden crossbows. A table and four chairs sat in a corner, and a warm fire burned in the hearth.

Not exactly the Ritz, but definitely a step up from the boozepit next door. Willow pulled off her cloak and took a seat close to the fire, crossing her arms and stretching out her stiff legs. Brand and Malvin did the same, collapsing in their chairs with thuds and tired groans.

"Looks as though you have had quite a journey there, Squire," said Pirate-Eye, smiling. "Nothing, o' course, that a cold ale tankard and my Marta's quail stew wouldn't fix up. Rest yourselves, then, and I'll be back in a wink."

Willow waited till he closed the door, then turned to Brand. "*Squire?* I thought you said you were a knight?"

A sullen red crept over Brand's face. "'Tis in the Game that I am a Knight. And I would be a knight at court as well, except for ... " He paused, undoing the clasp of his cloak. He let it fall against the chair back.

"Except for ... ?"

"Except for nothing! Stop plaguing me with your endless questions!"

Willow glared at him. In the last hour she'd been mobbed, lost and sexually harassed. She'd definitely reached her crap limit for the day. "Jeez! What *is* your problem?! You've been nothing but a big stupid pain since we left the castle. And I'm sick of it! And I'm sick of you! In fact ... " righteous indignation was beginning to grow, "I think I'd rather just return to Carrus!" She shoved back her chair and started to take a step toward the door but found that her whole body had suddenly frozen as stiff as a statue.

Brand and Malvin watched her curiously, both waiting for her to do or say something.

"Can't ... *move*," Willow finally managed to croak. "Something's wrong." Her eyes circled wildly around the room. "Brand! Help me!"

Brand quickly jumped to his feet. "Calm yourself, Highness. I think I know what it is." He stood in front of her and told her to take deep breaths.

Willow inhaled and exhaled until she could do it without hyperventilating. "Okay, now what?"

"Repeat after me," said Brand, *"I am going to Keldoran."*

"What?" said Willow, staring at him in disbelief. "I'm, like, *paralyzed,* and you want me to change my mind about Carrus?! Are you nuts?!"

Brand shook his head and clutched her shoulders. "Listen to me," he said, looking straight into her eyes, "it is that you are a Pawn in the Game. Pawns cannot move backwards. So, if you wish to unfreeze your body, say *I am going to Keldoran.*"

"I am going to Keldoran," said Willow through gritted teeth. Instantly, she felt her muscles and joints loosen and she fell forward. Brand steadied her, but Willow pushed him away and stomped over to the fireplace.

"You knew about this all along, didn't you?" she spat at him. She swore beneath her breath, kneading an angry foot into the flagstone hearth. *Damn. Damn. Damn.* She glanced over at Brand and Malvin and their sheepish faces. Unbelievable. Those two rats planned this, and now she was stuck here whether she wanted to be or not.

Willow kicked another hearthstone, ready to give the two boys a furious tongue-lashing. But just then Pirate-Eye burst through the door, carrying a huge platter of food. "Alright, my friends! Feast first and we'll chew the fat later."

"But first of all," said Brand, leaning back in his chair and avoiding Willow's evil look, "explain to us this new brand of customer, that rabble out there."

"Ah Brand, my lad," sighed Pirate-Eye. He smoothed out his grizzled beard. "Things have changed since your last visit, I fear. All my fine mage-brewed ale is gone. The only stuff that I have now is what I can brew myself, and, as you know, 'tis not fit for human consumption. Only that lot out there," he poked his thumb behind him, "will drink it. And rabble or not, I still need gold, or copper at least, to fill my purse." He noticed Willow lurking over by the hearth. "Now lad," he boomed, "shall you introduce me to your friends, here, or must I do so?"

Willow found herself pulled back to the table by an over-exuberant shoulder hug and deposited back into her chair, as Brand made the round of introductions. Despite her foul mood, she listened with interest to their host's colourful history.

Pirate-Eye, whose name was actually Trumble Quillondale, had been an arms master who'd ridden in King Ulor's army, a captain of his guards and even, at one point, the king's own personal protector. He'd been Brand's first sword and lance teacher and one of the best horse trainers in three kingdoms. The inn, which he now ran with his wife and four daughters, had been his retirement gift from the king.

Trumble raised a mug to Willow. Brand had just told him the truth about her identity, and, to his credit, she'd only caught a slight widening of his good eye and a minimal cough. "Well then, Princess," he said, bowing his head respectfully. "I would like to drink to your good health. And may the gods be with you on your quest." He took a deep swallow from his cup and slammed it to the table, urging them all to drink up. Brand and Malvin smiled weakly. They clicked mugs, then let them drift back to the table.

"You do not think that I would give you the grog that's out there, now, do you? This is the real stuff, lads. I've still a small cache hidden away. Just enough for a treat every now and then. So drink up! You're not likely to find another mage-brewed ale till you reach Keldoran."

Willow sniffed at the white foam in her mug. Didn't they have a drinking age here? This was the second time in two days that an adult had given her liquor. She watched Brand and Malvin quaff back theirs and took a small sip. Cold bitterness filled her mouth. She grimaced and swallowed it down, not wanting Trumble to notice her distaste.

The quail stew, however, was different. It went down fast and easy, like a hamburger and a side of fries. She shovelled it in, savouring juicy bits of meat and soft chunky vegetables, amazed at what being outdoors could do to the appetite.

An hour later, after a tasty dessert and a hot bath, Willow found herself tucked into a cozy, clean bed, playing a game of chess on her laptop. She stared at the computer screen, shocked by the Black queen's death shriek. Crimson silk billowed all around her as she fell to a chess square. The fair-haired White queen, wearing pale blue and holding a laser beam sceptre high in the air, stood over her a moment, then lowered her arms. The White queen resumed her dignified stance, watching impassively as the Black queen vanished from the board.

Sickened, Willow quit the game, not bothering to save it. Her grandmother was the Black queen. She'd just killed her grandmother.

Willow snapped shut the lid of her computer. She'd brought the laptop out to fiddle with the strategy again, only this time she'd let herself play both sides, making sure that Black made stupid moves until she and Brand had reached the back rank. Then she'd started playing for real, using her new queen like a mob hit man. But the scream had stopped her, reminding her of something she was trying to avoid thinking about. *King Ulor thought death was the only way to capture.* A cold chill ran up her spine. She shoved the laptop under the bed, hoping she'd never have to test that particular belief.

Yawning, Willow snuggled back beneath her covers, burrowing her head into the soft pillows on top of her feather bed. She smelled the fresh spot where her damp hair had just been. Well, there was one thing to be glad about. At least she was clean again. It'd taken over an hour of toting and heating, but Trumble's wife and two of his daughters had managed to ready a bath for her. She stretched her toes down into the coolness of the sheets then huddled them back up beneath her shift. She hadn't realized how much dirt and stink could accumulate in two days of horseback riding. Or how much her morning showers had been taken for granted.

She turned over onto her back again, then to her other side. She still couldn't fall asleep.

Toss. Turn. Toss. Turn. Willow tried sticking her head under the covers. She tried clamping her eyes shut. Part of her sleep problem, she realized, was due to her other problem — the glow problem. Her bath had washed away the sticky powder stuff that Brand had plastered over her and now her skin was as bright as a nightlight. Every time she closed her eyes, it was like trying to sleep with the morning sun shining in her face.

Finally she sat up, looking around at the bare, white-plastered room. The other part of her problem was her grandfather's worried face. She'd been trying to forget about it by playing chess, but obviously that hadn't worked. Guilt crept through her again. King Ulor had looked so weary in the image globe. Weary and worried.

She stared into the fireplace, watching golden flames lick

around the log pile, wondering what Nana would say about all this if she were still alive. Willow smiled. There'd be a lecture first, of course, about the perils of running away and worrying your elders. Then there'd be the dire don't-slouch warning. Willow pulled back her shoulders. And then the You're-A-Kingswell speech followed by Kingswells-can-do-anything-if-they-put-their-minds-to-it.

Willow felt her shoulders slump again. Nana had always been overconfident of Willow's abilities. Always so sure of her strength. It had been hard to contend with sometimes, having to live up to all that expectation. She'd never wanted to disappoint Nana.

Fat, slow tears began to trickle down her cheek. She missed Nana so much. Missed her warm comforting hugs and practical advice. Willow clenched her body at the sudden pain, struggling to control it. But a sob escaped, and then another, and she finally gave in, crying her rage and pent-up grief.

A little while later, a light tap sounded on the door. "Princess? Is everything well? Do you need anything of me?" It was Malvin. For a second she wondered if he'd peeked at her with the image globe, but then she remembered that he and Brand were right next door. He'd probably heard her.

"No, I'm fine."

There was a long pause, and then she heard the door open.

"Might I ... might I speak to you for a moment?" Malvin's frizzy head poked through the opening.

Willow sniffed and wiped at her eyes. "Look, I'm kind of tired right now. And ... "

"'Twill only take a moment."

Sighing, Willow nodded and pulled her covers up around her neck. Malvin stood at the edge of her bed, eyes pinned to the floor in embarrassment. Willow almost felt sorry for him. "Listen, if it's about the backwards thing ... "

"What you said downstairs is true," Malvin blurted out. "Brand and I both knew Pawns were not able to move backwards. And 'twas deliberate that we did not tell you about it. But we were not trying to deceive you, I swear it!" He raised earnest blue eyes to Willow and clasped his hands together, panting nervously. "Our plan was to tell you tomorrow. A-after we left Graffyn."

"Malvin," Willow smiled gently at his worry-stricken face, "calm down. It's okay. You don't have to do this." She reached for his hand and made him sit beside her on the bed. "I mean, I know why you guys did it. I understand about protecting the king and everything. If you'd told me, I probably wouldn't be here right now."

Malvin lowered his eyes again and picked at fringes on the bedspread. "Are you ... will you then still come with us to Keldoran?" he asked. His gaze stayed pinned to the bed fringes.

Willow stared, surprised at his question. *There was a choice?* A fireplace log shifted suddenly, crackling and shooting off flickering spark trails. Of course, thought Willow, her attention drawn to the fire's warm glimmer. She could stay here if she wanted to. Trumble would look after her. She looked around the room again, at the clean white walls and the comfortable feather-stuffed bed. The lemony scent of Mrs. Quillondale's freshly scrubbed floors and linens filled her nostrils. Yeah. She wouldn't mind staying here at all.

"Princess ... ?" Malvin was looking at her, waiting for an

answer to his question. Willow rolled her eyes. She couldn't say no to him. Not when he reminded her of a sad-eyed basset hound. "I ... I," she stammered, but then something else occurred to her. *Where the heck was Brand?* And why wasn't *he* in here apologizing, too?

"Where's Brand?" She narrowed her eyes, steeling herself against Malvin's niceness. "Does he know you're here? No; let me rephrase that. Did he *send* you in here?"

"I ... I ... " Now it was Malvin's turn to stammer. He swallowed hard, making a harsh little choking sound.

"I *knew* it!" Willow huffed, slamming her hands against the bedspread. "He knew I'd tell *him* to go jump in a lake, so he sent you instead. Well, you can tell him ... "

"Princess, wait," Malvin said, interrupting her tirade. "Yes, he did indeed send me in here. But that does not change things." He gave her that soulful basset hound look again. "If you do not come with us, it will be but a matter of time before King Ulor's men find you, and then Sir Baldemar shall force you to go with him."

Willow fell back into her pillows. Her grandfather's weary face had popped into her head again. "Fine! You can tell Brand that I'll go. But he'd better watch his step." She stared down the tip of her nose, watching Malvin's quailing fuzzy head nod up and down. Jeez! Being angry at Malvin was like trying to be angry with a puppy. She couldn't do it.

"Listen," said Willow, her voice softer. She sat up and touched the top of Malvin's hand. "I'm not mad at you, okay? I'm just ... I don't know," she sighed. "It's been hard for me here. It's been a hard time."

Malvin smiled shyly and looked into Willow's face. "'Tis the right choice you have made," he whispered. "Now, we should be getting to sleep. Another long day awaits us."

Flickering light from the fire turned Malvin's hair into a golden halo, making him appear like an angelic Einstein. Willow smiled back at him. She wondered if she would've been friends with him on Earth. Probably not. She would've thought he was too geeky. She studied her glowing fingers as they lay on top of Malvin's. For the first time she was glad she wasn't on Earth.

"Goodnight, Princess." Malvin withdrew his hand and stood. "Sleep well."

"Malvin?" Willow squinted up at him. "You and Brand are friends, right? How did ... I mean ... how did you meet?"

Malvin stood silent for a moment and then sat back down on the edge of her bed. "Is it how we met that you wish to know? Or is it how someone like me might be friends with a person like Brand?"

Willow felt her cheeks redden. "Umm ... well, now that you mention it ... I — I mean, you are really ... different." Dang! That didn't sound right. She wondered if her glow meant that her face was even brighter than it felt.

A big grin spread over Malvin's face. "On Earth is that what they would call me — *different?* 'Tis not so bad. 'Tis much better than *freakish weakling* or *Malvin the Milksop.*

Willow grimaced and hung her head, picking at the wool lint on her blanket. "Well, I don't know about that." She side-glanced at Malvin. "They used to call me *Willow Weenie* and *Spaghetti Girl.* So I'm sure they would have come up with something equally clever for you."

"Yes," nodded Malvin, smiling. "In all the worlds some things remain the same."

"So, you and Brand. You, like, met at the castle, right?"

"Yes, but 'twas in the stables, in fact, up to our elbows in horse dung."

"What!" Brand shovelling horse poop! Now that was a scene she could enjoy picturing.

"We were both twelve, and 'twas our first day of training. He was a page training to be a squire, and I was a first-year apprentice training to be a mage. How was either of us to know that a student couldn't correct a headmaster in front of the class, or that knocking a fellow page unconscious with a well bucket was not permitted?"

Willow blinked and nodded. "Uh-huh. Good first day of school," she dead-panned.

"Very much so," said Malvin, laughing. "Plus, 'twas late summer and the stalls were full to bursting with visiting courtiers' horses. If not for magic, I fear our mucking-out punishment would have lasted a full two days."

"What do you mean? You mean you magicked out the horse poop?"

Malvin nodded. "And not a headmaster suspected a thing. You see, apprentices aren't supposed to know how to work their powers. But no one knew that I had learned at home with my older brother's cast-off magic books."

"Wow! So you made it disappear, just like that?"

"Not all of it. We saved a bit for the bed of the page who'd called Brand a greenhorn clodpate. And I saved a chunk for Headmaster Ewert's morning walk around the courtyard."

"Malvin, I never knew you were such a shit disturber. And I mean that literally!"

"Yes," grinned Malvin, "I have many talents you know nothing of." He stood back up and leaned close to Willow, a serious look on his face once more. "'Tis four years now that

Brand and I have been friends," he said, tucking blankets up around her chin. "And he's always been true. If you give him a chance, he shall not disappoint you."

Willow brushed hair out of her eyes and regarded Malvin skeptically. "Well, I'm not making any promises, but I'll try and get along with him."

"'Tis all anyone can ask, Your Highness." Malvin bowed to her and said goodnight, and then he left, closing the door behind him.

Willow yawned and nestled her head deeper into the soft feather pillows. Maybe Brand wasn't so bad. Malvin sure stuck up for him. And if *he* liked him ... She felt her eyelids begin to droop, her thoughts floating away and scattering.

Just before she fell asleep, she saw Brand sitting on a white horse, wearing gold armour. He was holding a gauntleted hand out to her and smiling with teeth so white that they blinded her. She raised her hand, but as she reached out to him, he vanished.

A pair of huge eyes blinked open in the dark space where he'd been. They stared mockingly at her for a moment then winked shut, leaving her in darkness. Her dreams after that were of skittering mice and eyes — hungry, wild eyes.

CHAPTER 11

WILLOW WOVE HER FINGERS together, careful not to rub off any of the thick, sticky makeup powder she was wearing again. She waited in tense silence for Brand to agree to the terms of her peace treaty. Malvin had already accepted, but Brand was busy staring into his eggs.

It had been a long, mostly sleepless night. She'd had lots of time to sort through her feelings and make sense of them. And somewhere between the hungry-eye dreams and watching the fire burn, she'd decided to make the best of things. She knew it was what Nana would have wanted — what Nana had sacrificed her life for. If she hadn't left Mistolear to take care of Willow, Nana would still be a feisty woman in her sixties. She'd given everything up so Willow could become the princess she was meant to be. And Willow was determined now not to let her down.

The peace treaty was her first attempt to change things, but so far Brand hadn't gone for it. Willow watched him from the corner of her eye as he continued to study his eggs. Finally, he rolled his gaze up to meet hers.

"I accept," he began slowly. "But first ... I wish to apologize. I — I acted badly last night."

Willow smiled her relief. "It's okay," she said, reaching out her hand to him. "I wasn't exactly at my best, either. But from now on, we're a team, right?"

Brand's warm powdered fingers gripped hers, sprinkling a dusting of makeup over the table. He grinned at her sheepishly, nodding his head. Malvin raised a water glass and said, "To the quest!"

Willow laughed, a heavy weight suddenly dissolving. Now that she'd made up her mind to accept the reality of her new life, her imagination had been working overtime, turning every bad thing that'd happened so far into an exciting adventure. "So, what's the plan? Are we heading for Keldoran today?" She moved in closer and the three of them pressed their heads together.

"We shall need to pick up supplies first," said Brand.

They had a small argument about whether Willow should accompany them, but in the end she won out. The three of them, along with two of Trumble's bulgy henchmen and a pack horse, strolled over to the west market, where they purchased vegetables, dried fruits and meats, nuts, flour, oatmeal and several small packets of spices. Brand also selected small blades for Willow and Malvin that could be concealed in their boot tops, and slim ivory-handled daggers for their belts.

Willow rested her hand on the hilt of her new dagger, surprised that she liked its cool smooth feel against her palm. She hadn't wanted the knife. The thought of stabbing into someone's flesh sickened her. Yet knowing it was there, close to her fingertips, somehow reassured her.

Her eyes roamed over the other people milling in the market square. A sparse crowd today, due, no doubt, to the overabundance of threatening guards positioned along the streets and between the merchant booths. She bit into a pear that Brand had handed to her, wondering what had happened to all those poor hungry people that had swarmed her yesterday. She'd asked Brand about them this morning, but had only gotten a shrug and a disinterested, "'Tis not my business."

Juicy sweetness filled Willow's mouth as she chewed thoughtfully on the pear. Maybe she could get Brand to buy some extra food and donate it to a shelter or something. Her gaze fell to the purse of dwindling gold coins buckled to the side of Brand's belt. She sighed. Every purchase he'd made had cost them dear. There was no way he'd be open to any suggestions of charitable giving.

They rounded a corner leading away from the market. All the extra guards must have been making Brand feel they were somewhat safer than yesterday. He was actually leading them somewhere fun, the place where the gamers and street buskers entertained.

Lively music and the smell of fried pastry in the air jogged Willow's memory. She remembered her one and only trip to the Home County Fair and Exhibition with Nana. There'd been crowds, rides, bright kaleidoscopic colours and lots of people trying to sell stuff. Busker Alley reminded her of that.

Their first busker stop was an emaciated contortionist. Willow stared at him in horrified fascination. "That-is-so-gross! I can't even watch it." She shielded her eyes, blocking out the hand-walking man with his legs wrapped impossibly around his neck.

Brand laughed and steered her in the direction of a shrill chittering sound. "Take your hands away. Don't be concerned; you'll like this one."

Willow peeked between her fingers and squealed her delight as a tiny monkey dressed in a silver vest and hat danced and scampered on a little red stage. His owner was decked out in a matching silver outfit and played reedy music from a bulbous flute. Brand and Malvin tossed copper coins onto the stage and laughed as the monkey ran around, scooping them up in his little pillbox hat.

After a bit they moved on, passing by the fire-eaters, the jugglers and a red-footed coal-walker. Willow noticed a huge crowd gathering at a wooden platform at the edge of the market. "Oh, let's go see!" she begged. "I bet it's dancing bears or something!"

Brand grinned and signalled Trumble's men to guide the pack horse over to the stage. Willow smiled back and felt her cheeks flare as Brand's arm went protectively around her waist.

Shyly, she glanced at him. His long dark hair was tied in a tight ponytail. She could see the brightness in his black eyes and the cute curve of his smile. She marvelled at the change in him. Since their peace treaty, he'd been downright nice to her.

"The king cares not!" someone roared out, startling Willow from her Brand assessment. "Our children starve. There're blighted crops and no guild work. And what does the king?"

Willow blinked and looked around in confusion, wondering where the voice had come from. Brand pointed at the stage. She could see the speaker now. A short, heavy-set man, dressed in rich fur-lined clothing. Not exactly the destitute beggar she'd been expecting. "I shall tell you," he yelled. "He wars with the Keldorians to ruin us!" A skeptical murmur went through the crowd. "You believe not?" The man shook his gloved fist at them. "Who Captured the Keldorian princess? Who conspires with that elf witch, wagering his own granddaughter?" More murmurs. "'Tis King Ulor, I tell you, that we must blame for our troubles! King Ulor and his band of Game Players." This time a few cries of approval came from the crowd.

The man continued on, railing against King Ulor like a fiery evangelist against the Devil. Brand touched Willow's arm. "We must leave here at once. I know that man. He is ... "

Suddenly there was silence all around them. The man on the platform pointed accusingly. "See there! *See there!* 'Tis the White Knight! One of the Game Players! Arrest him! He will be our persuasion for the king. Our opening gambit!"

A group of men in the crowd sprang forward.

Brand didn't say a word. He grabbed Willow's hand. He didn't look around. He didn't hesitate. He just ran for everything he was worth.

CHAPTER 12

WILLOW STRUGGLED FOR BREATH, her heart beating frantically as she and Brand rounded a street corner. "Wait! I need — I need to stop." She tried to pull free from Brand's firm grasp, but he held tighter, dragging her along after him.

"I have a plan." He glanced back to make sure Malvin was keeping up, then pulled her even harder.

A blur of shops and startled people raced past Willow as she brushed sweat from her eyes and struggled to keep up. For the last five blocks, they'd managed to outdistance their pursuers by weaving in and out of dark alleys, but in the process had lost Trumble's men and the pack horse.

"Catch the White Knight!" someone cried.

"They're just up ahead!" yelled another.

Willow staggered and pressed a hand to her painful side, alarmed that the voices were sounding closer.

"We are almost there. Come now; you can do it." Brand slowed down a bit, helping her to catch her breath. Then a little further down the street, he yanked her and Malvin through a side door, closing and barring it from the inside.

Willow, aware of nothing but a pleasant smell, sank to the floor, gasping and wheezing. Malvin keeled over beside her.

"Good goddess!" cried a familiar voice. "Ye look as if the seven beasts of hell are chasin' ye!"

Willow looked up to see Gemma come bustling round a

floury countertop. Gemma squatted down beside her, trying to help her up. "I can't." Willow pulled away and flopped bonelessly against the closed door.

Brand, who'd somehow managed to stay on his feet, assisted Gemma in hauling Willow and then Malvin to standing positions. "We need a place to hide," he told her. "And quickly!"

"They've ducked into a shop!" came a loud yell. "You check that side. We'll check this one."

Gemma peered out the window for a moment, then turned back with a determined look on her face. "Come on. We can use the smugglin' bins." She led them to the rear of the pastry shop where six large wooden barrels lined a side wall.

"Hunker down real low. And I'll put the flour pans overtop ye." She pulled a lid from one of the bins and lifted out a round, basket-shaped pan full of flour, explaining that Master Swinton used the barrels for hiding black-market mage ale.

Willow climbed into the first barrel and Gemma replaced the flour pan, plunging her into darkness.

"Ye see," explained Gemma in a muffled voice, "the pan makes it appear as if the barrel's full to the brim with flour." Willow heard thunking noises as Gemma helped Brand and Malvin into their barrels and replaced the lids.

"Now, just keep quiet in there." Floorboards creaked as Gemma moved across the room. Willow heard the door bar lift and Gemma's spry steps behind the counter. She shifted carefully in the narrow barrel, her knees and arms straining uncomfortably against her chest, her face twisting at the sour smell of old mage ale and the wet feel of it seeping through the seat of her pants. Small bits of flour sprinkled down from the flour pan, resting like white dust against her shirt sleeve. She peered at the bright specks, suddenly realizing that it wasn't just her game-glow that was casting light. There were tiny cracks along the barrel's upper portion where the damp leather lining didn't quite reach.

Willow moved herself up to a squatting position, pressing her eye to one of the narrow openings. She could see the door and part of Gemma's display window.

Two men — one tall, the other short — and a pimply teenage boy suddenly burst into the shop. "Have ye seen the White Knight, girl?" said the shorter man, breathless from running. "He's dressed in black like the knave he is, and runnin' with a red-haired witch and a tall, thin-legged lad."

"The White Knight?" echoed Gemma, true surprise in her voice.

The pimply-faced boy pushed forward, his eyes bright with excitement. "Aye, Lord Radnor's callin' for his arrest."

Willow thought she heard a doubting snort come from Gemma.

"Well did ye see him or not, girl?" growled one of the men, the tall one this time. "We've no time for yer prattle."

"Nay," said Gemma. "I been here the whole mornin' and haven't seen a soul run by but a messenger lad or two."

The tall man grinned dangerously. "Ye won't mind us takin' a little look-see then, will ye?" Willow saw him scan the back room, his eyes settling on the barrels. He strode across the shop, not waiting for Gemma's permission.

Willow ducked away from the crack, her body quivering with fear. They'd called her a witch. Did that mean they really thought she was one, or were they just calling her something mean? Either way, she doubted her treatment would be any better than Brand's if she were caught.

Wood thunked and scraped as lids were lifted and quickly replaced. "Nothin' but flour," spat the man. "C'mon, lads. Let's check the shop next door." The floor trembled beneath his stomping footsteps as he and the other men left the pastry shop.

"Good," Gemma whispered, coming across the room, "now it's safe to come out." She pried the lid from Willow's bin and pulled out the flour pan.

Willow squinted from the sudden brightness and stood up, stretching out her cramped legs and taking deep breaths of the fresh air. Gemma hurried to the barrel next to hers and freed Malvin, who came up sneezing in short, rapid bursts.

"Gods! 'Tis lucky ... *achoo* ... I can hold my — my ... *achoo* ... breath for so long."

Brand came up next, covered head-to-toe in chalky white flour, his coated eyelashes blinking like powder puffs. "I do believe mine had a leak," he said dryly, brushing away flour.

Willow coughed a chuckle behind a closed fist.

"C'mon, c'mon," Gemma said. "The master'll skin me if the shop's closed for more 'an a minute. Ye can hide upstairs till the ruckus dies down."

"Is there a rear door?" asked Brand. "We could probably circle back round to Trumble's now."

Gemma shook her head. "Nay. They've left men behind to watch the shops, and no doubt they're watchin' the alleyways as well. Yer best bet is to hide out here till it's safe." She grabbed a pie off the countertop and headed toward some stairs.

Brand hesitated a moment, then followed, shaking a huge flour cloud from his head as he went. Willow and Malvin, both trying to contain their laughter, straggled behind him, leaving smudgy prints in his flour trail.

The room Gemma led them to was small and dingy, little more than an animal stall. Willow wrinkled her nose at a shabby rag bed in the corner, wondering how anyone could sleep on it with all the straw sticking up through the rips in the fabric. Malvin started sneezing again. Dust was thick in the air, dancing in thin light shards that squeezed through cracks in the window shutters. The floor was dirty, too, and had gaping spaces between the boards.

Gemma beckoned them in. "Ye'll be safe enough here," she said, pushing a basin off a rickety chair and setting down the pie. She turned to them with a worried frown. "The master'll be home soon. Ye mustn't make any noise, or he'll have me guts for garters." She backed toward the doorway. "Now, help yerselves to the pie. And I'll keep me eyes open and let ye know when it's safe."

Willow watched her close the door and listened to her footsteps thumping down the stairs. Brand went to the one tiny window in the room and carefully opened a closed shutter.

"She's right," he said. "There are two men searching the alleyway." He slipped the shutter closed again, leaning his head against the wall. "I am sorry. This is all my fault. I swore an oath to protect you, but I've done naught but lead you into danger." His chin fell to his chest. "You may wish, Princess, to wait for the king's men. 'Tis better that you have a contingent of knights to escort you."

Willow gaped at Brand. She didn't know what to say. She'd never seen him act this way before. "But I thought," she began slowly, "I thought you said we couldn't leave King Ulor unprotected. He needs those knights. He's under siege, remember." She pressed her hand to Brand's arm. "We can do this. I know we can."

"She is right, Brand," added Malvin. "We cannot turn back. We are past the area of battle now, and once we are past Graffyn, there's but Thorburn Wood. Then the worst will be behind us. And besides, what happened at Thorburn ... "

Brand whipped around, grabbing Malvin's tunic front. "Don't!" he said, gritting his teeth. A tearing sound came from the fabric, which seemed to make Brand come to his senses. He quickly let go of Malvin's shirt. "Mal, I am ... "

"It matters not," said Malvin. He turned away from Brand, a hurt look on his face.

Willow managed not to pipe in with questions about Thorburn. She didn't want to jeopardize their truce, and what with Brand's outburst last night, and now this one, he was obviously touchy about something. She went for the pie instead.

"Hey, I don't know about you guys, but I'm starving." Her new ivory-handled knife cut deeply into the pie's flaky crust. "Mmm, cherry. My favourite." She scooped up a big piece with her hand and bit into it. "Oh, this is so-o good! You guys have to try it."

First Malvin, then Brand came over, slicing out pieces and eating them till there was nothing left but crumbs.

Willow slid her finger along her knife blade and then licked off the cherry goo. "Now that was a great pie," she said, turning the knife over and then licking off the other side.

"'Twas indeed," agreed Brand. He groaned and rubbed his stomach, falling back against the straw bed. Malvin copied him, groaning even louder.

The pigs. Three slices each! They deserved to be sick.

Willow rolled her eyes at them and tucked her knife back into her belt. Well, at least they weren't fighting. She plopped onto the straw bed, pushing them both and laughing at their moans. "C'mon, you big pigs. Get up. I want to ask about something."

Malvin sat up and straightened out his tunic. He seemed a bit embarrassed. "Umm, you have a question, Your Highness?" he asked, brushing away the straw dust.

"You know," said Willow. She folded her arms. "You probably shouldn't keep calling me that. I mean, if someone heard you, they might get suspicious."

Brand leaned on his elbow and nodded. "Aye, I was going to mention that the other day. 'Tis best, I agree, not to use our titles." He sat up and looked at her thoughtfully. "The name Willow is elvish, though. People might get suspicious over that, as well."

"What about just Will?" suggested Willow. "That was my nickname back home."

"Will," said Brand slowly, thinking about it for a moment.

"Could be short for Willa or Wilda," Malvin advised.

"Alright then, we shall call you Will." Brand stood up and moved over to the window again. "Blast, there's still someone down there. 'Twill probably be nightfall before we are able to leave here."

Willow touched the swan shape beneath her shirt. "Well, let me ask a question then," she said, pulling it out for the boys to see. "Can you tell me more about this?" Brand and Malvin stared at her chest. "What?" she said. "What's wrong?"

"Queen Cyrraena's gift!" breathed Malvin. He lifted it gently from Willow's hand, clearly in awe. "Where did you get this? I thought you had left it in Earthworld?"

Brand moved in for a closer look. "Oh, but this is truly good fortune. 'Tis the proof we need for King Tarrant." He reached out to touch the pendant. "With this, he will never doubt that Willow is his granddaughter."

Malvin dropped the pendant and Willow tucked it back down her shirt front. "Make sure you keep it hidden," Malvin warned. "You saw what happened when they saw the White Knight. If they knew we had the Princess Pawn with us as well, we would have the whole countryside after us."

The Princess Pawn. That seemed an apt name for her role in all this. Willow covered her hand over the pendant again. "Is it magic? When I put it on the last time in Carrus, I'm sure I felt something. It was, like, hot, and made me feel real focused."

"Oh indeed," said Malvin, "'tis magic alright. 'Tis your nethergift. The emblem of Queen Cyrraena's protection. This means ... " he pointed at the pendant, "that the elf queen is watching over us. She is lending us her support and protection. 'Tis indeed remarkable, since she has hidden herself completely from humans since your trip to Earthworld. For in truth she is not permitted to intervene in any of this. But thus far, she has risked much to help us."

Willow glanced at Brand. She decided to take her own risk. "Who was that Lord Radnor guy who got the people in the marketplace to chase us?" she asked, hoping this wasn't another one of Brand's touchy subjects. She saw a quick warning look pass from Brand to Malvin. "He is ... "

"What's this!" a voice suddenly roared out. "You lazy, fat sow! There's a half crown missin' from the till and only five pies sittin' on yonder table. Are ye eatin' me profits again? I'll

teach ye to steal from me, ye thievin' wench!" A sharp slap cracked against the silence, followed by another and another.

Willow crawled across the floor over to a corner where she could peer down into a part of the pastry shop. "Oh my God," she whispered, "he's beating her."

CHAPTER 13

W ILLOW HAD SEEN VIOLENCE on TV, but it was nothing like this. There were no censored shots left out for young viewers. No shots away from the victim. Each time the man struck her, she could see the shock to Gemma's skin and the instant red blotches. The vicious cracking slaps kept time with the man's heavy breathing and resounded through the room. She could see his large bull-like chest and the muscular arms that pounded back Gemma's efforts to shield herself. She could smell sweat mixed with fear and hatred.

And something else.

She peered closer at the man. At the evil smile stretched over his face. Revulsion swept over her. *He enjoyed this.*

Willow couldn't bear it. She felt the scream gathering force in her lungs, but then Brand and Malvin were kneeling beside her, pulling her away from the crack.

"Do not look," whispered Brand urgently. "Do not look." He sheltered Willow's face against his shoulder and hugged her tight. "We cannot reveal ourselves. 'Twould only make it worse."

"Cyrill, leave the girl be now," ordered a gruff voice from below. Willow pulled herself away from Brand to stare down the crack again. "There's a whole pile of dishes that needs washin', and I don't need the little chit laid up for a week like last time." An obese woman stomped into view, her grey wool dress straining over her girth. "Come now." She tapped the man's arm with a wooden spoon. "There's payin' customers out by the window."

With a shrug of his big shoulders, the man stalked off. The woman moved in close to Gemma and said something. Willow couldn't hear her words, but she could see the tightening of Gemma's cut mouth and the contemptuous glare from her eyes. Gemma said nothing to the woman, but swished disdainfully past her with head held high.

Willow marvelled at her courage. These people treated her like garbage, but Gemma hadn't cringed or cried or any of the things that Willow probably would've done. She'd just walked past that woman like nothing had happened. Her gutsiness reminded Willow of someone else. Someone else who held her head high.

Abby.

"I think she is going to be alright," whispered Malvin.

Willow stood up and moved slowly back to the straw bed. She felt numb. Brand and Malvin sat beside her, hanging their heads and not speaking.

They sat like that for a long time. It grew dark and no more muffled sounds came from down below. Finally, Gemma climbed the stairs, her tread slow and tired. "It's just me," she whispered, opening the door and closing it behind her. She had the hood of an old blue cloak pulled low over her face and was carrying a basket in one hand and a flask in another.

"Thought ye might be needin' another meal," she said, handing Willow the basket and flask. "It's just a bit of bread and cheese, and this here's got cold well water in it."

Willow sat staring dumbly at the food and water. Gemma, who'd been punched and beaten, was still worried over *them* and whether or not *they* were hungry. She shook her head and handed the basket and flask to Malvin. "Gemma," she said, standing up, "we saw that man beat you. Are you alright?"

"Oh that," tsked Gemma, trying to brush off Willow's concern. "It weren't nothin'. Master Swinton, he just loses his temper sometimes, is all. He don't hit that hard." The blue hood trembled as she spoke, hiding her face in shadows. Willow reached over and gently pulled it back.

"Oh, Gemma," she whispered, shock taking her breath away. The other girl's face was red and swollen, with one eye puffed shut and a nasty bruise on her forehead. Her cut bottom lip protruded painfully.

Gemma let her look for a moment, then slowly drew the hood back up. "There isn't time to worry about me. Somethin's goin' on down at the main gate, so the streets are mostly clear now. Where is it that ye need to go?"

Brand stood up, followed by Malvin. He untied his money pouch and clasped it into Gemma's hands. "This isn't very much. But I hope 'tis enough to thank you for all your help." Willow knew his words meant that he didn't want her risking herself further. But Gemma handed the pouch right back to him.

"That's not necessary, Master Brand. If ye're the White Knight like they says, then I figure it's my duty to help ye." She pulled a woolen scarf out from under her cloak. "Here," she said, tossing it to Willow. "To cover yer hair with. If anyone does happen to be out and about, they'll be lookin' for three people, not four. And I know the city well. If ye tell me where ye're headin', I can likely find ye a shortcut."

Brand held the money pouch in his hand, clearly debating with himself whether to argue with her or not. Finally, he tied the pouch back to his belt. "We're heading for the Staff and Dagger. Along the west-end market."

Gemma's hooded head bobbed up and down. "Aye, I know it well. Mistress Quillondale's a good customer."

Gemma's shortcut consisted of a nose-plugging race along a refuse-clogged canal that flowed behind the pungent tanner district where, between the stretched-out animal skins and stinking vats of liquid, Willow had thought she'd stumbled into some small section of hell. The section, she was sure, reserved only for smelly polluters and public farters.

They reached the Staff and Dagger just as a servant was lighting the oil lamps that hung on either side of the inn's large entrance door. Trumble was waiting inside, angrily relieved to see them.

"Where've you been, lad?! I've had me men scourin' the city lookin' for you all afternoon! The whole town's in an uproar, lookin' for the White Knight."

Brand quickly told their story and introduced Gemma to Trumble. "This end of the city, at any rate, seems deserted. 'Twould be best if we pack the horses now, and try to leave by the south gate."

"Aye," agreed Trumble, "I've had your horses and supplies ready for near twenty minutes now. Seems as though King Ulor has sent some knights after you. A whole herd of them just rode in through the main city gates. O'course they weren't expectin' to be greeted by the mob that's a searchin' for you, too."

"What do you mean?" asked Willow with a worried

frown. Was anybody getting hurt because of her?

Trumble patted her shoulder. "Now, don't worry, lass. The people here in Graffyn are always lookin' for someone to blame for their troubles. They switch scapegoats like me Marta changes bedsheets. And once they see they're no match for mounted knights, they'll hightail it outta there lickity-split. C'mon, now, let's get you and the lads back on your way, because crumbcakes to crowns those knights'll be comin' here first to search for you."

Brand retrieved the image globe and Willow's laptop from Mistress Quillondale's strongbox. Willow said her goodbyes. She was about to say them to Gemma when Gemma side-stepped her and went over to Trumble. "Ye know the guards aren't going to let ye through, don't you?"

Trumble nodded. "Aye. Lord Radnor's got the city closed tighter than a drum. 'Twill take, no doubt, a pouch o' gold to change their minds." He jingled a heavy money pouch tied to his belt.

"My father was captain of the guards for the south gate," Gemma told him. "If ye take me with ye, I can make sure ye get through."

Trumble stared at Gemma, trying, it seemed, to see under her hood better. "Well," he said slowly, "you might save me my bribe money. Can you ride?"

Gemma's hood nodded up and down.

"Well enough, then. You there, lad, give her your horse." Trumble stalked through the hallway and out the back door into the stable yard, where torchlight revealed ten saddled horses milling over the cobblestones. Trumble and five of his men mounted up. "We shall be your escorts as far as the gate," he told Brand. "Then we'll hightail it back to the inn and see what can be done to stall them knights." He winked at Willow with his good eye and then grinned wickedly.

They set off at a fast pace toward the south gate, Trumble and three of his men leading the way. The streets were dark and mostly deserted, with only the odd indifferent citizen or two to watch their progress. Far to the north end, Willow heard the sounds of a skirmish and saw dim lights peppering the darkness. Ruby's ears pricked nervously, and Willow sighed, sliding her hand along the horse's smooth neck. She hoped that the knights weren't actually killing anybody, just trying to scare them away.

She still had her eyes downcast, concentrating on the horse tail swishing back and forth in front of her, as the sand-coloured walls rose and the party came upon the narrow edifice of the south gate. Brand's horse brushed up against her as they slowed to a stop beneath the gatehouse window. Two guards stuck their heads out, giving them a good look-over. Finally one of them growled, "State yer business," while the other one moved his spear point into view.

Gemma drew back her hood so that the guards could see her mouth, though not her whole face. "Tully?" she called out. "Tully Tupper? Is that you?"

The guard that had spoken to them tipped further out the window. He was lean and muscular with a ferocious-looking blond moustache that hung below his chin and twitched when he talked. "Who's that callin' me name?"

"It's me, Tully. Gemma Fletcher."

The man peered down at Gemma. "Aldwin's daughter is it? From the pastry shop?"

"Aye." Gemma cupped her hand around her mouth. "How's yer little boy doin'? Did he like the pie I brought him?"

A bushy blond smile lit the guard's face. He seemed sure now that Gemma was Gemma. "Oh, aye," he yelled back. "The lad lit into it like a priest off a fast day. And the swellin's down to nothin' now. Lad's as good as new." Tully looked around questioningly. "Where're ye off to, lass? Ye're not leavin' Graffyn, now, are you?"

"Aye," said Gemma. "These are my mother's people. They've come to take me south with them. To Trahern, where my aunt lives."

"Well, we'll be sorry to see ye leave, lass." He gestured to the other guard to open the gate, but the other guard was pulling on his arm. Willow could hear snatches of their conversation. "We can't ... but Lord Radnor said ... alright, alright ... " The heavy iron gate slowly began to rise. Trumble sidled his horse up to Brand's.

"I'll be leavin' you now, lad," he said in a low voice. He clapped his huge hand onto Brand's shoulder and turned over to Willow. "You've a fine Knight here, Your Highness. If anyone can get you to Keldoran, it's Brand here. Just put your trust in him." He turned back to Brand and shook his hand. "I envy you, lad. What I wouldn't give to be off on an adventure. Ah well. The missus made me promise." He smiled and tipped his head to both Willow and Malvin, then reined his horse around. "C'mon men! We've some knights to befuddle."

Willow smiled and waved at him. "Thanks," she called out. The gate was all the way up now, and Brand took the lead as Dusk sauntered through the narrow passage. Willow and Malvin and then Gemma followed him, their horse's hooves clip-clopping over the stone road. On the other side, once they were clear of the gate and drawbridge, Brand steered his horse around and trotted back to Gemma.

"We must now take our leave of you," he said. A tiny stream along the road trickled quietly, echoing Brand's solemnity. He took Gemma's hand and gallantly kissed her fingertips. "You have risked much for us, milady; and for that, the entire kingdom of Gallandra will be eternally in your debt."

Gemma gently pulled her hand away. "I think there's been a bit of a misunderstanding," she said, smiling broadly. "I'm not goin' back to Graffyn. I'm comin' with you!"

CHAPTER 14

RAND'S WARM SMILE turned frigid as he stared disbelievingly at Gemma. "Now look here," he said, clenching his jaw. "We are indeed most grateful for your help, but we cannot take you with us. 'Tis by far too dangerous. We ... "

"Look, the princess here needs someone to tend her, and I've made up my mind it's to be me." Gemma turned and nodded politely to Willow.

Willow glanced from Malvin's surprised face to Brand's accusing one. "Don't look at me," she said. "I didn't tell her anything."

Gemma laughed and shook her head. "Nobody needed to tell me. A halfwit could've figured it out. Ye said yer name was Willow, right? Captain Quillondale just called ye Yer Highness, and ye're gallivantin' around the countryside with the White Knight, here. And so, I just figured the rumours must be true, and that ye're the princess Willow aged by dimension travellin'. Not to mention ... " She leaned over in her saddle, gently touching a loose wisp of Willow's hair. "This makes ye look an awful lot like yer mother, the princess Diantha. I seen her once, ye know, ridin' through Graffyn with the prince. I wasn't up close or nothin', but I could see her hair. Everyone could see it. It was like a cloud of fire. Just like yers was today in the sunlight." Gemma folded her arms and gave the three of them an assessing stare.

Brand didn't agree with or deny Gemma's theory. He made another attempt to discourage her instead. "We've three days of hard riding still ahead. There are knights chasing us, knights hoping to turn us into chess pieces, and an elf prince who may or may not kill us, depending on the mood he is in."

Brittle windswept leaves suddenly leaped into the road, sending a rush of prickles clawing up Willow's spine. Ruby's head tossed in the air as she stamped an anxious hoof. "Ssh," soothed Willow, stroking the horse's mane and frowning at Brand, whose dismal scenarios were now even starting to scare the animals.

Gemma, though, still refused to be deterred. She drew back her hood, exposing her bruised and scabbed face. "I've nothin' to go back to," she said quietly. "So, if'n ye don't mind, I'd rather be takin' my chances with ye. Besides, I know how to cook, I'm handy in a knife fight, I can use herbs for healin'. And ... " she smiled at Brand, "I can dab yer powders on, so ye don't look so much like an undertaker's cadaver."

The wind whipped up the leaves again, swirling them into a wild dance. The horses snorted and milled nervously. Willow stared at Gemma's round, hopeful face. The other girl was waiting for her to say something. To stick up for her.

Willow's mouth opened but no words came out. She lowered her gaze.

Brand broke the awkward silence, making up her mind for her. "Keep up," he growled, "and you can come." He whipped Dusk around and galloped him down the roadway.

Willow urged Ruby forward past Gemma and the hurt look on Gemma's face. *That was nice*, she told herself savagely, *real nice*. Wimping out on people was starting to become a habit. She spurred Ruby faster, riding into the biting cold and letting it sting against her unprotected face.

Overhead the wind howled. She watched it whip angrily at the towering treetops, her own emotions roiling with it. It wasn't fair. She hadn't done *anything*. And yet every single person seemed to have all these expectations. Gemma, Brand, her grandfather — they were all the same. All wanting her to save them. And where was Nana when she needed her the most? Willow wanted to scream. Let loose and pound them. Pound them all into the ground and ...

A sudden image of Gemma's awful beating flitted into her mind, extinguishing her bitterness. Shame flared instead. The other girl had helped her to escape and had asked nothing in return — except to be her friend.

Tugging on Ruby's reins, Willow sidled close to Gemma.

"Gemma," she began hesitantly, "I just wanted to let you know that ... that I'm glad you came with us."

White teeth flashed in the dim light. "I'm right happy being with you as well," said Gemma, beaming a big smile at her. "It's been a long time gone, Yer Highness, since I've been where I wanted to be."

A new thought struck Willow. She glanced ahead, making sure Brand and Malvin were out of hearing range. "Um, Gemma," she said softly, "what about your mom and dad? Aren't they going to be worried about you?" She knew there was no way the pastry cook and his horrible wife could be Gemma's parents.

Gemma seemed surprised that Willow wanted to know. "Why, I'm an orphan, Yer Highness," she said, smoothing her cloak self-consciously. "I've been one for three years now. Me ma died back when I was ten, and me da a few years ago, when a horse trampled him in the marketplace."

"Oh. Sorry." Tears stung Willow's eyes. With Nana gone, she felt like an orphan herself.

"Da died a hero, though," went on Gemma. "He saved two little boys from being run down in the street, and bein' a soldier and a guard and all, it's how he would've wanted it. The whole town came out to pay their respects. Even the mayor." Moonlight flickered beneath the heavy cloak hood, exposing her dark bruises and an oozing scab that had crusted over her split lip.

Willow winced at the raw sight. "Why did you stay with that baker and his wife?" she asked, her eyes falling uncomfortably away. "Couldn't you have found someone better?"

Gemma seemed to ponder for a moment, gingerly feeling the sore spots under her hood. "I wish it'd been as easy as that," she finally said. "Ye see, after they died, I had nothin'. Not a penny to my name. Me da owed money to a local lender, and seein' as I was the last survivin' member of my family, his debt fell to me. Mistress Swinton helped me out. She was kin to me ma, and said I could come and live with her and work off the debt till it was paid for." Gemma fell silent for a moment, her hands holding tightly to the reins.

"He started beatin' me," she rasped, "soon as I moved in."

"What?" Somehow Willow never figured Gemma as the type to just let someone hurt her like that. "What about the police? Didn't you tell them?"

Gemma lifted her head and stared at Willow. "Don't ye understand? Mistress Swinton paid off my debt. She owned me — like a purse or a new dress. It didn't matter a whit what she or her husband did to me, I was their bought and paid for property. They could do with me what they liked. I did run away, though, once. Sheriff Tilford brought me back." She reined in her horse, opened her cloak, and pulled down the shoulder of her dress. An ugly purply-black circle puckered the soft whiteness of her skin. "They — they branded me," she said hoarsely. "And if — if they were to catch me this time ... I lose a foot."

Willow flinched. It was unspeakably cruel. How could they treat people like that? How dare they? And how was it that Gemma was so brave? She'd actually risked losing a ...

No! Willow brushed the image of a severed foot from her mind. She didn't even want to imagine such a thing. She grabbed the end of Gemma's saddle horn. "No one will *ever* hurt you like that again. I can guarantee you that."

Gemma pressed her hand over Willow's, squeezing it and smiling her big, beaming smile. "Thank ye, Yer Highness. Thank ye kindly." She wiped tears away and straightened her hood. "I'll be a good servant to ye. Loyal and honest."

Servant! Willow shook her head no. That wasn't what she'd meant. "No, Gemma, you're my friend. I want you to be my friend."

Gemma stared at her, blinking and wiping at her nose. "Forgive me, Yer Highness, but ye're a princess, and I'm nothin' but a peasant lass. It wouldn't be quite fittin' now, would it?"

"Well, I'll make you a lady then." Why not? If a king could dub a knight, why couldn't a princess dub a lady? Willow placed a hand on Gemma's shoulder. "Gemma Fletcher of Graffyn, for bravery and daring beyond the call of duty, I now dub thee Lady Gemma." She dropped her arm back to her side. "There, now we can be friends."

"I — I," stammered Gemma, "I don't know what I should say."

"Say yes."

"Yes, please do," said a mocking voice.

Willow and Gemma spun round to see Brand eyeing them skeptically. "If you two *ladies* are finished with your heart-to-heart, we'll be on our way." He flicked Dusk around and trotted away from them, ignoring their stifled snorts and giggles.

After a short but torrential rainfall and another two hours of slow riding in thick pine trees and near blackness, Willow found herself huddled under a fur blanket, staring at star patterns in the inky sky. According to Malvin's last globe check, the Black Rook, Lord Garnock of Grisselwait, was patrolling this area with a company of twenty knights. The same Lord Garnock of Grisselwait who had captured both her father and grandmother. Willow blinked uneasily at the speckled sky, imagining the Black Rook skewering her like a juicy shish kebab. What if Garnock believed in slicing and dicing and asking questions later? What if he ambushed them? Or what if ...

Brand coughed into a gloved fist, his chain mail clinking as he repositioned himself against the wide tree trunk. He was keeping watch, his sword glinting dangerously on his lap. Willow sat up, crawling past Gemma and Malvin's sleeping forms to sit closer to his reassuring presence.

He tilted his head, squinting at her in the dark. "You should be asleep."

"I know." Willow wrapped her blanket tight around her. "But I can't stop thinking about the game."

Brand nodded and settled against the tree trunk, waiting for her to continue. Willow took a deep breath, gathering her courage. "Okay — have you ever captured anyone? Do you actually have to *kill* them to do it?"

For a minute, Brand didn't answer. He fingered the bare sword blade, making it flicker eerily with the red glow of his knight skin. Finally, he heaved a tired sigh. "I was there when your father and grandmother were Captured."

An owl hooted in the distance. Willow swallowed hard and hugged her knees. "You mean ... you mean, you saw it happen?"

"Yes." A pained look came into Brand's eyes. "We were on our way to Keldoran with news of the princess' Capture. 'Twas there Lord Garnock found us — in Thorburn Wood. He pretended to be our ally at the first, then he ambushed us when we were not expecting it." Brand's jaw tightened. "'Twas the prince he did first. Told him that King Tarrant wanted for the queen to know what it felt like to lose a child."

Willow felt bile rise in her throat. This man, this King Tarrant, was her grandfather. How would she face him now, knowing what he'd done? Knowing how cruel he'd been?

"They dragged Prince Alaric from his horse," Brand continued, "and tied him to a tree. With his sword, Lord Garnock drew a thin cut on the prince's neck. That was all that it took, a tiny cut, little more than a pinprick, and Prince Alaric was changed into a chess piece. Your grandmother he cut on the cheek."

"So, he didn't actually kill them, then?" Willow had thought only death would work in a capture.

Brand shook his head. "No. He only drew first blood."

Willow exhaled slowly. She felt some relief knowing no one would actually have to be killed. "So what if someone who *isn't* part of the game cuts me? What happens then?"

"Well, from what we have learned, drawing first blood

only works if 'tis done by a Player on the other team. If another does it, Malvin or Gemma for instance, nothing happens. You would still be a Player."

"And if the cut's more than just a cut? What then?"

"Well, you *can* die. The Game does not make us invincible. But if you are killed, and 'tis not by another Player, then the Game will find a replacement."

"A replacement?"

"Yes. A Player who has been killed by chance soon has his place taken by another who is not part of the Game. Your own nurse was a Pawn before she died. And after her death, one of the blacksmith's sons awoke with the pawn glow."

Willow considered this new twist on the rules. It meant that she might have to defend herself. Might even have to hurt someone. Her hand strayed down to her leather boot top, trembling nervously against the knife that was hidden there. The reality washed over her. This was not a game. It was deadly real.

Brand must have seen the fear in her eyes, for he set aside his sword and pulled her beneath the damp, heavy wool of his furred cloak. His arms encircled her protectively, and she lay there, warm and comforted, till another thought began to niggle at her.

"Brand," she whispered, "you're part of the game. Why didn't Lord Garnock capture you, too?" But Brand didn't answer. He was fast asleep.

CHAPTER 15

WILLOW CAME AWAKE with a startled gasp. The eye dream! She'd had the same weird eye dream again. Only this time she'd been so close to the glittering turquoise iris that she'd seen a reflection in it. Not her own, though. It'd been someone else's. Someone with peach-coloured skin and long silvery hair.

Shivering at the strange thought, Willow snuggled against a warm, bumpy lump that suddenly groaned and shifted beneath her. She froze, eyes springing open. Brand's red-glowing face grinned sleepily down at her. "Sleep well?" he asked, shaking out the chain-mailed arm that had pillowed her head.

Willow jerked away from him, cheeks flaming. Ohmigod! She'd spent the night sleeping on Brand! This was totally beyond embarrassing. "Um," she faltered, searching for something normal to say, "your um ... y-your powder's all off."

"Aye," he said, pointing at her own bright face, "yours is off, too. We had best get Gemma to redo us." He jumped lightly to his feet and strode over to the horses, rummaging through his saddlebag for the powder pouch.

Willow stood up too and began folding her blanket. She cast a furtive glance around their small clearing, hoping no one had seen her and Brand sleeping together. Malvin and Gemma were both busy, Malvin studying the image globe, and Gemma setting out bread and cheese for breakfast.

Neither seemed the least bit interested in where she'd spent the night. Willow brushed twig-bits and dirt from her cloak, the burning sensation in her cheeks starting to subside.

A sharp cry from Malvin made her twist in his direction. The young mage had leapt to his feet and was hurriedly returning the image globe to its leather bag. "Mount up! Mount up! Garnock is upon us!" Then, before anyone could respond, a horn blast moaned through the woods. Mounted men with full armour and brilliant blue and gold tunics flashing burst from the forest into the clearing, surrounding them. Dazzled by the spectacle, Willow could only stare, wide-eyed and gaping.

An armoured man rode toward them. Willow quailed. Beneath his plumed helmet, the man blazed with the phantom blue glare of a rook.

"Well, well," he growled, "what do we have here? 'Tis not the White Knight again, now, is't?" His fierce eyes raked over the clearing, noting the pearly glow of Willow's skin. "And a young Pawn to boot." Gravelly laughter rumbled up from his throat. "Weren't thinking of sneaking your Pawn through to the back ranks, now, were you, boy?"

Brand didn't answer. He scanned the circle of knights, looking, Willow thought, for a way to escape.

A second man rode forward to join the other two, drawing a curse from Brand and the hint of a smile from Willow. He was like a medieval Liberace, all curled hair and fancy beribboned clothing.

"*Varian!*" Brand snarled at the flamboyantly dressed man. "I should have known all along 'twas you in league with Lord Garnock."

"Squire Lackwulf, you would find it best to address me as

Prince Varian," the man retorted. "And, yes, Lord Garnock and I do have a suitable arrangement in place." He laughed and cocked his head toward the blue-glowing man. "The boy doesn't learn his lessons very well, eh Garnock? Looks as if you'll have to teach him again."

Willow blinked at Prince Varian, the name suddenly ringing a bell. Wasn't her great-uncle named Prince Varian? The one she was supposed to have met up with in Thorburn Wood?

A metallic hiss answered Varian's veiled threat. Willow turned to see Brand pull out his sword. Her heart began to hammer. But then something else caught her eye. Something that made fear rise in her throat like vomit. Varian was gazing at her, his icy blue eyes as cold as winter. And that's when she saw the signal, the almost imperceptible nod of his head.

Then a savage cry cut the air, and a young man ploughed forward, aiming a crossbow bolt directly at Willow. "For Wren and Keldoran," he shouted, setting loose the arrow.

Silence. All Willow could see was the Black player's face. The clear white of his pawn glow. The anguish in his eyes.

Then the sound came rushing back. *"No!"* she heard Brand roar. Something pushed into her, knocking her to the ground. Horse hooves circled dangerously close to her head. "Shoot the girl! Shoot the girl!" Varian kept shouting, while Malvin yelled, "No, 'tis the princess Willow! 'Tis the princess Willow!"

Finally, she raised her head. Brand was beside her, a crossbow bolt sticking out of his shoulder. "My fault," he said weakly. "Should've told you the truth. I'm sorry." Suddenly he began gasping for breath and his eyes filled with fear. Willow, terrified, grabbed at his flailing hands, trying to calm him.

Trying to keep him from striking at the crossbow bolt. But his hands, already hard and turning white, had begun to shrink.

Willow rubbed her eyes. No, it couldn't be. She rubbed them even harder, not caring that it hurt. But it didn't matter, he was still there, his tiny bewildered head poking up through the grass. She reached out for him, her heart beating painfully in her chest. He was dressed in armour, holding a shield in one hand and a sword in the other, sitting on top of a horse. The crossbow bolt had disappeared, leaving him tiny and perfect.

Gemma squeezed her shoulders. "Ye're not past harm yet," she whispered, pulling Willow to her feet. "Look." She pointed to where Varian and Malvin were standing with Lord Garnock, arguing over her identity.

"I swear 'tis true!" cried Malvin. "That girl is the princess Willow." He turned and pointed at Willow.

Varian calmly shook his head. "The boy is addled, Garnock. The infant princess is dead. I saw her body with my own eyes. This *girl*," he sent a mocking look Willow's way, "is but a stray peasant that the Game chose in her place."

Willow raised her chin and closed her dusty cape regally over her sleep-rumpled tunic front. Gemma grabbed onto her arm. "Don't do nothin'," she advised, brandishing her knife. "They'll have to come through me first, a'fore they can get to you."

Willow held Brand out to her. "He saved me," she whispered brokenly. She kept her gaze on the creamy chess piece and away from Gemma's sad eyes. They both knew Willow couldn't let Brand's capture be for nothing. She had to stick up for herself.

"Arrest him!" Varian ordered suddenly. Two burly men

moved in and grabbed Malvin's arms.

"No!" yelled Malvin. "I speak the truth!"

Varian snorted dismissively. "The boy's making sport of us. Come now and let's finish this business." He gave Lord Garnock's shoulder a friendly clap and attempted to turn him away from Malvin.

"No, wait," Malvin insisted. "I have proof."

Varian stopped. "That's enough, boy." His unblinking eyes were deadly spears. "Speak another word and 'twill be your last." Ten crossbows were instantly at the ready, pointing at Malvin's heart.

"Here, now!" bellowed Lord Garnock, brushing off Varian's arm. "I'm in charge here." He clanked over to Malvin and glared down at him, his blue glow darkening to black. "Well, boy, this proof of yours had best be good."

Malvin swallowed convulsively. "Sh-show him," he said finally. "Show him the gift."

As Willow pulled out the pendant, heat tingled against her fingertips and then seared into a sudden flash of light. She jerked her hand away, staring down at her now brightly lit swan.

"By the gods," cried Lord Garnock. He strode over to Willow and cupped her chin. "'Tis truly you, then," he muttered. "'Tis truly you."

"Great Alcina and Myra, Garnock!" burst out Varian. "The girl is near full grown! How is it possible that she is the princess Willow?"

"Beggin' yer pardon, milords," interrupted Gemma. She squeezed in beside Willow and did a quick curtsy for Garnock. "But I think I can answer yer question. Her Highness was dimension-aged and has only just returned to Mistolear a few days ago."

Willow collected her wits, giving Gemma a grateful smile. "Yes. I'm trying to get to Keldoran to stop the war, because, as you can see, I'm not dead. So no one needs to be fighting over me."

"She lies!" Varian pushed Garnock aside and grabbed for Willow's pendant. "See, I ... *ahhh!*" His hand jumped back as if it'd been burned.

"Oh, someone's been lying, alright." Garnock drew his sword from its scabbard and pointed it at Varian. "And I would say I've got the knave right here." He pressed his sword tip to Varian's throat. "Thought we'd do all your dirty work for you, eh? Didn't you, Varian? Start a war. Eliminate the heirs. Checkmate the king. You had the whole blasted scheme planned from the beginning."

Varian's men rattled their weapons in a weak show of intimidation. They were out-bladed by at least three swords to one. They stood and watched as Varian's throat bloomed a small blood patch.

"Come now, Garnock." Varian tried to back away from him. "There's no reason for this. Our plans have not changed."

Garnock followed him, keeping the sword tip firm against his jugular. "How so? To me it would appear that everything has changed." Another blood patch sprouted on Varian's neck.

"Do you not understand? Tarrant is not about to forget Diantha's Capture — whether *that girl* is the princess or not." Varian dabbed a leather glove calmly to his throat and smiled. "So you see, my services are still very much required."

Garnock snorted, shaking his head. "By the gods, man, you've more shameless, boldfaced gall in you than a swaggering peacock!" The sword tip fell away from Varian's smug face and plunged back into its well-oiled scabbard. "I'll not kill you today, Farrandale. But if our paths meet again ... " His voice trailed off meaningfully, while Varian's smug face struggled with confusion.

"Release the boy," Garnock ordered, turning to Malvin. "'Tis my belief he speaks the truth."

"Wh-what are you doing?" sputtered Varian. "You cannot mean to disavow me now! After all that I have done for you. After *all* that I have done for Keldoran!"

Garnock stroked the ends of his grizzled beard, staring coldly at Varian. "Enough talk. Take your men *now*, Varian, and leave — before I change my mind."

Fear goosepimpled Willow's skin as Varian's murderous blue gaze raked hatefully over her, his fingers itching above his sword pommel in obvious deliberation over whether or not he should kill her himself. Willow's legs took an involuntary step closer to Lord Garnock.

Varian smiled at her, his look quickly changing back to a mildly pleasant one. Then he bowed in elegant defeat, his long curls cascading over his shoulders. "You win, milord," he said, lifting his head and saluting Lord Garnock. "I will withdraw." He signalled to his men and began to move from the clearing.

Halfway across, he stopped. "That is, till our paths meet again." His Cheshire cat smile filled his face, so Willow couldn't tell whether it was meant for her or Garnock, but the hairs on the nape of her neck stood straight up anyway.

Gemma asked the question that Willow had been thinking. "Why are ye lettin' him leave? If it were up to me, I'd be arrestin' him in a heartbeat."

Lord Garnock gave her a wry look. "Arresting a prince is

not a simple matter. He has lords and knights aplenty to go to war for him. Better, I say, to let the Gallandrians deal with their own traitors. Besides, he has not harmed us Keldorians. King Tarrant wanted him to deliver Players and ... well, that is exactly what he was doing."

"What do you mean?" asked Willow, a bit bewildered by what had just gone on. "You mean King Ulor's own brother has been helping him to lose the game?"

"Aye. And helping himself as well," said Lord Garnock, frowning. "He wants King Ulor's crown and figured to gain it by using the Game against him. You see, when your mother, the princess Diantha, was Captured, 'twas Varian that sent us word that King Ulor had given the order for it."

Malvin gasped at this information. "But 'tis not true. King Ulor would *never* do that!"

"Aye, I believe you, lad," said Lord Garnock. "I always had my doubts about your Prince Varian. He gave us no good reason for Princess Diantha's Capture and was too quick in offering up the whereabouts of Prince Alaric and Queen Aleria."

"Then why capture them?" asked Willow, feeling even more confused. "Why not talk to them first?"

"I had my orders."

Brand had said that King Tarrant wanted Queen Aleria to suffer as he and Queen Morwenna had. Willow couldn't help but remember it.

"You must understand," said Garnock, seeing the aversion on her face, "Princess Diantha was the sun and moon to King Tarrant. When Queen Morwenna had to tell him that their daughter's chess piece held no life force, he was filled with more grief then I've yet seen in a man. He could not see Varian's deception. He could only see his own pain."

Lord Garnock placed a hand on Willow's shoulder. "I tell you all this, Your Highness, so that you shall not judge your grandfather too harshly. He did what he did out of love for your mother, and what he thought was a wrong against her. When he hears the truth, though, he shall listen to reason. I can give you my word on that."

Willow still wasn't sure what the truth was. "Do you think then that it was Varian who captured my mother?" This seemed to still be a loose end.

"He is not part of the Game," said Lord Garnock, "so he could not have done it directly. My guess, though, is that he did have a hand in it. Which reminds me ... " he glanced to where his men held the young player who'd shot Brand, "I wonder what young Terrill Longbottom has to say about all this?" He marched over to the boy, ordering him to stand up straight. "Well, Squire Longbottom, I assume you have a reason for disobeying my orders. I should like to hear what it is."

The boy hung his head. "Yes, milord," he whispered.

"What's that?" Lord Garnock barked. "Speak up, boy; I can't hear you."

"I said *yes, milord!*"

"Good. Let's hear it, then."

Squire Longbottom raised his head and looked guiltily around him. "I — I talked to Prince Varian, milord. And he said ... he said that girl there was the Player that Captured my brother, Wren. He said it was my duty as a brother, milord, to Capture her back."

Willow squinted at Squire Longbottom, surprised at his

accusation. She'd forgotten that two pawns on the Black side had been captured by White. This boy's brother must have been one of them.

"So what you are saying, then," said Lord Garnock sarcastically, "is that for your own personal affairs, you jeopardized the life of Princess Willow and disregarded my orders."

The boy's head hung back down again and his lips trembled. "Yes, milord. I'm sorry, milord."

Lord Garnock sighed heavily and waved his hand at Squire Longbottom. "I shall deal with you later. Now, mount up! We must get the princess to Keldoran and put a stop to this blasted war!"

Willow squeezed her hand around Brand but couldn't bring herself to look at him. His face still had that horrible bewildered expression. She couldn't bear to see it again. She set him gently in her pocket.

"Just call me Alice," she mumbled, "for 'tis off I go to Wonderland."

CHAPTER 16

"TELL ME THE TRUTH," ordered Willow, settling herself down beside Malvin. "What really happened between Brand and Prince Varian?"

She'd been thinking about that question all day. Even when the first winter snows finally came skirling down around them and the bitter winds had made her eyes water and her lips chap, she'd still clung to Brand's marble figure, wondering what truth he'd wanted her to know.

Malvin blinked at her, surprised. He'd been staring trans-fixedly into the fire and hadn't noticed her approach. It was late at night and all around them rugged Keldorian men slept beside their swords, their fur-mounded bodies looking like dozens of small snow-fuzzed hills. Other fires dotted the spaces between them; other eyes, those of the watchful guards, followed her curiously.

Willow waited, the cold air around her and Malvin filling with the silence of the falling snow. Malvin looked down at her hands, where he could see Brand clutched in her gloves. He reached out to gently claim the figure.

"Brand revered your father," he whispered, seeming to ignore her question. "Hearkened to his every word."

Willow nodded patiently, trying hard to imagine her father. Nana had always painted him as tall and handsome, the hero in a story, the knight that saves the princess.

Hero-action Dad! That's how she'd thought of him. She remembered playing Barbies and pretending the Ken doll was the father, always swooping in and saving Barbie with a tinfoil sword. A half smile twitched across her lips. Her father and Brand had probably been a lot alike.

Malvin studied the polished white face that gleamed golden in the firelight. "When Queen Aleria decided to take the sad news of your mother's Capture to Keldoran," he began, in a low storytelling voice, "King Ulor was against it. He knew King Tarrant and, more precisely, King Tarrant's temper. And he did not trust him to act with reason. The queen refused to listen. Just sending a message was cold and heartless, she told him. It had to be done by a family member. She convinced Prince Alaric of this as well, and together with two regiments of King Ulor's knights they set off for Keldoran."

Willow tucked cold, stiff legs close to her chest and rested chin to knees, pulling her cloak tighter. The half smile twitched across her lips again. Her grandmother sounded an awful lot like Nana. Both big sticklers for doing the right thing.

"Brand, of course," continued Malvin in the same dreamy story voice, "was also required to go. As squire to the prince, he set off from Carrus riding proudly at his side." Malvin turned suddenly, holding Brand out to her. "If you could've seen him that day, you would never have believed he could betray Prince Alaric. He would have died for him!" Tears sprang to Malvin's eyes, and he brusquely wiped them away.

Betrayal? Willow took back the cold white figure. Brand had mentioned nothing about *betraying* anyone when he'd told her of Prince Alaric's capture. "He told me what happened in Thorburn Wood," she said softly, "but nothing about betraying my father."

Malvin stared into the fire again. "Brand was the only Player who returned to Carrus that day," he said, composing himself. "Someone started a rumour. They said 'twas Brand who had Captured Princess Diantha and that 'twas him who set up the Capture of the queen and prince."

"*What?!* You're kidding, right? Why would anyone think that?"

"'Tis a long story, but to begin it, I must tell you that Brand and your mother were scarcely speaking to each other at the time."

This was turning out to be more complicated than Willow had thought.

"Brand believed that the best strategy for the Game would be to queen each and every Pawn, both Black and White. We could then use their combined magic powers against Nezeral."

"But that's a great idea!" So great, in fact, that Willow was surprised she hadn't thought of it herself. She did the math. Sixteen pawns plus two queens. That would've been, like, eighteen players with magic powers, instead of just two.

Malvin nodded. "I know. I thought it a good strategy as well. But Princess Diantha did not. She opposed Brand, saying that his plan held far too great a risk."

"Why?"

"All the Pawns, except for the princess herself, were either ordinary folk like the blacksmith's son or older people like your nurse. They might have been hurt. And they would not have known how to use the power. Like your other grandmother, Queen Morwenna, they might have caused more harm than good."

"Queen Morwenna caused harm?" No one had mentioned that to Willow before.

"Aye. Your Keldorian grandmother was not a mage before the Game and could not properly harness the magic of the Queen Player." A grin inched across his face. "She caused a fair bit of havoc for near six months. She has improved much since then, however. Doesn't make her court ladies bald or turn them green anymore and doesn't cause hail storms in the summer. But still, to think of all those Pawns unaccustomed to magic and all that power ... " Malvin shrugged. "Well, you must understand our dilemma."

Stifling a chuckle, Willow swept away her sudden vision of bald green court ladies. "But what about my mother? You said all the pawns except her had no experience of magic." Then she thought of something else. Something she'd never even considered before. "And what about me? Do *I* have magical powers?"

Malvin stared down at his booted feet, clearly uncomfortable with the question. Finally he cleared his throat and flicked a guilty glance at Willow. "To answer your first question, yes, your mother was a mage before the Game spell. But when the Game first started, she married Prince Alaric and very soon was pregnant with you. She did not want to be queened because ... because she did not know for certain what would happen to either her or to you, her unborn child." His eyes fastened back to his boots. "No one has yet attempted the queening move," he admitted with a weak smile. "I fear we learn the intricacies of the Game as we go along."

Willow took a moment to digest this new information. They wanted to queen *her*, didn't they? Did that mean she would be used as their guinea pig?

"And as to your second question," added Malvin glumly,

"I do not know. Your mother and paternal grandmother have power. So you might have inherited it as well. But then again, you might not. 'Tis hard to say."

"So getting back to Brand," said Willow, trying not to think about all the alarming possibilities scrambling around inside her head, "who started those rumours?" As soon as the words left her mouth, though, she knew the answer. *Varian.*

Malvin angrily flung a stick into the fire, watching as flames ate at its curling bark. "I was never certain until this very day," he spat out bitterly. "But now it all makes sense. It had to be Prince Varian who started those rumours to draw attention away from his own plotting."

Varian's cold blue eyes surfaced in Willow's thoughts, right alongside Brand's earnest glare and deep dimples. How could anyone have distrusted Brand when they had someone like Varian around?

"At least we know the truth now," Malvin said dryly. "Varian must have bribed one of our White Players to Capture Princess Diantha. He sent word to King Tarrant, claiming that White did it deliberately, told the king where he could Capture Prince Alaric and Queen Aleria. Then he started the rumours about Brand — all in a bid to win himself a crown." Malvin paused, a new idea dawning on his face. "And that man we saw — Lord Radnor — creating unrest in the marketplace yesterday, he is one of Prince Varian's men and must also be part of his scheme."

Something clicked in Willow's head. The "truth" that Brand had wanted her to know was that he had never betrayed her father. In fact this whole get-her-to-Keldoran mission was not just a way to protect the king, but also a way for Brand to prove to everyone that he wasn't a traitor. "Brand was helping me, wasn't he, so people would see that those rumours aren't true?"

Malvin nodded agreement. "He did it for your father, too, because he thought he owed him something."

Willow stared down at Brand's glowing white face. She understood him now. Understood why he'd been so touchy in the beginning. He'd seen her disbelief in him.

"I'm sorry," she said over the lump in her throat. "You know, about giving you guys such a hard time in Graffyn. But Brand made me so mad, and I ... " Willow glanced shyly at Malvin. "Did he ... I don't suppose he thought much of me?"

Malvin didn't answer. The thick quiet of the snowy night crept into his silence, prompting Willow to look up. She found him smiling at her, a glint in his eye.

"You are fond of him, aren't you?"

A hot blush raced over Willow's glowing cheeks, staining them, she was sure, an embarrassingly bright red. "No, I ... " The words seemed to dangle off her tongue. She didn't finish them, because she knew they weren't true. She'd been thinking about Brand all day — and *not* just about what truth he'd wanted her to know. She'd been grieving for him. Worrying if they'd ever find a way to set him free.

"'Tis nothing to be abashed at." Malvin looked down at his feet, sparing her the huge grin on his face. "I asked Brand the same question about you."

The furred hood around Willow's head was suddenly suffocatingly hot, its fine soft hairs tickling her cheeks unmercifully. She brushed at the fur, making an effort to appear cool and calm.

"He said that you were the bravest, most bad-tempered and stubborn girl he had ever met, but that when you smiled, you reminded him of a Zuriel Blagdon painting."

Willow grinned. "A Zuriel Blagdon painting; that's like a *good* thing, right?" She snuggled closer to Malvin and held Brand up between them. "Brand told me that when Lord Garnock captured my father and grandmother, he only pricked them with a knife. And Brand was only wounded in the arm. None of them were actually killed. So you know what I think? I think he's alive in there. And that he can hear us."

Malvin stared thoughtfully at Brand's small figure. "'Tis possible. Mayhap there's some other reason why Queen Aleria saw no life force in your mother's Pawn piece." He pitched a few twigs into the fire and smiled at Willow. "Mayhap they can be rescued. 'Twill be something to ask Queen Morwenna," he said, "and something to hope on."

Willow rested her cheek on her knee, close to Brand. She warmed him against her flushed face, imagining that she was sending him telepathic messages. *You are alive in there, I know you are. Just hold on a little while longer, okay, and I promise I'll get you out.* She felt Malvin's arm slip gently around her shoulders and her eyes began to drift shut.

❦

Brand stirred. Someone was talking to him. Willow's soft voice whispered in his ear. *I'll get you out,* the voice promised. *Just hold on a little while longer.* Then the voice was gone. A terrifying blackness surrounded him.

He tried to feel for walls or a floor, but there was only empty air. Was he hanging from a rope? How could there be no floor? There had to be a floor!

Suddenly he remembered. He remembered the crossbow

bolt and the boy who'd tried to kill Willow. But there was nothing there. No bolt. No pain. *No shoulder!*

Brand panicked inside, twisting and turning, trying to feel something. *Anything* that would prove he was still alive. His thoughts flailed as a terrible realization set in. He'd been Captured. He was inside a chess piece. That was why he had no body. That was why he couldn't see anything.

He strained to hear Willow's voice again, but the silence around him was just as profound as the darkness.

"Willow!" he called out. *"Willow!"* The name echoed around him. How, he didn't know. He called her name again, hoping that if he had heard her, that she in turn would be able to hear him.

There was no answer.

The last memory Brand had of Willow was her white face framed by a red tumble of hair.

⁂

Seersey's Peak, on the outskirts of Tulaan, Keldoran's capital, provided an amazing aerial view of the city. Willow blinked, still not used to the brightness outside of the sheltering forest. After their second day of riding, it had finally stopped snowing and now both the sky and landscape were a clear, sparkling white. She shielded her eyes to look at the setting sun, which was just beginning to dip behind a range of snow-capped mountains. Pink and gold deepened to brilliant scarlet, painting the jagged peaks into a toothy red smile. Weird, but kind of beautiful at the same time.

At the foot of the mountains, but up higher than the city, was a huge storybook castle. Willow stared in awe. It had been dark when she'd left Carrus. She had seen nothing of it but stone walls and a postern gate. But even in the shadow of the great mountains, she could see that the Keldorian castle, with its hulking grey-stoned walls and towers that rose a hundred feet, was immense.

Willow's gaze followed along the walls that stretched out from the farthest towers. They formed an enormous square that encompassed the entire city of Tulaan. She could see the winding streets and all the little snow-covered, boxy houses with their pale wattle and daub walls. Here and there a merchant's rich home or a large inn or a stone-spired church jutted above the crowded, jumbled-together rooftops. It reminded her a bit of Graffyn, except that Graffyn seemed small compared to this place.

"Crumbcakes! What a view!" Gemma whistled under her breath. "Who would've thought a city could look so grand?"

Willow agreed, smiling. She noticed that Gemma's bruises were beginning to heal. They were only a dull yellowy brown now.

Brand's warhorse, Dusk, whinnied and head-butted impatiently at Malvin. Since Brand's abrupt change into marble, his big charger had become mule-stubborn and skittish as a colt, calming down only when Malvin's little brown mare was near. So, consequently, poor Malvin had gotten stuck leading him.

"Dusk! Stop it!" Malvin gave Dusk a firm stare, then moved in closer. "Aye, 'tis a grand city. Almost as big as Carrus."

"Ah, Your Highness, look," said Lord Garnock, pointing down at the castle. "The banners are flying. His Majesty must have received my dispatches."

Willow stared at the blue and gold pennants that whipped and waved from each tall tower. She'd been in shock when she'd met her first grandfather, and everything had been so chaotic. Nothing had seemed real to her then. But now it was different. Excitement tingled through her like a live current. This was real. Very real! There were people down there, relatives, *family*, who really wanted her. The pennants seemed to stream their happiness. With each flap and flutter she knew that they would love her.

A gloved hand patted Willow's arm. "Come then," said a smiling Lord Garnock, "your family awaits you."

At the city gates, an honour guard bright with banners and shining armour had been sent to meet them and lead them through the main thoroughfare. Willow, tense with anxiety, barely noticed the crowded buildings or gawking crowds. All she could think about was meeting her grandparents.

"Are ye nervous?" asked Gemma, excitement trembling in her voice. "Because I swear if ye're not, I'm nervous enough for both of us." Her blue eyes widened rapturously. "To think, *me*, Gemma Fletcher, is goin' to see the inside of a castle. Why, it's enough to make me pinch meself to see if I'm really awake!"

Willow laughed. She'd gone way past pinching. It was the reality/acceptance stage that was the real kicker. Jackhammer heartbeat, cold clammy hands and mouth so dry she couldn't find spit to swallow. She leaned over to Gemma. "That's nothing. Try meeting a family you never knew existed. Now *that's* what I call nervous!"

Gemma's eyes goggled in mock horror. "Cripes! Yer Highness, ye must be near to faintin'!" She leaned over and reached into her saddlebag. "Here." She handed Willow a leather flask. "Drink this. It'll give ye courage."

A spicy apple smell wafted from the small container. Willow tipped it up and took a sip. It tasted kind of good. Like a cross between cider and Trumble's mage-brewed ale. She took a bigger drink. "Hey, this isn't bad," she said, swishing it around her dry mouth. "Where did you get it?"

"A soldier gave it to me. He said it came right from yer own grandmother's apple orchard and that she mage-brewed it herself."

Willow took another big swallow and handed the flask back to Gemma. *Her own grandmother*. The words sounded strange and familiar at the same time. They stabbed her with pain, making her eyes burn. "You know, I had another grandmother who ... who died just before I came here. I ... " Willow blinked, surprised. She hadn't meant to tell Gemma about Nana.

Gemma stared at her, waiting patiently for her to go on.

"I ... I ... just miss her is all." Willow looked straight ahead, not sure she trusted herself to hold the tears in.

After a block and a half of silence, Gemma asked timidly, "Was she the one who looked after ye in Earthworld?"

Willow nodded and lowered her chin.

"I'm sorry. I know what it's like to lose someone. Me da and I were pretty close. I thought I would never get over the missin' of him." She paused for a moment, then leaned over and added in a whisper, "Ye know, I talks to him sometimes. When I'm feelin' lonely or scared, I pretend he's watchin' over me. Helps me, ye know, not to miss him so much."

"Really," Willow said, turning to look at Gemma, "that really helps?" She'd used her imagination on everything else — why hadn't she thought to use it on Nana?

"Oh aye. And next thing ye have to do is to pretend they answer back. Then it's like they really are there helpin' ye."

A hesitant smile came over Willow's face. It felt strange talking about her problems to someone other than Nana. Strange, but kind of nice. "Thanks. Maybe I'll give it a try." She turned from Gemma and stared at the high grey walls of the Keldorian castle that were coming into view at the end of the street.

Well, Nana, she said inside her head, *we're here. We finally made it, and I'm going to have a family again.* She could see Nana smiling, her soft white curls pinned into a neat bun, her dark eyes bright with approval. She was riding a sturdy little brown mare and wearing a thick wool cloak. *'Tis proud I am of you, my sweetling,* Nana beamed. She reached a frail, tender hand to Willow's cheek. *To find your courage is no small feat.*

Willow felt her eyes prickle. Nana's skin felt warm and alive. *But I haven't really,* she told her grandmother. *I'm scared all the time.*

Nana smiled. *But you go on anyway, right? And isn't that what real courage is all about? And another thing,* she looked over to where Gemma rode, oblivious to Nana's presence. *You've made a friend. Let those tightly locked feelings of yours out for a little airing. Well, at least now I can rest easier.*

A shrill trumpet blast echoed over the street. Willow blinked, looking up to see six long narrow horns draped with blue and gold ribbons overhanging the castle gatehouse. The wooden drawbridge was lowered, and as their horses clattered over top it, the trumpeters let go another deafening blast.

Willow stared into the murky moat water, trying to collect herself. What had happened there? That was more than just a fantasy. She'd actually *seen* Nana. *Touched* her!

The water moved at a sluggish pace, thick and oily look-ing, its fungus smell permeating the air. Willow looked away, peering at the sharp tips of the gatehouse portcullis and into the dark walkway beyond it. She was in Black's back rank now. Maybe that had somehow affected her.

The gatehouse tunnel ended and Willow came out into an empty snow-covered courtyard that faced the four front tow-ers of the castle. She pulled on her reins, stopping to stare through the long narrow opening between the two biggest ones, considering Nana's words. Her fate was on the other side of that opening. Did she truly have the courage to go through there?

Malvin sidled up next to her. "I wish Brand were here," he said, smiling sadly. "'Twould have eased him greatly to know you've arrived here safe and sound."

"Yeah." A hard-squeezing lump made it impossible to say more. Willow slid her hand into her pocket and held tight to Brand.

Nana was right. She had made friends. Good friends. She flicked her reins, moving her horse toward the inner portcullis.

Now it was time to meet her family.

CHAPTER 17

*T*HEY STOOD IN THE INNER COURTYARD, bundled up in rich fur cloaks, straining overtop one another to catch a glimpse of her. Willow watched as the honour guard ahead of her split into two lines, six riders on each side, to form a path for her to ride through. Behind, high up on the second gatehouse, more trumpets blared, and Lord Garnock appeared at her side to lead her toward the spectators.

Willow rode slowly, her heart thumping against her chest, painfully aware of how she must look. She'd tried earlier to do something with her hair. But without a brush, all she could manage was a bushy ponytail. She pulled her cloak bottom forward, edging it over torn pants.

At the end of the guard line, Lord Garnock stopped and dismounted, bowing to the crowd. Willow scanned their faces. No, she thought. Not bowing to the crowd, but bowing to *them,* the two people in the middle wearing the gold crowns.

A hand touched Willow's wrist. Lord Garnock was waiting to help her dismount. She slid her leg over, letting herself fall into his arms and land gracefully on the ground. He took her hand, holding it high, as if he were going to walk her down a wedding aisle.

"Your Majesties," he said gravely, "I present to you your granddaughter, the princess Willow." He then bowed low again and moved aside, leaving Willow all alone.

No one budged or tried to speak. They were all staring at her, entranced. Finally, a small regal woman who glowed like a golden sun — her grandmother, Willow reminded herself — broke away from the others and ran forward. She flung possessive arms around Willow and squeezed her tight.

Willow stared at sparkling blue sapphires and blood-red rubies and down at the top of her grandmother's gold-crowned head. Oh God, she was like a giant next to her. The crown shifted, pressing into her face. Willow hugged back, blinking and holding her cheek away from the dangerous jewel-studded spikes.

The queen broke the embrace first and looked up at Willow, grasping her arms firmly. "Welcome, my dear. Welcome home."

"Th-thank you." Willow couldn't get any more words out. She was lost in the green pools of her grandmother's soft eyes, her lovely unlined face and her happy smile.

Another arm wrapped around her, and she was pulled close, this time with her face pressed into a masculine shoulder. "You are safe now," whispered a deep voice. "And at home, where you belong."

The proprietary way he said that — *where you belong* — made Willow feel slightly uncomfortable. Being a pawn was bad enough. She did not need to be someone's possession on top of it.

The king stepped away from her and gripped her arms as the queen had done. "Look at her," he said, winking down at the queen. "'Tis plain to see the Somerell blood."

Willow didn't know what he meant at first, but as she stared past his purple glow, it soon became clear. Chocolate brown eyes, pale skin and thick hair the shade of a cherry tomato — she and her grandfather had the exact same colouring.

"Well, now that we have done with the introductions," said King Tarrant, folding her into a shoulder hug, "let us get you inside out of this cold. 'Twould seem, from what Garnock has written, that a warm hearth and a hearty meal would do you some good."

"Now my lord," interrupted the queen, claiming Willow's other arm, "she needs a bit of time to herself first." They began leading her toward one of the towers. The crowds followed in their wake, a long train of quietly swishing cloaks and dresses. "There are new clothes and a nice hot bath awaiting you. Then ... " the queen smiled brightly and squeezed Willow's hand, "we've planned a lovely feast, all in your honour."

"Aye," agreed King Tarrant. "Cook tells me he's even managed to snare a peacock or two. A rare delicacy in these parts."

Willow smiled, basking in their warm, excited chatter. It felt good to be wanted. To have someone else in control again. She ignored a twinge of uneasiness that prickled through her. Tonight, she was going to be happy. She was going to forget about the game and just enjoy being part of a family at last.

Inside the castle, Willow's new-found grandfather gave her another quick hug and set off, saying he needed to take care of some matters with Lord Garnock. Queen Morwenna, after shooing away her clustered courtiers, led Willow to her rooms.

There was a wooden tub filled to the brim with hot, sweet-smelling water sitting in front of a blazing fire. Her grandmother and three servants quickly stripped off Willow's clothes and immersed her in the deep tub.

Willow sat back and relaxed, letting the older ladies natter and fuss over her. They soaped and washed and oiled her, till she came out gleaming like a seal. They slipped her into a royal blue dress with gold silk edging the neckline and sleeves, and delicate gold embroidery decorating the skirt.

"You're a vision," sighed the queen, dabbing at her eyes with a handkerchief. "'Tis almost like seeing my Diantha again. That blue always did suit her so."

Willow stared down at herself, suddenly aware of a slight breeze. The dress was pretty, but it fell well above her ankles. She stretched out her arms, noticing that the sleeves and waist were also too short and that the front had a little more space to fill than she could naturally manage.

One of the ladies tried to fit some blue slippers on her feet, but only got as far as the toes before giving up.

"I could wear my boots, maybe," offered Willow, trying to hide her horror of just such a possibility. She might be a princess, but she doubted she'd be setting any fashion trends with dirt-stained boots and blue velvet.

Her grandmother laughed, a high tinkly sound that made her seem like a young girl. Willow looked at her, wondering for the first time how old she was. Beneath her golden queen-glow, she had long honey blonde hair wrapped into a chignon, no wrinkles or grey hair, and a smile that puckered an impish dimple in the corner of her mouth. Maybe mid-thirties or early forties, Willow guessed. Definitely a weird age to be calling someone Grandma.

"Oh, no, no," said Queen Morwenna when she caught her breath. "I knew the dress would not fit you, dear. I was planning to alter it." She stepped toward Willow, placing her hands lightly on Willow's slim waist. "This won't take but a minute."

Willow's mouth gasped into a small, surprised "o" as Queen Morwenna's dainty hands slid down to her hips, the too-short fabric sliding and stretching with them.

"Now, lift here," said Queen Morwenna, raising Willow's arms. She touched her sides, and the fabric around Willow's chest magically shrunk to the proper proportions. Her sleeves were next, and then Queen Morwenna knelt to deal with the hem length. She put her whole arms around the dress and began to lower them, the dress hem obediently expanding and following.

Holy cow! It had totally slipped Willow's mind that her grandmother could make magic. "That was amazing!" She felt her hips where the fabric now fitted snug and comfortable. There were no tears or patches or even a loose thread. It was as if the dress had been made that way.

"Yes, 'tis quite startling the first time one sees true magic." Queen Morwenna brought the blue slippers back to Willow's feet. "'Tis also quite startling," she added, her hands magically stretching them to fit, "the first time one performs it. My first achievement was to pass my hand through an oak table, and I must say, it was quite a shocking moment."

Willow smiled and helped Queen Morwenna to her feet. "What else can you do?" she asked, thinking about all those old TV shows like *Bewitched* and *I Dream of Jeannie*. "Can you disappear, or turn me into a bird? Can you *fly?*"

"No, yes, and sort of," said Queen Morwenna, laughing. "I haven't learned to disappear yet. I *could* turn you into a bird. And I can't fly in my physical state, but I can sort of float a little. I'm still just a beginner, you know. It takes years and years to really excel at it."

Willow picked up her swan pendant from the table where

she'd set it before her bath. "My elf gift," she said, holding it out to the queen, "you know about it, right?"

Queen Morwenna's chin trembled slightly. "I never attended your christening, dear," she whispered. "I never even got to see you as a babe. But yes, I did hear about the gift."

Willow swallowed hard. She'd been about to ask about getting her powers, but now found she couldn't. All along she'd been so busy dealing with her own feelings about having a new family that she hadn't once stopped to consider what *they* were dealing with.

Her grandmother sniffed and dabbed at her unshed tears, and Willow was suddenly engulfed in her pain. Queen Morwenna had missed out on her only granddaughter's whole childhood. Had never seen her first steps or heard her first words. Had never fed her, never played with her, nothing.

"You must have been a beautiful child." Queen Morwenna pulled back Willow's hair and helped her to fasten the necklace. "Your mother's hair was this red," she said, running the long strands through her fingers, "even as an infant."

She picked up a brush and began to slide it through Willow's hair. "I know what the pendant means," she said after a few moments.

Willow waited for her to continue, feeling badly now that she'd ever brought it up. It was obvious her grandmother was upset.

"It means," she finally went on, "that you are the elf queen's netherchild and will have to be queened. And — that you will have to leave me again to go into battle against Nezeral." She set down the brush and pulled Willow into a tight embrace. "I don't want to think about that tonight. Let's pretend it doesn't exist. Just for this one evening."

Her shoulders are so narrow, thought Willow as she hugged Queen Morwenna back. *So narrow and fragile.* She pushed her many questions to the back of her mind, determined to grant her grandmother's wish.

Willow pulled away, looking down at Queen Morwenna. "Grandmother, there's something that I really have to know."

"And what would that be, dearest?" said the queen, sniffing and smoothing out her skirts.

She didn't seem offended at being called an old-lady name, so Willow took her arm and began to walk toward the door. "What exactly does a roast peacock taste like? And what do they do with all those feathers?"

Queen Morwenna's silvery laughter pealed all the way down the hallway.

CHAPTER 18

*L*AUGHTER AND EXCITED CHATTER could be heard outside the doors to the feast hall. Willow paused. Her stomach started to spiral as though it were oral presentation day at school. *Oh great, that's all I need — to be sick, clammy and breathless in front of a bunch of strangers.* She smoothed sweaty palms against her dress, trying to relax.

Queen Morwenna glanced at her, taking in her white face and nervous gestures. "Are you alright, my dear? You look a little shaky. Mayhap 'tis too soon for a party. Would you prefer another night?"

"No, no. I'm always nervous when I meet new people. Don't worry. I'll be fine. Just need to take a couple of breaths, is all."

Merry laughter burst from the feast hall, echoing around Willow and Queen Morwenna. Queen Morwenna poked her head through the open doorway. "No need to fear tonight, my dear. Come and see." She waved at Willow to look in with her.

Willow hesitated, then peered around her grandmother into the feast hall.

"See," said Queen Morwenna. "They're festive and well into their cups. A good combination. 'Tis only when they're quiet that you need fret."

Festive wasn't the word for them. Willow blinked in wonderment. *Magical*, maybe. Or *fantastical*. Explosive colour took her breath away. Blues and greens and the brightest scarlets, yellows and purples and browns, all in their truest, deepest shades. Her eyes raced over the crowd, taking in their silks and furs, their glistening jewels and their huge elaborate hats.

Too much, she thought. *This is too much.*

The room was alive with her fantasies.

"Just imagine them all in their smallclothes," said Queen Morwenna, looking back at her. "'Tis a trick your grandfather taught me."

Willow blinked down at Queen Morwenna. "What?" She wasn't sure, but she thought her grandmother had just told her to imagine the feast crowd in their underwear.

"Imagine them in their smallclothes," repeated Queen Morwenna, smiling. "They won't seem so intimidating then."

Willow grinned, glancing into the room again. *Her* idea of underwear, she was sure, was not the same as her grandmother's. "Okay," she whispered. "I'm ready."

Queen Morwenna signalled to a man across the hallway who stepped into the room and blasted on his trumpet, settling the crowd and grabbing their attention. All eyes turned to the doorway. Willow felt her legs go wobbly.

"Her Majesty, Queen Morwenna," the man bellowed, "and the princess Willow."

Queen Morwenna waited in the entrance long enough for her husband to stand at the front of their table, then she hooked her arm through Willow's and marched, dignified and confident, into the great feast hall.

Step. Step. Step. Hey, this wasn't so bad. Willow concentrated on her grandmother's slow, steady steps. No worse, at least, than that day she'd walked to Melissa Morrison's cafeteria table with everyone staring holes through her. She lifted her head and smiled at the people around her.

When Willow and her grandmother reached the other side of the room, King Tarrant nodded to his wife and claimed Willow's hand. He led her up the steps of the dais where their table was placed and turned her around to face the crowd.

"Lords and ladies of Keldoran," he said in his big, booming voice, "your king and queen welcome you." Cheers and clapping erupted from the assembled guests. "This eve," he continued, after they settled again, "brings us much to celebrate. Diantha's daughter, *my* granddaughter, is returned home to us. Thus our quarrel against Gallandra has been settled, as we now have reason to believe that King Ulor may *not* be held responsible for our dear Diantha's Capture." He paused as more cheers echoed throughout the room. "And now," his hand guided Willow forward, "I present to you the princess Willow!"

This time the applause was thunderous. People climbed to their feet, clapping and cheering. *The Gifted One!* some cried out. *Death to Nezeral!* others shouted.

Willow blanched a bit at their enthusiasm. She'd forgotten that it wasn't just Brand she had to help. Two whole kingdoms were counting on her. She wished that she could forget, just for a moment, that she'd been chosen as Queen Cyrraena's champion, that it was up to her to somehow defeat the elf prince. But the crowd obviously wasn't going to let her.

King Tarrant's hands went up, palms toward the audience, quieting them. "And now, let the feast begin!" Another cheer arose and people dropped back into their seats, resuming their gossip and merriment.

"You did well," said King Tarrant, patting Willow's shoulder. He steered her around the table to their seats. "Don't you think so, Morwenna? Did you see those courtiers?" he said, not waiting for her answer. "They haven't been this rowdy since the last tourney. I think the child has done wonders for their morale, don't you?"

"Yes, dear," agreed Queen Morwenna, smiling. They were seated in comfortable gold cushioned chairs, with Willow nestled between them.

Willow looked around the room again, her eyes drawn to the bright colour splashes that jumped out at her everywhere. Blue, gold and red were the main ones. They were in tapestries and banners, tablecloths and carpets, all depicting in some way the boar's head and crossbow, which were clearly the symbols for her grandfather's coat of arms.

The other guests, she now noticed, were seated at tables lower down and spread from either end of hers in an enormous U-shape. They sat on low wooden benches and were crowded together on both sides of the table. She could see Malvin to her far left, but couldn't see Gemma anywhere. She scanned the room, wondering if Gemma had been too tired to come.

"'Tis quite a sight, is it not?" King Tarrant leaned in close, engulfing Willow in a beer-scented breath.

Willow sat far back in her plush chair, pretending to stare up at the ceiling. "Incredible. Absolutely incredible." She hadn't noticed the ceilings before. They were as high as a church's with enormous vaulted beams that looked like the rib cage of some great beast. Iron chandeliers hung from them, dangling from long, thick chains, flickering with hundreds of dancing, smoking candles.

"What was your feast hall in Earthworld like?" boomed King Tarrant. He tipped back in his chair to look up, too.

"Was it as big as ours?"

Willow blinked at him. "Ah, not quite. We just had a small dining room." She omitted the fact that by small, she meant probably the size-of-the-king's-closet small. "There were just the two of us. My nana and me."

King Tarrant's laughter echoed around the room. "You jest with me, Granddaughter," he snorted, clapping her back so hard that she spilled wine on her gown. "What about your servants and guards and cook?"

Willow didn't answer; she patted at the wet spot on her lap. Her grandfather, she realized, was a bit drunk and wasn't too likely to be able to understand her frugal life on Earth.

The food arrived, carried in, platter by platter, by an army of white-aproned servants. First came the meat dishes. Roasted venison, grilled rabbit, chickens glazed in orange sauce, swans and peacocks resplendent in their redressed feathers, even a fire-breathing boar's head that brought oohs and aahs from the crowd of onlookers. Each sumptuous tray was paraded around the room and then brought to the king's table for inspection and the first cut.

Soups, puddings, vegetables, breads and sauces were placed on every table. Wine and ale were poured by servant boys posted along the walls, and musicians, placed inconspicuously in a far corner, played slow, relaxing dinner ballads.

Willow picked at her food, trying to ignore her grandfather's increasingly intoxicated condition. Difficult to do, though, when he spilled salt on her meat and spit pieces of carrot at her. She gazed longingly at Malvin, wishing she could sit with *him* instead.

Finally, after what seemed like an eternity, a troop of brawny servants started to clear off their table. King Tarrant reached over to squeeze Willow's shoulder. "The nobles wish to meet you, my dear. We're setting up a receiving line."

For two hours, Willow stood uncomfortably between her grandparents, putting up with King Tarrant's loud voice and over-tight shoulder grasps, greeting so many Lords of This and Ladies of That that by the end of the receiving line she just smiled, thanked the person for coming, and didn't even try to remember their names. Finally, after the last guest had bowed and introduced themselves, King Tarrant ordered the dancing to begin.

Willow sank gratefully into her seat, wondering if, as the guest of honour, she would be allowed to leave. She looked around for her grandmother, but saw that she was busy talking with a group of ladies. King Tarrant caught Willow's eye. Quickly she glanced away. But it was too late. The king started toward her, dragging a young man behind him.

"'Tis my granddaughter," he bellowed, pushing the boy at her. "Dance with her! Dance with her!"

A blue eye winked at Willow's red face and a blond head bowed over her hand. "Your Highness," he said politely, "may I have this dance?"

Wanting to get as far away from her grandfather as possible, Willow allowed the young man to lead her onto the dance floor. Once there, she pulled her hand away. "I'm sorry, but I don't know how to dance. Could you please just take me over to my grandmother?"

The boy nodded sympathetically and guided her to the queen's table. "The king," he said in a low voice, "doesn't usually drink this much. 'Tis the excitement, I think, on meeting you, that has him in such a state."

Willow gave him a wan smile. It was good to know that

her grandfather wasn't a drunkard, but still that didn't help her present embarrassment.

"Your Highness," said the boy, bowing to Queen Morwenna and backing away.

The queen, her golden game-glow brilliant in the candle-light, acted the proud grandmother as she drew Willow into her circle of ladies. "You see, Lady Lyris," she said to an elegant, green-gowned woman, "'tis as I told you: my granddaughter has my nose and chin."

"I'll wager she has your smile, too," added a short woman in a feather hat.

Another woman, one with thin lips and narrowed eyes, gave Willow's swan pendant a hard stare. "And when does Your Majesty plan on the queening ceremony?" she asked bluntly. Faces paled and lips pursed shut all around the circle of women. Obviously, this was not a topic normally up for discussion. Willow eyed her grandmother curiously, her interest piqued. No one had ever explained a queening ceremony to her before.

"Well, Countess," said Queen Morwenna icily, "a decision has not as yet been made. The princess, as you know, has only been in our world for a few days. She needs some time to recover her strength. I am sure you understand."

"Of course, Your Majesty," said the thin-lipped woman tightly. She lowered her head in a deferential bow, eyes sparking with anger. "And I'm sure that *you* understand that my son, Wren, has been a Captured Pawn for over a week. And now Lord Garnock has put my other son, Terrill, in jail for trying to avenge him. The queening, I believe, should be sooner rather than later."

This time gasps went around the circle of ladies. Willow

guessed that speaking your mind to a queen wasn't a particularly good idea.

Queen Morwenna's small stature seemed to increase as her chin lifted imperiously. "I, too, have a Captured Pawn for a child. So I will forgive your impertinence." She turned to the green-gowned woman. "Lady Lyris, please escort Countess Longbottom to her chambers. I believe she requires a rest."

The two women bowed and started across the room, the countess struggling not to cry.

Willow stared after the two women, a sudden realization jolting through her. Countess Longbottom was the mother of Terrill Longbottom — the boy who'd captured Brand. Her sympathy for the woman flared into anger then simmered back down again. It wasn't Countess Longbottom's fault — or her son's fault — that Brand was now a chess piece. It was the stupid game's fault. And the fault of the one who'd started the game in the first place — Nezeral.

The queen placed a hand on Willow's arm. "What is it, dear? You look upset."

Before Willow could answer, the music stopped and a voice thundered over the great hall. "Lords and ladies," King Tarrant bellowed, "I have another announcement to make." He searched the room till his eyes found Willow. "Granddaughter, come up here, please."

Willow glanced at Queen Morwenna, who shrugged her shoulders uncertainly. "'Tis nothing I know about," she whispered, a worried look in her eye. "He's had much too much to drink tonight, though."

"Come, come," said King Tarrant, waving Willow impatiently up on the stage.

Queen Morwenna patted her arm. "Go on, 'tis probably

nothing more than another speech to welcome you."

Willow swallowed hard. Everyone was looking at her and waiting. She began moving toward the platform, a tight knot forming in her stomach. She should just ignore him. Turn around and walk right out the door. But Lord Garnock's words niggled at her. He'd said not to judge King Tarrant too harshly. That his grief had made him distraught.

Willow kept walking toward her grandfather, a seed of pity growing inside her. She thought of poor Countess Longbottom and her two sons, King Tarrant and his daughter and King Ulor and his son. They'd all suffered so much, were still in the midst of their grieving. The least she could do is forgive King Tarrant a few too many drinks.

When she came to the dais stairs, the king took her hand and helped her to climb the narrow steps.

"I have come to a decision," he announced suddenly. "From this day forth there shall be no more Game playing!"

Willow blinked. What did he mean by that? No more game playing. A frightened whisper went around the room, and people crowded in closer to the dais to listen.

"That is right. No more Game playing. I have decreed that war with Gallandra is at an end. My granddaughter is returned to our arms. We must now move ahead, and release from our hearts our losses. It is what my dear daughter Diantha would have wanted. *Her* daughter shall not be sacrificed on the same altar. We must accept what is. We shall learn to love our lives such as they are, without magic." He motioned to a man who was holding a covered tray. The man stepped forward and pulled off the linen cloth, revealing a beautiful jewelled crown. Willow heard gasps of horror, and then the crown was being set on her head.

"As her mother, the princess Diantha, was before her, I now proclaim the princess Willow heir to the throne of Keldoran. And as such, she shall never be queened in this cursed Game. Never shall she be forced to do battle with the elf prince, Nezeral."

"No!" screamed an anguished voice. Countess Longbottom, restrained by Lady Lyris, thrashed around like a wild animal. "You cannot do this! You cannot allow my son to perish like this!" With a sudden kick, she broke away from Lady Lyris and flew across the hall and up the dais steps to Willow. Kneeling at her feet, she clutched Willow's gown. "I beg you, Your Highness, *you must save my son!*" Two burly guards appeared. Holding an elbow each, they hustled her out of the room.

From the platform, Willow stood frozen as the crowd began to mutter more and more loudly. King Tarrant stood imperiously beside her, silent, his face growing more and more red. Finally Queen Morwenna came up on the stage and raised her arms. Something crackled from her fingertips and then there was silence. People's mouths were still moving but nothing was coming out.

Willow felt in her pocket, clutching hard at Brand's chess piece. Fear trembled through her. How could she defeat Nezeral all by herself, without Brand? She couldn't plan attacks or use a sword. She couldn't even survive by herself in the woods.

Fear leaped into panic. Still clutching Brand, Willow raced down the stairway and through the now silent crowd. She knew the answer to her question. She had always known the answer.

She couldn't do it. She could never defeat Nezeral.

CHAPTER 19

IT WAS MORNING. Daylight streamed through the windows. Real windows this time, Willow noted. She lay pillow-propped in her blue and gold canopied bed, thinking about her options.

Option Number One: Do what her grandfather wanted for her. Stay the way she was and grow up here in the castle.

She imagined King Tarrant and Queen Morwenna as doting grandparents. She'd get to wear pretty dresses, go to balls. Maybe learn to dance and sing and whatever else princesses did. And maybe Nezeral would just get bored and go back to wherever he came from.

It seemed like a pretty sweet set-up, and if she were honest with herself, a big relief.

Relief. That's exactly what she'd felt when King Tarrant had declared the Game over and made her his heir — once the shock had worn off, that is. And oh, how she wanted to let it happen. Just be a good girl and obey her grandfather, letting him look after and protect her.

"But I can't let him, can I?" she whispered to Brand. She held his smooth white figure to the light, tracing over him with a tender fingertip. She knew she couldn't live with herself if she at least didn't *try* to save him. Him and who knew how many others? Maybe even her own parents, her grandmother, *if* they were still alive in those chunks of marble.

Most of the night she'd attempted to talk herself out of such a decision. Her arguments ran along the lines that she didn't know how to use magic, she was scared to death of Nezeral, she had no idea how to find him and, most importantly, she didn't have a clue as to how she would defeat him. But talking it all out with Brand's chess piece had seemed to make her braver. She'd imagined Brand giving her encouragement, telling her she could do it, she *could* stop the game spell and defeat Nezeral. She saw his dark looks, his dimpled smiles. She saw him step, without hesitation, in front of the arrow meant for her. And she knew she had no choice. She had to save him. And the others. It was what Nana would have wanted her to do. She just couldn't let them down.

"So, I guess that leaves Option Number Two," she sighed, "make them queen me, and go find Nezeral."

※

Brand knew it was Willow. Her voice was so clear and real, as if she were whispering in his ear. He'd been calling out to her over and over again, but the words he heard her speak were not in response to anything that he said. She was promising to help him, to get queened and find Nezeral on her own.

Dread took hold of Brand. He'd never told Willow his true plan. Of how her Queen powers, once she had them, were meant to aid *him,* not her, in getting through the magical Game barriers. She was supposed to be safe and sound in Tulaan, while *he* was the one who defeated Nezeral and rescued *her.* At least, that's how he'd always pictured it.

He let himself drift into his hero fantasy, to the part where he returned to Gallandra after having defeated Nezeral and ended the Game spell. It always started with a parade through the city, with teeming crowds cheering him and Dusk all the way to the castle. The king and his father and all the great Gallandrian lords would be there in the courtyard to greet him, with smiles and honours and no shadowy rumours of treason in their eyes. And Willow ... she would be there also.

He saw her the way she'd looked that first day in Carrus, tall and fragile, hair unbound like a child's, her wide tawny eyes sparking in fiery pride. Only, in his courtyard scene, her eyes weren't angry. They were soft and filled with admiration.

Brand shook the images away. His foolish dreams of hero-ism had endangered the princess. Because of him, she would try to fight Nezeral on her own. He flinched inwardly at the thought. Nezeral, he knew, would destroy her. Would, in the end, destroy them all.

༄

A light tap sounded on the door. "Willow? 'Tis me, your grandmother," said Queen Morwenna in a low voice. "May I come in?"

Willow pushed back her coverlets and quickly tucked Brand back beneath her plump feather pillows. "Yeah, sure. C'mon in."

Queen Morwenna swished into the room looking slim and elegant in a simple red dress. Her crown was gone. In its place, she wore a gold hat studded with pearls and rubies. "Did you sleep well, dear?" she asked as she lay a green gown onto a chair back.

Willow shrugged and swung her legs out over the bed, sinking her bare feet into a furry piece of carpet. Across the room, the fire that the queen had magically lit last night was still blazing brightly. Warmth spread over her like sunshine.

Queen Morwenna sat down on the bed beside her. "I am truly sorry for what happened last night. Your grandfather ... well, he is only doing what he thinks best."

"It's okay," Willow mumbled. She wanted to say more, to ask if Queen Morwenna agreed with King Tarrant's decision, but she didn't. She looked down at her knees instead, where a thin golden-glowing hand had reached over and was smoothing the creases in her soft linen nightgown.

"I want to show you something," said Queen Morwenna, rising from the bed. She took Willow's hand and led her from the room.

It was a bit chillier in the hallway, with the cold floor stones biting into Willow's bare feet. But they didn't go far, only to the room next door, where the hearth fire was blazing like a hot summer day.

Willow looked around the empty bedroom, wondering what her grandmother wanted to show her. Then she saw it, hanging over the fireplace, in brilliant blues and golds and reds. A portrait of a woman who looked so much like her that they could have been sisters.

"Your grandfather loved Diantha very much," said Queen Morwenna, putting her arm around Willow's slack shoulders. "I think the sight of you in that dress last night was more than he could bear. He simply couldn't risk losing you, too."

The woman in the portrait, Willow noticed, was wearing the same blue dress that she herself had worn at the feast. It suited her. Her waist looked tiny in it and the blue colour was just the right contrast for her bright coppery curls and creamy skin.

She stepped away from her grandmother, moving to the fireplace for a closer look. Their features, hers and the portrait lady's, were slightly different. The lady's were finer, more delicate.

But her eyes ...

Willow stared at the portrait. Large. Creamy chocolate. She knew those eyes.

Her eyes.

The eyes of her mother.

"How old was she? When that picture was done?"

"She was nineteen. 'Twas just before her marriage to your father."

Yes, thought Willow. That made sense. She looked beautiful and happy. Like a woman in love.

"Tarrant shall have to change his decree eventually."

Willow faced her grandmother. "What?"

"Tarrant *must* change his mind about queening you sooner or later. He is being stubborn about it this morning, though. 'Twill take a few more days, but I am sure he shall come to his senses eventually."

A thin stab of disappointment went through Willow. Somehow, she liked having Option Number One to fall back on, in case Option Number Two got too difficult.

"Well, come on, dear," said Queen Morwenna, slipping her arm around Willow's shoulders again. "I have brought you another dress to wear. And then after you have had a good breakfast, I shall show you around the castle."

Breakfast, due to the king's "ale-head," was a private, uncomfortable affair in the king and queen's chambers. The king was avoiding eye contact or any mention of the feast. Willow just picked at her food and answered his brusque inquiries concerning her sleep. After the servants cleared away the dishes, Queen Morwenna plucked up Willow's hand and hurried her out into the hallway.

"I fear a night of ale drinking turns him into a bit of a bear," she laughed, rolling her eyes. "But once he has had a nap, he'll be right as rain. Till then," she gave Willow a quick wink, "we'd best stay clear of him."

Queen Morwenna led Willow down carpeted hallways, up curving staircases and into large sumptuous rooms. She showed her dark, sombre pictures of her ancestors, rich tapestries embroidered with Keldorian history, and a library filled with shelf upon shelf of Mistolearian literature.

Willow stood, holding one of the heavy leather-bound books, staring at a map of Mistolear. In Nana's stories, she had heard only of the two countries of Keldoran and Gallandra. But Mistolear was clearly much more than that. There were continents and islands and mountains with exotic names like Issander, Tuumagia and the Mountains of Doomriel. There were oceans, lakes and rivers. There were deserts and forests. It was a world, Willow realized with surprise, much like Earth.

Her hands carefully placed the book back on its shelf, and she gazed out a window at a distant line of snow-covered trees, vivid and stark against a blue horizon, wondering exactly how far the game spell spread.

Queen Morwenna followed her gaze, guessing at her thoughts. "That row of trees," she said, pointing eastward, "is one of the borders of the Game spell."

"Borders?"

"Yes, in the beginning, when we were still in the midst of trying to make sense of the Game, your grandfather and his knights set off for the east to see how far the spell extended.

They could go no further east," Queen Morwenna said, shading her eyes, "than that tree line. There is a magical barrier, you see, that keeps us enclosed in the spell. It encompasses both Keldoran and Gallandra, but nothing beyond." She turned away from the window and sighed. "We have heard no news from the outside world for over a year now, so we must assume that the barrier, as well as keeping us in, keeps them out."

Willow knew the game spell stretched between Keldoran and Gallandra, but she'd never heard anyone mention a barrier before. A question she'd always shied away from suddenly popped out. "Where *is* Nezeral? Is he inside the spell or outside it? And if he's outside it, how am I supposed to find him?" Brand's and King Ulor's plans had only gone as far as her being queened. No one had talked about what would happen next.

Queen Morwenna looked back to the window again, staring out at the distant horizon. "There is a castle, a hunting stop for Tarrant, that lies ten leagues beyond those trees. Nezeral, we believe, is there."

"But then that means he's on the other side of the spell. So what can I, or anyone else, do to stop him? Is there, like, a way through the barrier or something?"

The queen looked uncomfortable with the topic of conversation. "No. We could find no way, magical or physical, to go beyond the barrier."

"Then how the heck am I supposed to get through?!" Willow threw her arms up in exasperation. The more she learned about this crazy game, the more complicated it became.

"Well ... well, we — we do not really know, dear. But you ... you are the elf queen's champion. So mayhap that shall make a difference. Or ... " Queen Morwenna stopped, her lips pursing tight.

"*Or?*"

A trapped look clouded the queen's eyes. "Or, he will come for you as he threatened to do when you were born."

This was definitely a new twist on things. Willow stared hard at her grandmother, waiting for her to explain herself.

Queen Morwenna moved away from the window, running shaky fingers over a tan silk chair back. "He swore that the very moment you were queened ... he would ... he would ... destroy you."

Willow breathed out but couldn't seem to breathe back in again. No wonder the plans never went beyond her queening. There *was* no beyond! "Does everyone know about this?" She was beginning to see King Tarrant in a new light. By refusing to queen her, he was the only one who seemed interested in keeping her alive.

Queen Morwenna nodded at her question. "Cyrraena, the elf queen, is not unmoved. Do not forget that she is your protector. She swore she would not let him take you before ... before you were ready." Her arm stole around Willow's shoulders. "I am sorry. I would do anything to take this burden from you. But ... "

"Why me?" Willow shrugged away from the queen's embrace. "Why did she pick me for the champion? I'm just a kid. I don't know anything about magic or elves or *anything!*" Anger crashed through her like a tidal wave. *Who were these elf people anyway, playing with her life as if she were a toy!*

"I am sorry, child. I cannot answer your question. The ways of the elves are a mystery to us. You are her choice. 'Tis all I know."

"Well, where is she? I mean, I know how Nezeral got here, but how did this Queen Cyrraena get here? How is she protecting me?"

"The elf queen is Mistolear's guardian. She abides in her own realm of Timorell, which is a part of Mistolear and yet ... not a part. This, I am told, is like the faerie stories of Earthworld, where humans could enter the faerie realms only through the will of the faerie folk. Here we are the same. We cannot see Timorell or Queen Cyrraena unless she wishes it."

"What is she then — like *God* or something?" said Willow sarcastically.

"No, not a god, but a being like us." The queen perched on the arm of the silk chair and tapped her chin thoughtfully. "I have been told that in Earthworld there are only two types of beings, human and animal. Well, this is not so in Mistolear. We have many types of beings here. Human, elf, dwarf, gnome and pixie — to name just a few. You have seen only humans because Keldoran and Gallandra are human countries. Outside our borders, though, lies a vast diversity of life. Dwarf mountains in the north. Pixie forests to the south. Even the lakes and oceans have their own water nymphs and merpeople. But elves are the most advanced of all our races. They do not grow old, and their magic is many times more powerful than ours."

Willow listened to Queen Morwenna with growing fascination. Pixies. Merpeople. Dwarfs. *They really existed.* If only the game spell were already broken! Then she could explore Mistolear and see all of these amazing creatures for herself. But as she touched the cold figure of Brand, which was tucked away in her pocket, she focused back on her questions.

"Okay, I understand about elves and that this Queen

Cyrraena has been protecting me. But what I want to know is, is she going to help me stop Nezeral?"

"That, my dear, is a good question." Queen Morwenna stood up from the chair arm and patted Willow's shoulders. "As I said before, the ways of elves are a mystery to us. She may help, or she may not. We can only wait and see. For now, though," she took Willow's hand, "my ladies await us in the solarium. 'Twill do us both good, I think, to let these matters lie for a bit. 'Tisn't every day, after all, I get to spend a whole morning with my granddaughter."

Willow let her grandmother lead her from the library and down another carpeted hallway. *Letting matters lie for a bit* didn't bother her. Her brain felt like a big sponge that couldn't possibly absorb anything else, even if she wanted it to. They passed by a table draped in black velvet and covered in white roses.

"Wow," said Willow, stopping to touch one of the silky petals. "Where'd all the roses come from?" As far as she knew, even in this world, flowers still grew in the summer. "I bet they're magic, aren't they?" She bent over to smell their wonderful fragrance.

"They are ... they are for Diantha," said Queen Morwenna quietly. "Tarrant would not allow any funeral ceremonies. He still hoped ... well ... they are my reminder of her. I've kept them blooming since her Capture."

Willow's eyes widened. *Funeral ceremonies.* Her hand fell away from the rose she was touching. Guilt stole over her. The woman in the painting, her mother, had been captured and maybe killed not for fourteen years, but only for a few months.

She tried to imagine that she'd grown up with Diantha as

her mother, that she felt a daughter's grief. Her eyes grew hot. She couldn't do it. The woman in the painting was a stranger.

Only Nana had ever been her mother.

"I'm sorry," she whispered. "I shouldn't have ... "

Queen Morwenna plucked one of the roses and held it under her nose. "Please, do not be sorry. I should have sent them back to the greenhouse before your arrival. At any rate," she slipped the rose back into its vase and brightened her smile, "my solarium is just around the corner. Come, we shall listen to harp music and chat some more."

Listening to harp music was about the last thing Willow felt like doing, but the queen insisted, imprisoning her arm again and leading her down the hallway to a large bright chamber crowded with girls and ladies who were either working on embroidery or practising a slow, twirling dance. A musician sat among them with a golden harp, providing a steady flow of soft, undulating music.

The queen's entrance caused a flurry of curtsies. "Ladies, ladies," said Queen Morwenna, "please continue with your sewing and dancing." She signalled to the harpist to continue playing and led Willow over to two comfortable chairs by a sunny window.

Willow sat studying the fluid movements of the dancers. She'd watched them for a bit last night and had admired their gracefulness. Today, though, with sunbeams catching their colourful gowns, the young women looked like bright jewels swirling around the room.

"Why don't you join them?" said Queen Morwenna, nodding at the dancers. "I shall call Lady Tavia over to give you a lesson."

"No, no. I'm afraid that when it comes to dancing, I'm too

tall, and I've got two left feet. Two *big* left feet."

"Nonsense! Your grandmother Aleria was at least an inch taller than you, had a size nine foot, and she danced beautifully. It just takes time, is all. And lots of practice."

Time and practice. Willow sighed. Two things she might never have. She looked down at her own gold-slippered size nines, wishing they were an un-clod-like size six.

"You know, dear," said Queen Morwenna, speaking low so that only Willow could hear her. "I could cast a dancing spell on you so that you would know all the steps."

"Really? You can make me dance like that?" Willow looked at the laughing girls holding hands and dancing in a loose ring. They reminded her of Melissa Morrison and her friends, so carefree and happy.

"Yeah," she whispered, "it'd be cool to dance like them."

The queen's hand gripped Willow's, sending a startling jolt through her.

"Then 'tis done," she said simply. "Your wish is granted."

CHAPTER 20

W ILLOW FELT ALL TINGLY. She looked down at her feet. Still the same klutzy size nines as always.

"Go on, give it a try." Queen Morwenna clapped her hands, telling the dancers to stop and allow her granddaughter to join them.

A pretty girl with bouncing brown curls who was playing at being a boy giggled and bowed before Willow. "May I have this dance, Your Highness?" she asked, proffering her an open palm.

Willow hesitated, not wanting to make a fool of herself in front of all these people, but with the queen prodding at her back and the brown-haired girl clasping her hand, she rose to her feet. "Okay, okay," she said, allowing the girl to lead her to the dance circle.

Queen Morwenna clapped again and a lively harp song filled the room.

At first Willow felt nothing; her feet peeping beneath her gown were their usual leaden selves. But then the spell ignited. A surge of energy rushed down her legs and crammed into her toes, making them move of their own volition. And suddenly she was doing it. She was dancing! And not just swaying to the music either, but actually stepping and twirling and making complicated moves that suggested she knew what she was doing.

Faces and kaleidoscopic colours flew by as she danced in giddy wonder in a circle. She remembered how much she'd hated dances in grade school. All those horrible afternoons when she'd either cowered at the refreshment table or stayed in class pretending to do homework. She crossed nimble hands with the brown-haired girl. If only she'd known that it would be like this. That it would be such *fun!*

The dance slowed. She completed a graceful turn that touched her hand to a new partner, who smiled and said, "You are an excellent dancer, Your Highness."

Willow grinned and pirouetted. For the first time since she'd arrived here she felt like herself again. Just a regular teenager with no fears of elf princes or game spells. No worries about people depending on her. She was just a girl dancing with other girls. A normal-ordinary-everyday girl.

When the music stopped an hour and a half later, Willow wasn't ready to let the real world come crashing back in. She collapsed against the other girls, giggling and laughing as if they were old friends. It came to her then that she was a *princess*. That these girls respected and admired her. She gave them all a brilliant smile. "*That*," she panted, "was the best fun I've had in a long, long time. Thank you so much."

The girls nodded and curtsied. Queen Morwenna came up behind Willow, hugging her shoulders. "Lovely dancing, ladies. Just lovely. Now," she steered Willow toward the doorway, "we must hurry. The noon meal awaits us."

The feast hall was again filled with courtiers and their families, only this time no one looked excited or happy. A dark cloud of gloom rested over them. Willow stepped into the room with the queen and her ladies. People stared and whispered, obviously still upset over the king's no-queening policy.

Willow let her eyes find King Tarrant's. He sat tall in his chair on the raised dais, shooting daggered glances at his unhappy courtiers. No change of heart there. King Tarrant still looked stubborn and mulish, though not quite so green around the gills anymore. He must've had that nap that the queen had mentioned.

"Why don't you sit with the younger ladies this time?" said Queen Morwenna, who must have noted King Tarrant's sour demeanour. "'Twould help you to get to know them better." She signalled to the pretty brown-haired girl. "Tavia, dear, escort the princess to your table, please."

Tavia bowed and led the way to a table to the left of and just below the dais. Willow sank into a chair, relieved not to have to sit up high with her grandparents, the centre of everyone's glowering attention.

Servants brought in roast chicken, apple tarts and leftover peacock in raisin sauce. Willow began to eat as Tavia made a round of introductions. The girls, not seeming to notice the oppressive atmosphere, smiled and chattered, each trying to vie for her attention with their questions about Earth.

"Is it true," asked one delicate blonde girl, "that your Earthworld is a material realm with *no* magic?" She said the last part as though Willow had grown up in some primitive caveman place. Willow chuckled at her. "It's not like you think," she explained, sipping at some water. "We had stuff there that you don't have here. Stuff that's almost as good as magic."

"Oh, I know what you speak of, Princess," interrupted a girl with wide green eyes. "My uncle is a seer who has seen Earthworld in his visions and tells tales of horseless carriages and mechanisms that produce pictures and voices."

"Yes, those would've been cars and television sets." The girls seemed astonished at the strange new words.

"Then 'tis true," said the green-eyed girl eagerly, "that Earthworlders live in castles that stretch to the sky and can fly in the stomachs of great metal birds?"

Castles that stretch to the sky? Willow's brow wrinkled in confusion.

"*Desma!*" cried Tavia, glaring at the green-eyed girl. "Do not start pestering the princess with your uncle's ridiculous notions of Earthworld." She turned to Willow, rolling long-suffering eyes and sighing dramatically. "Please forgive Lady Desma, Your Highness. Her uncle grows senile and is beginning, I fear, to spout nonsense."

"No, wait," said Willow, starting to put it together. "She's right. Castles that stretch to the sky are called apartment buildings. And flying metal birds are airplanes."

The girl named Desma smirked at Tavia and said, "See! I *told* you." This brought on a whole new flurry of Earthworld questions. The girls wanted to know about everything from food and clothing to boys and dating. Willow answered their questions as best she could, surprised to find she was enjoying being the centre of everyone's attention.

After they'd finished eating, servants began clearing away the dishes. "Oh Tavia," Desma whispered, nudging Tavia's arm with her elbow. "Is the chamberlain hiring out of work players again? Look at the new clearing wench. She looks like Big-Bellied Bess from last year's winter pageant."

The girls who'd heard her comment glanced over at the next table to see the new clearing wench and giggled in agreement. Tavia smirked, too.

"Nay," she said, laughing, "'tis the princess here with the

overfed taste in servants, not the chamberlain. Tell us, Your Highness — where did you find such a porkling?"

Willow frowned, not having a clue what they were talking about. She glanced at the other table. Gemma, wearing a clean white apron, her hair hidden beneath a scarf, was stacking dishes onto a tray. *Her* Gemma. Not some clearing wench. Willow tried to stand, to go to Gemma, but found herself inexplicably glued to her chair. Magic prickled at her skin.

"Why, I found her in a *pastry shop*, of course," said Willow, the words spilling involuntarily from her mouth. "Where else?" Her hands flew to her shocked lips. Why had she said such a horrible thing?

The girls all smiled knowingly and a few of them went, "*Ssh! Ssh! She's coming over here!*"

Willow fought to move, but something continued to hold her fast to the seat. Her eyes widened. Queen Morwenna, she suddenly remembered, was known for magic spells that backfired. *Crap!* Willow wriggled frantically in her chair. The spell that had made her dance like the other girls must also be making her talk like them.

A hand shot between Willow and Tavia to scoop up an empty plate, and a voice rang out happy and loud.

"Yer Highness," said Gemma excitedly, "I'm that glad to see ye! How've ye been? Ye're lookin' right well in yer fancy new duds."

Willow's head jerked up and a cool smile forced its way onto her face. "Thank you, Gemma," she said, the words squeezing through her gritted teeth. "I see castle life agrees with you, too. You're also looking well." Willow winced internally. *God!* She sounded like a condescending creep. A few girls snickered and Gemma stepped back, her mouth quavering into an uncertain smile.

Willow could see her yellowy bruises and the scab on her lip, which was beginning to peel. *I'm sorry! I'm sorry!* her mind screamed out. *Please forgive me!* But what she said was, "I hope my family found you a job that you like."

Gemma's head bobbed up and down. "Aye," she whispered, "I work in the kitchens now." This answer brought on another wave of snickers. Gemma swallowed and gave a small curtsy. "I'd best be gettin' back to my clearin' now, Yer Highness. May I be excused?"

The tears were bright in Gemma's eyes and Willow felt herself crushed with shame. "Nn ... " she began, then stopped for a moment. She'd almost said, *No, don't go.* But the bespelled her stepped in quickly, smiling and nodding stiffly.

"Of course, Gemma. It was nice seeing you again." Then she watched as Gemma backed away and hurried out a darkened side door.

"She seemed a mite weepy," remarked Tavia. "Do you think mayhap she'd prefer working in the laundry? I could speak to the chamberlain for you."

Willow wasn't listening. She was using all her strength and every bit of willpower to move her legs. And it was beginning to work. Her foot had twitched. *I can do this! I can do this!* One whole leg moved. Then the other. She was starting to stand. Starting to walk, then run, toward Gemma.

"Your Highness, where are you going?" called out Tavia.

Willow didn't answer. She ran from the room and down Gemma's escape hall.

A dark figure glanced back, then disappeared around a corner. "Wait!" Willow cried out. "Gemma wait! I didn't mean it!" She rounded the corner at a dead run, nearly smacking into Gemma, who was leaning against the wall, breathing heavily.

"I'm sorry," Willow gasped. "I didn't mean it ... I ... it — it was a spell."

Gemma backhanded away tears and kept her hurt eyes glued to the floor.

"Oh Gemma." Willow touched the other girl's arm. "I'm so sorry. Please forgive me. Nothing I said out there was me. It was this spell my grandmother made. I think it had side effects. Anyway, I really meant what I said before. You're my friend, Gemma. Not my servant."

Rustling skirts could be heard swishing along the hallway. Willow turned to the sound just as her grandmother came hurrying around the corner.

"Willow, dear!" she cried, stopping short. "Whatever — " Her words were cut off as Malvin ploughed into her backside, nearly barrelling her over.

Willow leaped to steady her, clasping her arm to keep her from falling, but her grandmother weighed more then she'd thought, and the two of them went tumbling down in a big velvet heap.

"Oh Yer Majesty!" gasped Gemma as she and Malvin reached in to help Queen Morwenna to her feet. "Are ye alright? Ye're not ... ye're not hurt, now, are ye?"

Queen Morwenna patted her golden hair and smoothed out her skirts. "No ... I don't believe so. Everything seems to be in the right place." She frowned down at Willow, who was still lying flat on the floor.

"Granddaughter," she said, speaking firmly, "whatever were you thinking, running from the room like that?"

A breathy moan escaped from Willow's throat. A hand or

a sharp knee had rammed her stomach, knocking the wind out of her. She felt like a windshield-splattered bug.

Queen Morwenna's frown swiftly turned to a small "o" of understanding. "You there," she ordered, looking to Malvin, "help me to get her up. She's hurt."

Malvin reached beneath Willow's arms and lifted her gently to her feet, holding her against him until she stopped swaying.

"I'm okay. Just have to ... have to ... catch my breath ... is all."

Queen Morwenna waited a moment, then began questioning her again. "You must tell me what happened. Did someone at court do or say anything to upset you?"

"No, no; it was nothing like that." Willow stared around at the worried faces of her friends, suddenly feeling like a total and absolute jerk. She'd been here for a day now and hadn't even introduced them to her family yet.

"Grandmother, I want you to meet my friends." She linked an arm through Malvin's and pushed him forward. "This is Malvin Weddellwynd, a true hero and a Gallandrian mage apprentice. And this ... " she took Gemma's hand and pulled her over beside Malvin, "this is my best friend, Lady Gemma Fletcher. Without her and Malvin, I'd never have even made it here."

Gemma stared at her in astonishment then pinkened and smiled nervously. "Pleased t-to meet ye, Yer Majesty," she stammered, curtsying and bowing her head.

Queen Morwenna smiled back and graciously acknowledged Gemma and Malvin's greetings. Then she stared at Gemma's scarf and apron, a horrible realization suddenly dawning on her face. "Oh my dear child," she cried, touching

Gemma's white apron. "My chamberlain's made you a servant, hasn't he?" She looked up to the ceiling and shook her head from side to side. "In all the excitement, I never thought ... Oh, I am so sorry! We never meant ... I mean ... "

Gemma gave the queen one of her big, full-faced smiles. "Yer Highness, beggin' yer pardon an' all, but ye've got nothin' to be sorry for. I've been in much worser spots than in yer clean and tidy kitchens. It was scarcely a trial."

"Well, be that as it may, I shall endeavor to make it up to you." Queen Morwenna grasped Gemma's shoulders and, closing her eyes, slid her hands down the entire length of Gemma's body, changing the plain blue wool of her dress to shimmery blue velvet.

Slow fingers gingerly touched the soft fabric. "Yer Highness, it's ... it's ... " But the words wouldn't come. Gemma was too overwhelmed with wonder at the magical dress.

The queen reached under Gemma's chin and gently lifted her head. She stared at Gemma's cuts and bruises for a moment, a tight frown puckering her mouth. Then she reached out, tracing over each injury with a steady fingertip, erasing the yellowing bruises and the peeling scabs till Gemma's face was smooth and whole again.

Willow stared. Gemma was truly beautiful. She wondered why she'd never noticed how blue her eyes were before. Or how creamy her skin.

"Now," said Queen Morwenna, heading down the hallway once again, "we shall have dessert first. But then, Willow, I think I should like to hear more about the heroic deeds of your young friends here."

CHAPTER 21

FUNNY, BRAND SEEMED WARMER to the touch now, as Willow held him up in front of her. His expression seemed different, too. Somehow happier. During the private evening that she, Gemma and Malvin had spent with King Tarrant and Queen Morwenna, Willow had found the courage to ask her grandmother to look at Brand's chess piece. She wondered if maybe Brand had heard the queen proclaim that he was alive. That she could see his energy aura shining clearly all around the chess piece.

Willow stretched her toes closer to the hearth fire and leaned back on the plush carpeting, staring up at her mother's shadowed blue and gold picture.

After the three of them had told their stories to Queen Morwenna and King Tarrant, Willow had insisted that Gemma take her old room, while she had taken this one. The portrait, she knew, had drawn her here. Made her feel like her mother really had existed and wasn't just some heroine in one of Nana's stories. She rubbed her palms into the thick red carpet, suddenly realizing that Diantha had probably sat in this very spot, gazing up, as she was, at her painting.

Sparks crackled and popped noisily, drawing Willow's attention back to the magical flames. Queen Morwenna had added green and purple rainbow colours to them, showing her the way Diantha had liked her bedtime fires when she was little.

Willow snuggled deeper into a woolen blanket that she'd wrapped around her shoulders. All in all, she thought she'd done a pretty fair job of convincing her grandfather to rescind his no-queening order. He'd been quite impressed that she and her friends had made it to Keldoran without a full force of knights backing them up. Maybe he was beginning to have a bit more faith in her. But he still wanted a few more days to think about it.

Willow stood up, yawning. She stretched out her arms, shivered, then wrapped the blanket higher around her shoulders, gazing up once more at her mother's gentle face. The flickering firelight almost made it seem alive, the sweet smile growing then waning, as if she were about to speak.

"Goodnight," Willow said softly. She kissed a fingertip and touched it to one of Diantha's hands, adding a quick, whispered, "Mom," to her words. It felt right somehow.

She sighed, thinking for the first time that maybe everything was going to turn out okay. Well, almost everything. No magic could bring Nana back. Still, though ... Willow felt a surge of well-being. Nana would be happy to know she was back with her own family. Willow's fingertip drifted down Diantha's blue dress and settled on a squiggly black mark in the bottom corner. She peered at it. It was someone's name.

"Zuriel Blagdon," she read, laughing out loud — the artist who painted the smiles that Brand liked. She leaned in close to Diantha's painting, holding Brand out so he could see them both. "There," she said, stretching her mouth into a big, say-cheese grin, "is this the smile you were referring to?"

There was no answer from Brand's frozen lips, but a sudden urgent knocking on her bedroom door almost startled Willow into dropping him into the fireplace.

"Willow, dear," her grandmother said, striding into the room before Willow could answer. Her face, beneath the game-glow, was ghostly white, and she was wearing a velvet housecoat, her long blonde hair streaming down her back. "Please, you must come with me immediately." She grabbed Willow's hand and led her toward the doorway.

Willow followed, not resisting. Panic was in her grandmother's eyes. Panic and stark fear. "What is it?" she began in alarm, but stopped when she saw the tall, blue-glowing man waiting for them outside her bedroom door.

Queen Morwenna didn't pause to introduce them but continued down the hallway with Willow and the man in tow. She led them down two spiralling staircases and a low narrow passage that required head-ducking with a magic light that appeared from a jewel she was wearing. The passage led to another spiralling staircase and then, at its bottom, a large metal-braced wooden door with no lock or doorhandle.

Queen Morwenna paused for a moment, her hand hovering shakily over a gold disc in the door's centre. "Oh, Lachlan," she whispered, "I fear I cannot do it."

The tall man moved closer. He pressed the queen's hand to the gold disc. "You must," he said simply. His hand stayed pressed to hers till she nodded her agreement, then it dropped away.

A single guttural word fell from Queen Morwenna's mouth. Willow gasped as the huge door creaked and groaned, finally grating open with a greyish cloud of dust. Silent, gloomy darkness lay beyond it. Willow alternated between intrigue and terror. She waited outside with the man, peering in while Queen Morwenna entered and lit candles with her fingertips.

Walls appeared to suddenly shoot up to surprising heights with row upon row of thick leather-bound books that reached right to the ceiling. Queen Morwenna had lit an enormous brazier in the middle of the floor and was staring sombrely into its flames.

A firm hand ushered Willow into the room.

"Willow ... a dreadful thing has happened," said Queen Morwenna slowly, picking her words with care. She turned wide, frightened eyes toward her granddaughter and took a deep breath. "You must be queened. Right now — tonight."

Willow stared, suddenly afraid. Why was her grandmother acting this way? Something was wrong. Horribly wrong.

"'Tis Terrill Longbottom," Queen Morwenna continued. "You remember the boy who was put in jail after he shot the crossbow at your young Knight? Well, he's ... he's gone and hung himself."

"Now, that may not be entirely true, Your Majesty," said the tall man, stepping forward. "You did not give me a chance to finish earlier. The boy might not have done it to himself. Apparently a rope was used that the guard captain swears was not in the boy's prison cell an hour ago."

The queen looked stunned. "What are you saying, Lachlan? That someone murdered the poor boy?"

"Aye, madam. There was no chess piece, just the body, so anyone who was not part of the Game could have done it. My guess would be that it was a spy for Prince Varian, as he is the only person who seems to have gained by it. Although, from all accounts, the boy was in great despair. Adding a rope to his cell would have been all that would have been required."

Willow was hearing their words, but nothing they said was making any sense. What did Varian have to do with this

Terrill kid's death? And more specifically, what did any of it have to do with her? "Okay, would somebody please tell me what's going on here? I kind of think I have the right to know."

"Oh my dear, please forgive me." Queen Morwenna brushed back loose hair strands with harried fingers. "It has all happened so suddenly, I am afraid I am all amuddle." She took a deep breath and touched the tall man's arm. "Willow, let me present to you my mage knight, Sir Lachlan Montrose."

The tall, glowing man turned his fierce grey eyes to Willow and gave her a curt nod. "Your Highness, 'tis a great honour."

Willow smiled and nodded back at him. He reminded her of someone. Someone tall and bearded who wore the same type of black clothing. Then it hit her: he reminded her of Trumble Quillondale, minus the eye patch, of course, and the boisterous humour. She felt herself relax a little. Both Sir Lachlan and Trumble, and even Brand to some degree, had that trustworthy, honour-above-all kind of quality that made you feel safe around them.

"I summoned Sir Lachlan a few moments ago," continued the queen, "because I had felt poor Terrill's death. You may not know this, but as a Queen in the Game, I am able to sense when the Players are Captured or killed. And I know if they are replaced or not. And in Terrill's case, there was a replacement." She paused, a concerned frown lining her face. "You are in grave danger, my dear. Which is why we must act now."

"But why?" asked Willow. She remembered what Brand had told her about replacements. But she still wasn't getting it. "What does Terrill's replacement have to do with me?"

Queen Morwenna stared with narrowed unblinking eyes.

"'Tis Varian."

"Varian?" Willow didn't know why, but she felt surprised. Somehow, she'd let her uncle's veiled threat of revenge slip to the back of her mind. "But he can't hurt you, can he? He's miles away and ... " What had they said about Terrill's death? That maybe Varian had caused it. Oh God! She swallowed hard, feeling suddenly sick.

"No, Willow, dear. You don't understand," said Queen Morwenna. "'Tis not me he can hurt. 'Tis you."

"But if ... if ... " Willow blinked at the queen. *Me? How can he hurt me?* Then she understood. Varian was replacing Terrill. He was a Pawn now. A *Black* Pawn! All he had to do was prick her with a pin and she'd be toast. She'd ...

Queen Morwenna grasped the edge of the blanket which had slipped off Willow's shoulders. "'Tis alright," she whispered. She snuggled the soft wool back around Willow's chin, fighting to keep back her tears. "Varian's not in Tulaan, dear. He did not kill Terrill. Not directly, anyway. When I felt his change, he was at his castle."

Sir Lachlan shook his head wearily. "This Game does nothing but confound me. The prince is no Keldorian. Why would *he* have been chosen for Black? It makes no sense."

The queen sighed. "I do not know. But 'tis well known he delivered White Players to Tarrant. Mayhap the Game knows as well." Her fingers dug sharply into Willow's shoulders. "But Lachlan, we mustn't give up yet. This could be a favourable thing. Varian's castle is still a full four-day ride to Carrus. 'Tis not too late. If we train the princess tonight and all day tomorrow, that will still leave her with three days to find Nezeral before Varian becomes a threat. Maybe even four or five, knowing Varian." She smiled grimly. "Setting the trap, after all, is half his fun. King Ulor may not be his only, nor his first, target."

Willow was just beginning to realize what Queen Morwenna was saying. Varian didn't just want to hurt her. No, he was going for the gusto, the whole shooting match. If he went to Carrus instead of Tulaan, all he had to do was Capture King Ulor and there'd be no more brother, no more heir — no more problems. The Game would not only be over — Gallandra would be his, lock, stock and barrel!

"But wait," said Willow breathlessly. Another thought had just occurred to her. "Won't King Ulor know? I mean, about Varian being a Black Pawn? You knew and ... "

Queen Morwenna was shaking her head no. "He won't know in the same way that I did. Only the Queens feel the changes, and ... without Queen Aleria ... "

"But he's got a really big chess set," interrupted Willow. She wasn't going to give up hope. Not yet, anyway. "Won't he notice the change himself? I mean, I've seen his pieces, and the faces are incredibly clear on them. He's bound to notice his own brother's face!" Even as she said it, her heart sank. She remembered that he hadn't immediately noticed Nana's changed face. Varian was, apparently, just another Pawn. And now that the war was over, what reason did King Ulor really have to keep on watching out for them? He'd be lulled into a false sense of security.

"Yes, 'tis possible," admitted Queen Morwenna. "But we can't depend upon it. I don't know how often he studies his board or for how long. And who's to say, even if he does notice, that Varian will not find a way to checkmate him regardless. So you see my dilemma now, don't you, dear?" She turned from Willow and began waving her hands in wide, flanking circles. "No matter how I look at it, I must queen you. 'Tis the only way any of us will have a chance."

Willow stared at a spot beyond the queen to where a shiny ghostly image was wavering in and out of reality.

"Concentrate, milady. Aye, that's it! Just a little more." Sir Lachlan clapped his hands as an exact duplicate of King Ulor's chess set finally appeared — right down to the people-faced Players and the white marble pedestal. "Well done, madam! Well done! Your focus is most definitely improving."

A small smile flickered across Queen Morwenna's face, but then disappeared as she strode quickly to the pedestal. "There's no movement yet," she pointed out as she studied the board. "Varian's piece is still at mid rank. He'll probably wait till morn to set off. So we mustn't waste any time. Willow." She made a waving motion with her hand. "Come here, dear, and I'll show you what to do."

Willow's thoughts of Varian were suddenly slammed away by new ones of magic powers. Was she *really* going to be able to make things appear and disappear? Stretch out fabric, colour a fire, heal bruises and cuts — all with just the twitch of her hand? Tight with anticipation, she stepped toward her grandmother.

"Now, we believe all that's really required," Queen Morwenna explained, "is for you to touch it like this." She placed a hand palm down on the board's bare midsection. "See, there is nothing to it."

"Okay," said Willow. "I think I'm ready." She exhaled one really big breath, closed her eyes ... then slowly touched her hand to the board.

CHAPTER 22

WILLOW CLOSED HER EYES. She could hear her heart hammering, pumping adrenaline-charged blood at a tremendous pace. The marble felt cold and smooth against her fingertips. She edged them onto the board until her palm was fully touching it.

Suddenly her hand was on fire. On fire and burning up her arm. She tried to pull it away, but found Lachlan's strong blue-tinged fingers firmly over hers, keeping them crushed against the hot marble. A searing heat exploded inside her. Something was loose and free. Something incredibly powerful. Willow clutched at the board, struggling with all her might to control it.

"That's it," said Lachlan. "Tether it, Princess. *Command it!*"

Willow shrieked a terrible gut-wrenching scream, finally tearing her hands from the hot marble and Lachlan's heavy grasp. Her eyes flew open. She was shaking uncontrollably, her breath coming in great gasping heaves.

But the magic ...

She could feel it! It was flowing through her blood, hot and dizzying, like an ocean of mage-brewed wine.

"Well done, Princess. Well done," said Lachlan, smiling broadly. Sweat glistened on his forehead. "Never before have I seen such a surge of power."

"Is she well?" Queen Morwenna was at his side, white-faced and peering at Willow.

"For one who has just tethered in a surge of power the size of the Valandrean Mountains, Your Majesty, I would say she's doing just fine."

Queen Morwenna hugged Willow, a jubilant smile lighting her face. "Did you hear what he said? We have succeeded! Touching the board queened you!"

Willow stared at her grandmother. She could see her mouth moving. Even hear the words. But she was so absorbed by the new blue-white glow of Queen Morwenna's halo that nothing else was penetrating. She reached out and passed her hand through it. Little tingly vibrations licked at her fingertips.

Queen Morwenna moved back. "'Tis the aura of my energy. 'Twill fade in a few moments."

Willow peered down at her own hand. All around the circling new queen-gold of her Game-glow was a flaring green. She lifted her head to look at the room. The light — it was everywhere. She could see it surrounding the books in the cramped shelves. On the candles and in their flames. Even in the smooth stones of the floor and walls. She looked closer at the wall's niches and grooves. It didn't seem solid anymore. It was as if her hand could slip right through it.

She turned to Lachlan and Queen Morwenna. "What's going on? Why is everything glowing?"

"You are seeing the auras of energy, Princess," answered Lachlan. "Every living and non-living thing has one. 'Twill fade in a moment, and then you will not see them again unless you wish it."

Lachlan's new crimson glow glimmered next to Queen

Morwenna's soft blue one. "Your and Sir Lachlan's colours are different. Does that mean something?"

Queen Morwenna's face went slack and she stared at Willow vacantly. "Your green aura ... " she began but then stopped to blink her eyes back into focus. "Oh, I hate the way that feels," she said, still blinking rapidly. "'Tis like being cross-eyed." She gave her head a small shake and her eyes one final blink-test before continuing. "Each colour is a different soul gift. How does the rhyme go? *Green for the gift of wisdom and knowledge, blue the gift of compassion and calm. Red for strength and warrior cunning ...* " She paused, tapping her chin. "I cannot remember the rest, quite. There are many colours: yellow, purple, orange and hundreds of varying shades of each." She held out a hand to Willow. "Look closely, and you will see that as well as blue, I also have strands of yellow and green underlying my blue."

Willow reached out and held her grandmother's hand, studying the bright patterns of her aura. Queen Morwenna was right. If you looked past the gold of the Game spell, there were several thin strands of yellow and green wavering within the blue. It reminded her of the way a fire flickered or the sun shimmered if you looked at it too long.

"We each have many colours that define us." Queen Morwenna flipped her hand over so that she was now holding Willow's. "In you, I saw traces of red and bits of my blue." She smiled softly and let Willow's hand drop. "All the colours one needs to be a great ruler."

Not quite catching that last remark, Willow made a gesture at the stone wall and the bookshelves. "But I see light from *all* of these things. A white light with no colours. How can something that isn't even alive have energy?"

"I have some knowledge of your Earthworld, Princess, and I believe that you would call that energy — molecules." Lachlan stepped toward a bookshelf and pulled out a red leather book, bringing it to Willow to examine. "When you look at something with your inner vision, the structure of its life force, its energy, becomes quite evident. Here." He held the book close to her hand. "Try to pass your fingers through it. Because once you can see that inner structure, you should also be able to change it."

Goosebumps rose along Willow's arms and up the back of her neck. Her blanket had fallen to the floor, but she wasn't cold. Intense excitement had overwhelmed her. She could actually see the tiny, clinging molecules that had banded together to create the book. See them moving and breathing ...

Her hand reached out to hesitantly touch the red leather. It felt solid but not solid. And somehow she knew what to do. Knew that she had to picture those tightly packed molecules letting go of each other, parting to let her hand go through.

"By the gods," said Lachlan, his eyes wide in disbelief. "She did it."

"You didn't even tell her how," Queen Morwenna whispered.

Willow stared at the book that now lay on top of her hand. *She'd done it.* She'd actually passed her hand right through to the other side!

"It took me a month to learn that!" exclaimed Queen Morwenna. "How could she ... 'Tis not possible, Lachlan, is't?"

"Well, I would have thought not," he said, smiling. "But after today ... I suppose I stand corrected." He turned and passed the book to Queen Morwenna. "Here," he said, kneeling down by Willow's feet, "let us try a slightly more difficult task." He ran a finger over her cold bare foot. "Take the energy from the air and see if you can shape it into a pair of slippers."

Willow narrowed her gaze, trying to see the white aura of the air.

Yes ...

If she squinted just right, she could see nothing but light. It moved all around her, alive and pulsing. She let her eyelids drift shut and visualized her favourite green frog slippers. Imagined them in every detail, right down to their googly plastic eyes and the red-stained nose of the left slipper.

"What manner of footwear is that!"

Willow blinked until she couldn't see the light anymore. Queen Morwenna was right. It *was* like being cross-eyed. She gave her head a shake and focused on her grandmother. Queen Morwenna was staring at her and pointing at something on the floor.

"Do they require feeding?" she asked, a perplexed frown on her face. "One seems to have spit something up."

Willow glanced down at her bright green Kermit the Frog feet, the left one red-nosed from where she'd spilled ketchup on him. "I did it! I did it!" She squatted down, poking and probing at the green slippers to see if they were real.

They were.

Lachlan, still in his crouched position, was staring at her, astonished. "Never in all my years as a mage knight have I seen anyone arrange air energy on their very first attempt. 'Tis unheard of." He reached out to touch a plastic Kermit eye. "How did you do it? How did you know what to do without being taught?"

Willow was puzzled herself. He had a point, there. How *had* she known? She hadn't even thought about what she was doing. She'd just done it. "I don't know. Maybe it was just dumb luck or something. I mean, I imagined my slippers, and then there they were right on my feet. I have no idea how I did it."

"Evidently," said Queen Morwenna, resting a hand on Willow's shoulder, "you are a magical genius, dear. And the elf queen must have known it. Think of it, Lachlan. Why else would she have chosen to gift an infant?"

A light sprang into Lachlan's eyes. "Of course," he said, rising to his feet, "the rumours must be true, then, and *she*, not King Ulor, engineered the whole Earthworld trip."

Queen Morwenna nodded. "I know. I always thought that uncharacteristic of him. He is terribly protective of his family. It must have caused him such pain to let her go."

Willow stood up, bewildered. *Magical genius.* How could she be a magical genius? It had been so easy. Nothing more than using her imagination.

Suddenly, an old memory popped into her head. Nana had loved to quote this one Einstein saying — something about imagination being more important than knowledge. "Grandmother. Sir Lachlan. What makes the magic work? I mean how did I do it, technically?"

"I do not know how you did it." Sir Lachlan smiled rue-fully and shook his head. "I have never seen anyone below a sixth level mage arrange air energy. And no one on their first attempt."

"But how is it done? What process has to happen before the molecules will do *this?*" She stuck out a Kermit-slippered foot and waggled it in front of Lachlan.

"Well, it requires concentration," he said, running his thumb and forefinger over his dark beard. "A great deal of it, in fact. More than most young people your age are capable of. Then — and this is the next most important thing — the imagining of the visual construct. You must be capable of visualizing whatever it is you are going to do in complete detail. Then ... "

"I knew it!" Willow broke in. "I knew it had to do with imagination! That's why I can do it, isn't it?"

"What do you mean, dear?" asked Queen Morwenna.

"I mean, in my world, that's all I ever did — use my imagination. The toys I had ... my dolls, my books, chess, role-playing. Nana used them to teach me how to visualize. Don't you see? She trained me with toys and games! That's why I'm so good at this magic stuff. I'm not some kind of genius, I just had a good teacher."

"Being able to see a thing clearly is but a part of the process," Lachlan said. "A most important part, yes, but still only a part. The focus, the visualization and the degree of your talent all must needs work together as a whole. And 'tis only when all three are in such balance that the magic can work." He rubbed thoughtfully at his beard again.

"Your abilities are a great mystery to me, Princess. A mystery I am sure I shall wish to ponder further once the Game is over. But for now, our goal must be to prepare you.

"Here, have a look at the board. See what you make of it."

Willow gazed down at the large chess set, surprised to find that the lights and auras had faded. The marble figurines were lustrous now, with an orange glow. But it was from candlelight and nothing magical.

"Oh look, dear," said Queen Morwenna, picking up one of the pieces. "You have truly become a Queen."

A creepy feeling came over Willow as she looked at the new, taller version of herself carved into the chess piece; the same *Twilight-Zony* feeling that had come over her when King Ulor had shown her her Pawn face. Gingerly, she took the Queen from her grandmother, holding it at eye level. If she unfocused her eyes, the energy auras came flaring back into view.

The white figure had a soft, pale glow around it, the energy aura of the marble. Willow placed the piece back on its space in the back ranks of Black. The Game had changed somewhat. White had lost a Knight but had gained a Queen. There was some forward movement of the King and his Rook and Bishop. She wondered if they were planning on coming to Keldoran. Maybe they would bypass Varian and ...

She picked up the Black Pawn closest to her left. Varian's handsome face stared proudly back at her. He would, she knew, destroy her if he could — destroy anyone and anything that got in the way of his plans to become king.

With a shudder, she placed him back on his square, squelching the worms-slithering-on-her-skin feeling that had suddenly enveloped her.

And that was when she noticed that some of the White Players were different.

They were lined along the side of the Game, Captured pieces with glowing auras. Glowing *coloured* auras. She picked up the two White Knights with deep scarlet auras. "I have Brand's piece upstairs. How is he down here as well?"

"Those are not the true pieces," Queen Morwenna explained. "The Game manufactures these ones for ... for keeping track of things, I suppose. King Ulor has them on his board as well." She slipped past Willow and opened a drawer, pulling out a small silver tray. "These are the real ones. The ones we Captured. And this one," she pointed to a lone Black Pawn, "is our dear Diantha. Lord Garnock retrieved her from Queen Aleria and Prince Alaric on their ill-fated journey to Tulaan."

Willow stared at the tray. On it lined up like toys were a blue-auraed Queen and Rook, a red-auraed Knight, a few multicoloured Pawns, a green-auraed Bishop and the sad Black Pawn with no colour, just a white, lifeless glow.

She knew without looking who the red Knight was. She picked him up along with the Black Pawn.

Her parents. She was holding all that remained of her parents.

CHAPTER 23

WILLOW KNEW SHE SHOULD FEEL TIRED. She'd been up all night changing herself into cats and mice and birds, making things appear and disappear and memorizing the construct sequences for spell-casting. Construct sequences were, according to Sir Lachlan, the most important part of her training. They were a series of steps that — once remembered and understood — could be used in almost any spell, provided you had the corresponding magic talent to match it. And Willow, as they had all discovered, seemed to possess every magic talent imaginable and was a pro at visualizing constructs.

A yawn escaped her. Well, maybe she was a little tired. She stretched her arms up over her head and yawned again. It was early dawn, and the feast hall where she'd been practising her magic skills had not yet stirred with the morning breakfast crowd. Pale light in long, broad shafts illuminated the empty room, taking away the warm nighttime candle glimmer. Willow sighed and leaned into a light beam, watching as dust motes swirled around her.

She had tried to sleep earlier, had conjured warm flannel pajamas and a fire, but that was about as far as she had gone. Having magic was almost the equivalent of winning the lotto. You just couldn't turn the excitement off. And so she had dressed and wandered back to the feast hall again, somehow finding its great tapestried walls and smooth-tiled floors strangely comforting.

She settled in against the cushioned back of her chair, draping an unladylike leg over its arm. Memories of what she had done through the night came back to her. The crunch and grind of shrinking bones. Arms that spread into weightless feathers. A dizzying flight to the ceiling tops. Being a bird had been her favourite construct, the closest thing to being free from a body that she could imagine.

Footsteps and voices interrupted Willow's reverie. She lifted her head. Three servants had entered the feast hall and were snuffing out the candles on the wall and beginning to set the tables for breakfast. Willow slid back down in her chair. Could she fool these servants? Make them believe she was something else?

Shuffling footsteps came closer to Willow. She ducked beneath a table and waited patiently for a red-booted servant to pass by. A platter banged over her head, bringing drifting odours of bacon and fresh bread.

Willow peeked through an opening in the tablecloth. The place was now swarming with servants. This was going to be fun. What should she be? A bird? A mouse? Nah, those constructs would just freak people out. Plus, birds were cool, but mice were just gross. They had this totally disgusting need to squeeze into tight spaces. Willow shuddered at the squirmy memory of it.

She heard hissing noises down by the doorway and squinted. A servant shooed an angry grey tomcat out of the room. Willow grinned. Now *that* was a transformation she could handle.

The aura lights winked around her like sparkling stars. She focused on them and began building the cat construct in her head. She could see its small triangular face, sleek body and the short smoothness of its silky grey fur. Heat washed over her, liquefying solid bones and reshaping them, her skin molding over the lithe new skeleton with fluid ease.

Willow blinked. Sharp bacon smells made her new tiny nostrils twitch with anticipation. She arched her back, ready to spring up onto the chair and investigate, but a boot that poked at her from beneath the tablecloth brought her back to herself. She was Willow Farrandale and not Grisard the cat. It took a moment for her own brain to override the cat brain, and then she was off, padding across the feast hall and out through one of the doors that a servant held open for her. No one had noticed anything unusual.

The hallways, at her new ten-inch height, seemed unfamiliar. She started down one direction and then stopped. Map images of the correct route surfaced in the cat's mind. Willow loosened her control a little, allowing the cat's keen senses to guide her. She found the stairway and the corridor that went past Queen Morwenna's solarium and then the hallway that led to her own room.

Outside her doorway, she let the construct go, her own body shooting up miraculously from the cat's. Weariness hit her like a punch. The excitement, she decided, was finally beginning to wear off. Time to get back to bed. Sluggishly, she entered her room.

The velvet curtains were still drawn tight, and the inviting glow of the fireplace freckled her bedchamber with cozy shadows. Willow slipped onto the bed, not even bothering to cover herself.

She fell asleep instantly, but, in what felt like only minutes, suddenly came awake again. Her whole body from head to foot was flopping and jiggling like a fish out of water. There was no sound, but she thought she knew what had taken place.

Earthquake!

She tried to move, to warn everyone. But nothing happened. Her legs were there. She could see their outline under her dress. They just weren't moving. In fact, now that she could see clearly, nothing was moving, not even the bed. But somehow she could still feel herself shaking and bouncing.

"You are not fully out of your body yet," said a soft voice. "Do not be afraid. I shall help you." Light tingly sensations fluttered around Willow's hands, then tightened. She felt herself being lifted and then drawn up from the bed.

"There, you are fully out now. Have the vibrations stopped?"

Willow stared at the ghostly woman who was holding her hands. She was like a cloudy outline etched in shimmering gold. Her touch felt solid, though. Willow looked down at their clasped hands. A liquidy green outline was merged with the shimmering gold.

"What have you done to me?!" Willow spun around to the bed and gasped. She could see herself, still asleep and lying on top of the bed covers. She looked solid and alive. Not ...

One of her new see-through hands lifted into view, its shiny green fingertips glowing eerily. She floated it back and forth with a hypnotic sway.

"This, child, is your spirit body," said the woman, "the one you dream with." She smiled and reached out to take Willow's other hand. "Come, you have much to learn and little time."

A powerful sucking sensation engulfed Willow. It was as

though she were being inhaled up a straw. Inky blackness surrounded her. She could no longer see the woman or the walls
of her room. She was squeezed from all directions, suffocated.
She gasped in loud, panicked breaths.

Then suddenly it was over.

Bright sunlight dazzled her blinking eyes. Summery wood
smells and sweet trilling birdsong drifted to her, relaxing her
grip on the woman's slender hands. She could see the woman
clearly now. Dark russet hair the colour of shiny rain-soaked
tree bark, green tip-tilted eyes and a wide, sensuous mouth.
She was amazingly, almost inhumanly, beautiful, like some
ethereal faerie queen, or ...

"Are you ... are you ... "

"I am Queen Cyrraena, your nethermother." The woman
twisted her fingers into Willow's long gold chain and pulled
out the swan from beneath her bodice. "And you," she said,
setting the pendant gently against Willow's dress front, "are
the princess Willow, Restorer of the Balance and my own
beloved netherchild." A heavy sigh escaped her as she drew
Willow into an embrace. "I am sorry for all that you have suffered. If there had been any other way, I swear to you, I would
have taken it."

Willow pulled back, still awed by the woman. "Is — is
this a dream?" Her own hands and arms, she suddenly realized, were flesh again, and there was no golden Game-glow.
She looked down at herself, at her slippered feet and bright
blue gown. She *seemed* real enough, but somehow she felt
lighter, more airy, as if she'd float away when Queen Cyrraena
had released her.

"No, not a dream," said Queen Cyrraena. "But an awak-
ening. I have freed your energy from its physical bonds and

have brought you to the elf dwelling of Timorell. It was the only way to bypass Nezeral's shields.

"Come." She stepped away from Willow and spread apart some lacy tree fronds. "We have much to speak of."

Willow peered past Queen Cyrraena into the opening. She could see blankets and cushions and an array of food spread beneath an enormous willow tree whose long slim branches trailed along the ground, weaving an intricate breeze-ruffled wall around them. Queen Cyrraena's sheer green dress glimmered in its sun and shadow patterns, making Willow blink. For a moment the elf queen had seemed to disappear into the tree branches.

Willow blinked again. No, she was still there. She was on one of the gold pillows now, and easy to see. Willow edged her way through the branch curtain and sat opposite Queen Cyrraena, who was leaning comfortably against the willow's vast trunk.

"Would you like some refreshment?" Queen Cyrraena offered her hot buttered buns and a brimming silver goblet.

Willow shook her head no. Old legends about eating faerie food had come back to her. Something about how once you ate faerie food, you could never return to your own world.

Queen Cyrraena's lovely mouth curved into an amused smile, giving Willow the niggling feeling that Queen Cyrraena had read her thoughts. The food and wine disappeared with a graceful wave of her hand. "Perhaps you are right," she said in her soft low voice, which reminded Willow of whispering breezes and rustling tree leaves. "We have much to discuss. I hardly know where to begin." She faced Willow with a sad green stare.

Before Willow could stop herself, the question shot out of

her mouth. "Why me?" Queen Morwenna hadn't been able to tell her *why* the elf queen had chosen Willow as champion. She *had* to know.

Queen Cyrraena seemed to ponder this for a moment, somewhat taken aback by Willow's directness. "I see the wisdom name suits you well," she said finally. "You ask the most difficult question first." She looked away from Willow and up into the swaying tree branches. "There are many reasons why I picked you. Mostly, though, it was merely a matter of timing. I was not allowed to intervene myself unless Nezeral chose to break the laws. He broke the first law when he rigged the initial chess game so that King Tarrant could not possibly beat him." She paused and looked back to Willow. "It was then that I knew a netherchild must be chosen."

"But still, why me? I was just a baby."

"I needed someone Nezeral would not anticipate."

Willow let out a bitter laugh. "So you figured he'd never imagine me as an opponent, right?"

Another amused smile lit up Queen Cyrraena's face. "Precisely. But not for the reasons you are thinking. You see, he was expecting me to choose a battle champion. He wanted a fight, and, in the beginning, no one was agreeing to play his game. So I believe that he waited the year, hoping I would select a worthy opponent. When I chose you, he was enraged; I truly believed then that he would go back to Clarion. But, as you know ... he did not."

Queen Cyrraena's words sent a cold empty wave through Willow. More than one Game was being played here. And she was obviously a pawn in both of them.

"You chose me, then, because you hoped Nezeral would get bored and go home?"

"Yes. I know it sounds like a dreadful thing to use an infant in such a way, but I never dreamed Nezeral would go this far. Once the human war began, I had no choice but to train you into the battle champion he wanted. And, unfortunately," she said, reaching out to grasp Willow's hand, "I had to do it as quickly as possible. There was no other way."

Willow swallowed and took a deep breath. She was being used. Her childhood had been stolen to injure this elf prince's pride. Well, she had her own pride as well. And now she had a family to protect. It didn't matter if she was just a Pawn. Everyone was counting on her. She stared at the elf queen with hard determination.

"How can we stop him? What do you want me to do?"

"Willow, dearest," said Queen Cyrraena, shaking her head. "I do not know how to stop him. The answer to that question will have to come from you. All that I can do is tell you about his weaknesses."

Weaknesses? Willow sat up a little straighter, inching closer to Queen Cyrraena. Finally she was going to hear something that might actually help her.

"Nezeral is from an upper realm dimension called Clarion. I am also a Clarionite, but I choose to live here in the elf dwelling of Timorell to be a guide to the humans. You do, of course, know the story of King Tarrant's lung fever and how his mage summoned the higher power?" Willow nodded. "Well, it should have been to me that the mage made his summons, but he knew that even though I had the power to save the king, I would not. For my role as a guide does not include changing what must be. And the mage, who knew this, broke a great law by calling out to the upper realms."

"But, I don't get it," said Willow. What did any of this

have to do with Nezeral's weaknesses? She puckered her face. "Like, what's the big deal with upper and lower? He was just asking for help."

Queen Cyrraena let out a sigh. "To explain that, you will need to understand our history." She smoothed delicate fingertips over her lap in an easy, graceful motion that, to Willow, seemed strangely hypnotic. "Eons ago, before the magic laws were created, the elf people were free to journey through all realms — upper and lower. In those times, they lived side by side with humans. We tried to help them advance." Calm green eyes regarded Willow. "The problems started when some of the elf lords proclaimed that humans were not in truth spirit beings but merely physical beings. They believed that because the human lifespan was so short, humans were not capable of any true spirituality. They were, therefore, related more to non-rational beasts than to elves themselves."

Willow, who had held Queen Cyrraena's gaze up until the non-rational-beast part, looked away. The tale was an old one. Earth people, she knew, had used the same type of faulty reasoning to rationalize slavery and genocide. Only their excuse hadn't been lifespans. It had been skin colour and different belief systems.

"Those elves who were in general agreement with this way of looking at things committed dreadful acts against the humans. Pretending to be gods, they made slaves of the humans and convinced their leaders to make wars and to partake in other atrocities." Her hand reached out to touch Willow's knee. "Your own Earthworld was just such a place."

"What?" Willow's head snapped up, her eyes focusing intently on Queen Cyrraena's suddenly alien features. The elf queen stared back, unflinching.

"Think. All of Earth's mythologies are rife with gods and goddesses. Deities who demanded worship and temples and wars. Some who even decreed human sacrifice." Queen Cyrraena's eyes brightened with anger. "Nezeral's father, Jarlath, was one of the worst. One of his avatars required the sacrifice of human blood and hearts in order that the sun might rise each morning. He was the cause of death for hundreds of thousands of innocent people. And even after he had left the lower realms, it took more than half a millennium for his dreadful teachings to lose their power."

Willow's mind spun with Queen Cyrraena's words. *Gods and human sacrifice.* Just what had this elf queen gotten her into? She studied the queen's smooth features again. The woman looked about twenty. If Nezeral's father had been the source of an Earth myth, just how long did these people live, anyway?

"Jarlath was not the only one, though," Queen Cyrraena continued, her head bowed in what Willow thought to be shame. "There were many who shared his hideous views. So many that those of us who could not bide their barbarous actions formed an alliance and called a council. The debate was fierce and lengthy. It was decided that a vote must be held." The hand that still rested on Willow's knee tightened its grip. "The vote, of course, was in favour of the humans." Queen Cyrraena drew her hand away and leaned back against the tree trunk, a faint tremor passing over her. "It was a close thing. I tremble still when I think what may have happened had Jarlath triumphed." She turned to Willow, giving her an assessing glance. "Child, can you guess how Earthworld was changed then?"

Willow thought of all the old legends and faerie tales she

had read as a child. Had there been one about a change? She remembered Merlin from the King Arthur tales, how when his mistress Viviane tricked him into the faerie realms, it was said to have been the end of all magic. Had something like that really happened at some time in the past? Had all the old legends and tales been based on actual events? "It wasn't the end of magic, was it?"

Queen Cyrraena smiled. "It was exactly so, Willow. The council banished all magic and all magical beings from Earthworld. Furthermore, they cast a spell so that our magic would sicken if ever we were to come near iron. All material realms have iron cores. So now, were we to visit them, our magic should vanish and we ourselves become powerless."

So the elves were allergic to iron. What did that have to do with Willow? And, more specifically, what did *any* of it have to do with Nezeral's weaknesses?

The elf queen tilted her head, signalling to an attendant who materialized from among the willow fronds. He carried a long narrow wooden box thrust as far from his body as possible, stepping gingerly toward the queen as though what he held might suddenly explode.

Willow stared at him. She couldn't help it. He was like Queen Cyrraena, otherworldly beautiful, his moss-green clothing and bright robin-orange hair making him seem a part of the forest. A part of summer itself. Her eyes fell to his leather-booted feet as he carefully placed the wooden box between her and Queen Cyrraena. He then backed away, quickly disappearing among the lacy tree fronds. Willow caught a swift dapple of vanishing green that made her wonder if the boy had been real, or if Queen Cyrraena had magicked him out of the warm fragrant air. She turned to the elf queen, meaning to question her, but Queen Cyrraena was edging away from the box, a look of apprehension crossing her face.

"It contains a sword," she whispered, gazing steadily at the box. "An iron one. See if you can open it."

Queen Cyrraena wasn't asking her to do anything dangerous, yet Willow hesitated. The elf boy, as she recalled, had not been very happy about having to carry the box, and now the queen herself was starting to look queasy. "Why put a sword in a box? Is there something wrong with it?"

"There are four elements. Earth, air, fire and water." Queen Cyrraena's eyelids closed as though she were trying to gather strength. She moved even farther away from Willow and the box. "These elements," she continued, her eyes slowly blinking open, "are the elements of protection. The elements of life. The wood of the box is an earthen element. It helps to shield me, absorbing some of the iron's power."

Queen Cyrraena really wasn't looking too well. Willow leaned over the box and peered at her. "Are you okay? You look kind of sick."

A weak smile flickered over Queen Cyrraena's pale face. "The wood, as I said, only absorbs *some* of the iron's power. I can still feel its potency. It pulls at my magic and tires me. Do not concern yourself, child. I shall grow used to it. Go now. Open the box."

Willow's hand drifted to the carved wooden lid. She didn't feel anything weird or powerful. No pull at *her* magic. She glanced at Queen Cyrraena again. Could she trust her? What if, after all this, she was only being manipulated into another scheme? A thought prickled at the back of her mind. Something didn't feel right. Something ... Willow raised her head, looking past Queen Cyrraena to the thin swaying tree branches. It was too quiet. Where had all the singing birds gone? She saw bright glimpses of orange and green: the boy who had brought the box was still out there. He was watching her, nervously waiting as Queen Cyrraena was to see if she would open it. There were patches of crimson and gold as well. He wasn't alone.

Suddenly, she understood their fear. It was not whether or not she *would* open the box — but whether or not she *could!*

CHAPTER 24

WILLOW RESTED BOTH HANDS on the box's lid, narrowing her eyes until she saw the shining band of aura light. It was white and pure. Nothing to indicate any danger. A deep breath and a flick of her fingers, and the lid was lying on the ground. She leaned over the box, peering into it, momentarily surprised to find it filled to the brim with dirt.

Earth, air, fire and water. The four elements of protection. Wood alone hadn't been enough. The elves must have needed a double dose of absorption power. She dug her hands into the cool soil until she felt something hard.

In a gritty shower of damp earth, she pulled the sword, rough-grained and heavy, from the box. Willow stood, holding it up to a bit of mottled sunlight. It wasn't a pretty sword, all shiny and decorative, like the one she'd seen Brand carry, nor was it razor-edged like Lord Garnock's. It was dark and ancient, pitted with battle scars and dull from lack of use. A sword for a museum or a scrap heap.

"What ... what do you ... feel ... ?" Queen Cyrraena's lips trembled and her slack face was a sheet-white mask. Alarmed, Willow swiftly reburied the sword. *She* had felt nothing. The elf queen, however, looked ready to keel over. Willow knelt beside her and helped prop her against the tree trunk. "Your Majesty? Are you okay?"

Queen Cyrraena nodded, her eyes falling closed. The orange-haired boy appeared again, replacing the box's lid and then nimbly carrying it from the willow grove. Other elves scurried into the opening, fussing over their queen with fans and water goblets. A few moments later, Queen Cyrraena's eyes opened, colour like an ivory-gold sunset suffusing her skin.

"Forgive me," she said, her voice beginning to sound stronger. She shooed away the over-exuberant attendants and smiled sheepishly. "It has been many an eon since last I was exposed to pure iron. I had no idea my vulnerability would be so great." Suddenly she blinked, fastening her green stare to Willow. "You held the sword! I *knew* you would. My dear child!"

What was the big deal? So she'd held some rusty old sword. Was she supposed to be sensitive to it? What about everyone else on Mistolear? There was iron all over the place: weapons, armour, eating utensils, those brackets for holding candles — they were all made out of iron. If everyone from Mistolear was supposed to be allergic to it, how did people stand to have it so close to them?

"You know, I've been here for over a week, and, uh, you're the first person I've seen who's fainted from iron." Willow folded her arms, giving Queen Cyrraena a hard look. "How come?"

"Let me explain," said Queen Cyrraena. She sipped from a goblet that one of the attendants had left her. "As you know, not everyone in Mistolear has magical powers. Only in the upper realms is this so. In the lower realms, magical ability is inherited, like blue eyes or curly hair. And few are blessed with it. Since you and Queen Morwenna are now the *only* two humans in either Gallandra or Keldoran with magic, you are now the only two who should have a sensitivity to it. If there is no magic — there is no sickness."

"So how come *I'm* not sick?"

"You should be. Your magical powers mean that you should have the same sensitivity to iron that I do. You should not have been able to touch the sword."

"I know what it is! All those years on Earth — it's because I grew up on Earth, isn't it?" said Willow. "It's made me immune, right?"

Queen Cyrraena nodded. "I sent you there not only to age you, but also in the hopes that you would become safe from the iron sickness; become immune, as you say. You see, during the great Earth exodus, Ryanor, one of my elf folk, was left behind. For the love of a human woman, he purposely chose to stay, even though it meant the loss of his powers. Ryanor lived there for close to thirty years, until the woman died. He was then permitted to return to Timorell." Queen Cyrraena fingered the shiny surface of her gold drinking glass. "We all thought that he would be left powerless forever. But no sooner had he returned than his powers returned as well. We found out quite by chance about his iron resistance. We were attending a tourney hosted by your Gallandrian grandfather, and a stray piece of a broken sword fell into Ryanor's lap. He should have sickened as you saw me do, but it was not so. He lifted the iron shard as though it were no more than a windblown tree twig."

Willow stared at Queen Cyrraena's hands — hands that still trembled from being so close to the iron. Was this what the elf queen meant by Nezeral's weakness? Willow's mind spun with the dark implications. Was the iron sword to be her weapon? Did she have to *kill* him with it? Willow's stomach wrenched sickeningly. Maybe being Queen Cyrraena's battle champion was a whole lot more than she could handle.

"Am I — am I supposed to, like, kill Nezeral with that sword?" she blurted out, her voice high and squeaky. "Because if I am ... I — I don't think I can do it."

A heavy silence fell over the grove. Queen Cyrraena looked away from her, unable to meet the fear in Willow's eyes. "Nezeral's powers are intensified in this realm. You would not get within a league of him with a sword in your hand."

Relief flooded Willow. At least she wasn't expected to murder anyone. She only had to ... to *what?* She frowned at Queen Cyrraena, who was still studying the intricate green folds of her dress. "Exactly how *do* you expect me to stop Nezeral? Am I supposed to trick him or have a magic show-down or something?"

This time, Queen Cyrraena lifted her head and gazed directly at Willow. "You will know what to do when the time comes. You must believe this. You must believe in yourself."

"But ... but what if I don't? What if I fail? What happens then?"

"No, you can't ... " Queen Cyrraena paused, regarding Willow with frustration. Finally, she rose to her feet. "Do you see this tree?" She pointed at the thick willow trunk. "This is your name tree. It stands for the strength and wisdom that I have gifted you with. Look at it, Willow." She drew Willow up to stand beside her. "Do you see how firm and strong its trunk is? How steady?"

Willow nodded, patting the scratchy trunk bark with her hands.

"And yet its branches," Queen Cyrraena gestured behind her, "are supple and easy to bend. Wisdom works in this same way. You must be strong in your knowledge of who you are, but at the same time you must remain open to what is newly possible."

Nice sentiment. But hardly something that was going to help her defeat Nezeral. Willow sat back down on the cushion. "This isn't helping," she said dismally. "I don't mean to be rude or anything, but couldn't you just gift me with a magical plan instead?"

Queen Cyrraena stared for a moment and then suddenly burst into bubbling laughter.

Willow watched her, feeling a little angry. What was so funny? Was this some kind of joke to the elf queen?

"I'm sorry," said Queen Cyrraena. Her laughter became a contrite smile. "I did not mean to laugh." She sat back on the cushion, letting out one more stifled chuckle. "You may yet need to grow in strength, but you show no lack of being open to what is newly possible."

A puzzled look crossed Willow's face. She was *not* getting this elf queen at all.

"Not one person in this whole realm, human or elf, would dare to gainsay one of my gifts. It would not even enter their minds to *think* such a thing." Queen Cyrraena smiled and jiggled Willow's knee. "*That* is why you might yet best Nezeral. Your life on Earthworld — it allows you to see things very differently from us. You will examine every situation in a manner completely foreign to a magical being. Nezeral will not be expecting this.

"And the iron immunity ... " she looked at Willow thoughtfully, "he will not be expecting that, either. Somehow, all these things together are meaningful. It shall be up to you to determine how. My wisdom gift shall help you there. When the time comes, I promise you, you shall know what to do."

Willow didn't say anything. The whole thing seemed kind of hokey to her. *Just believe in yourself. When the time comes, you'll know what to do.* Queen Cyrraena was sounding like some New Age whacko from the psychic channel.

Willow rose from the blanket and stood at the edge of the swaying willow fronds, her fingertips trailing over the delicate leaves. She thought she was finally beginning to understand why Queen Cyrraena had picked her for the netherchild and why she'd been sent to Earth. But there was one thing that Queen Cyrraena had yet to explain. Willow let her hand fall from the leaves and turned back to the elf queen. "You haven't said anything about why Nezeral is doing this. I mean, I know King Tarrant's mage summoned the higher power, but why did he answer? Why would Nezeral, if he hates humans so much, even bother to come here?"

A pained expression clouded Queen Cyrraena's face. She looked at Willow as though gauging how much she should tell her. Finally, she lifted her chin and began to speak. "What I told you earlier regarding lower and upper realms is not entirely correct. There are mid realms as well. Mid realms that can potentially become upper realms." She too rose from the blanket, standing tall and erect. "Beings like Jarlath will stop at nothing to keep this advancement from happening. He sends his son here to create chaos. As that is what keeps humans from progressing. Chaos and war."

The grove had gone strangely silent again. Willow studied Queen Cyrraena's luminous forest-coloured beauty. She looked mostly human, but there was something else. A vague difference that hinted at her alien nature. Willow looked away, tears pooling in her eyes. Everything that had happened to her — losing Nana and Brand, growing up without her family, being exiled to another dimension — it had all happened because of something she couldn't change, something as uncontrollable as hair colour or body height — her humanness. Nezeral hated them because they were humans.

Gentle hands slipped over Willow's shoulders. "I wish," Queen Cyrraena said quietly, "that Nurse Beryl were here to see you. She would have been most proud. Your wisdom and bravery do her a great honour."

Willow blinked, swallowing back the lump that had just bunched in her throat. She turned to Queen Cyrraena. "Did you know her?" she asked. "Because she never mentioned you. That it was you who gave me this." Willow lifted the swan pendant, remembering Nana's story about it. *'Tis your mother's necklace*, she'd said. *One that has been passed down from generation to generation.* Nothing about it being magical or a gift from an elf queen. Willow let the swan drop back to her chest.

The elf queen looked sad. She lowered her gaze to the pendant. "Your nurse knew what I had done. That I had gambled your life on ridding Mistolear of Nezeral. It angered her greatly. It does not surprise me that she told you nothing of me."

A breezy sigh escaped Queen Cyrraena and she drew her hands away. "She was a good woman, your nurse. A very strong spirit. She visited you on the moat bridge in Tulaan. Did you see her?"

"You mean that — that really *was* Nana? I wasn't just seeing things?"

"The spirit realm is all around us," said Queen Cyrraena,

"only on another plane. If the want is great enough, the beings there can make themselves seen to those who need them. And as I said, your nurse is a very strong spirit. She gave me a message as well. She asked a favour of me."

Queen Cyrraena's gaze lowered and she reached out for Willow's hands. "This is something that you must think long and hard about." Her fingers squeezed Willow's. "Your nurse has asked me to grant you a gift. If you defeat Nezeral and come back unharmed, you will be allowed, if you wish it, to return to infancy."

Willow's mouth dropped open. *Return to infancy!* Her nana wanted her to be a *baby* again! "You — you can't be serious. Why would I want to do that?"

"She wants you to have a normal life. To grow up with a family and friends. To truly belong somewhere. But the decision is yours. She only requested that I offer such a choice. It is yours to decide."

The fine-boned hands that still clasped Willow's fingers tightened and then released their hold. Willow watched them fall to Queen Cyrraena's sides, mesmerized by their bird-like frailty. *The decision is yours.* The words burned in her head. All these decisions. They were too much. She didn't know what to say anymore or how to react.

"It is late morning in the human realms." Queen Cyrraena's voice drew Willow from her confusion. "I must get you back to your body before someone tries to awaken you." She drew Willow over by the tree and held her shoulders.

"There's one more thing I must tell you. Since you first arrived in Mistolear, I have shielded you from Nezeral with a magical barrier. But now that you have your powers, I can no longer do this. I can, however, grant you one last protection."

Her voice quavered and her eyes pressed shut. "Nezeral will not be allowed to enter your thoughts. Your mind will be closed to him." She took a deep breath and reached out to touch the swan pendant. Her eyes blinked opened. "And, of course, I will be watching ... "

The same powerful sensation that had brought Willow to Timorell suddenly engulfed her again, and Queen Cyrraena's beautiful face faded into blackness. "No! Wait!" Willow screamed. She wasn't ready. There were still questions that needed answers. But the tightness squeezed her breath away and sent her plummeting sickeningly downward.

CHAPTER 25

WILLOW'S EYES OPENED WIDE, her panicked cries still echoing in her head. She scrambled to sit up, to check her arms and legs. She was inside her glowing body again, Morwenna's magical fire warming her and casting soft rainbow-colours over the room. Anger flared inside her. Nice of Queen Cyrraena to mention the protection barrier. Especially at the last minute, when she couldn't ask her anything more about it.

So, what did it mean? Hesitantly, Willow scanned the dark-stone walls and murky end corners of her room. If Queen Cyrraena wasn't protecting her anymore, did it mean that Nezeral could see her? That he could move her around the same way Queen Cyrraena had? Another image filled her mind — that of the eye dreams. Maybe Nezeral had been watching her all along, sneaking into her dreams without Queen Cyrraena knowing.

The creepy thought propelled her out of bed. She went to the windows and threw open each shutter, letting pale light spill over the shadows. Outside, fresh snow blanketed the ground and powdered the bare branches of the bleak stunted apple trees that clustered below. Willow pressed her face to the glass, feeling its chill against her skin. Fear gripped her. For the first time she sensed the Game spell. Could see its thin wiry aura weaving a net all around her — all around everything —

making it terrifyingly clear just how powerful Nezeral really was.

She turned from the window, blinking away the aura lights. Dread made her heart pound and her mind race. What if she failed? What would Nezeral do to her? Kill her? Stick her in a chess piece? Make her a prisoner? What?

Willow hugged herself tight and sat back on her bed. Thinking about chess pieces had also reminded her of Prince Varian and the fact that he was poised to checkmate King Ulor. Her gaze fell to the gleaming pair of Knights that sat on her night table. She didn't need Nezeral to destroy her. If Varian succeeded this would be her fate. A tentative finger brushed over one of the chess pieces.

Stay and be Captured or fight and be Captured. There were no other options.

The realization numbed her, blocking out the fear. She squinted, unfocusing her eyes until she could see the air energy. She visualized herself in her warm green tunic and pants, the fur-lined cloak heavy on her shoulders and her leather boots sleek around her legs. When she opened steely eyes, she was ready to begin her quest.

She scooped up Brand and her father from her night table and plopped them into her pocket. If by some miracle she actually did beat Nezeral, the first change she wanted to see was theirs. Her face clouded. *Damn it!* She'd forgotten to ask the elf queen if defeating Nezeral *would* bring the Captured Players back. *Stupid. Stupid. Stupid.* She drummed a palm into her forehead. *How could she have been so stupid?!* What if she did all this, risked her life and defeated Nezeral, and Brand and her parents still stayed chess pieces?

She sighed. It didn't matter. Her options still were to stay or to fight. Whether or not the Players were released didn't alter these choices.

A metallic gleam drew Willow's eyes back to the night table. The pearl-handled knife that Brand had given her in the marketplace lay mirroring the flickering flames from the fireplace. She picked it up, running her finger over the sharp blade. Queen Cyrraena had said that Nezeral would know if she carried iron, that he would not let her near him if she did. No sword. Not even a little knife. So without a weapon, then how could she defeat him? She set the knife back on the night table, a new realization slowly dawning on her. Elves were immortal. Maybe weapons couldn't even hurt them. *Crap.* If she kept this line of reasoning up, she'd end up hiding beneath the bed or something.

She stood and walked over to her wash basin, splashing cold water onto her face and combing back her hair into a tight ponytail. She'd walked every path of the maze in her mind, and they all led here, to this decision. There was no choice but to fight.

"Okay, Nezeral. I'm ready whenever you are." She was ready. What would happen would happen.

"Well, now, Princess, I'm glad to hear that," said a voice ripe with laughter.

Willow spun around. No one was there. She felt her heart begin to hammer again, her breath shorten. Something itched in her nostrils and blackness began to creep in around the edges of her sight. She fell to the floor, striking her head hard against the stone tiles. A dry chuckle filled the room, then ... nothing.

Willow came to with a throbbing head, a tongue that felt like it was wearing a sock, and eyes that refused to open. Gingerly she massaged her temple, where a golf-ball-sized lump exploded with pain. She winced and forced an eyelid open, peeking out at a bright light and an even brighter yellow-coloured bed curtain. This was definitely not her room — on Earth or otherwise.

She closed her eye. So, this was it, then. No goodbyes to Gemma and Malvin or her grandparents. Nezeral had come for her and that was that. She pried open her other eye, alternating between the two until they could both open at the same time.

She felt strangely calm. Relieved, almost. Whatever was going to happen, she told herself again, was going to happen. She just wanted to get it over with.

Slowly and very carefully, she pulled herself to a sitting position. The room swirled around her for a moment, giving both her head and stomach a queasy lurch. She clutched the bedsheets, taking deep, fortifying breaths through her mouth until the sick feeling passed.

Jeez! What had Nezeral done to her, anyway? Her whole body felt weak and rubbery, like she'd had the stomach flu for a week. She pressed her fingertips to her temples again, rubbing them in slow circles, careful not to touch her painfully protruding bump. The pounding began to ease off. Willow slowly raised her head.

The room that swam into focus was large and circular. Probably a castle tower, she thought, glancing at the windows that all opened only to bare blue skies. That, or they were up on a mountain somewhere. She grabbed the bedpost beside her and pulled herself up, taking a wobbly path to the nearest stone-edged sill.

Bright sunshine burned her eyes. She squinted, ignoring the accompanying pain in her head, and pushed open one of the glass casements. A warm, flower-scented breeze washed over her, ruffling her hair and caressing her skin. Birds trilled their summer songs and down below a garden was in its full summer bloom.

From the top of the castle tower, Willow's gaze swept over the lush green landscape forested with leafy oaks and maples, her heart leaping. For a moment, she thought Queen Cyrraena had returned her to Timorell. But then she saw the white in the distance, a great serrated line of snow-covered winter spruces that rose incongruously behind the summery trees and curved to the east. It was only a small part, she knew, but a part nonetheless of the Game spell's invisible barrier.

Reluctantly, she turned from the window, her insides quailing again at Nezeral's immense powers. She could not even begin to imagine what kind of energy it must take to create a seasonal weather adjustment. More than she had, that was for sure. She sighed and leaned against the stone sill, letting her gaze roam the large room.

It was like most of the other castle bedrooms she'd been in, but somehow the furniture seemed different, dainty and elegant rather than big and ornate. She walked over to a richly brocaded couch and sat on it, stretching her legs up over its cushions. It was cool to the skin and feather-pillow plush. Willow laid her head against its armrest, noticing the high-curved ceiling for the first time. It vaulted over her with green twining vines that ringed the tapestry edges like a thick shady forest.

Wow. Whoever this Nezeral was, he definitely had

Lifestyles-of-the-Rich-and-Famous taste. She smiled sardonically and reached over to scratch an itchy wrist. There was a dull scraping sound. She blinked, looking down at her arm, which still held its queen-glow. Thin iron bands were tightly clasped around her wrists.

She pulled up her tunic sleeve and touched one. A strange hot wind blew against her face, making her blink again. She looked up. The wind hadn't come from the bands, but from across the room.

"Good midday, Princess Willow."

Willow sat up quickly. Whatever she'd been expecting of Nezeral, it certainly wasn't what had just appeared. She stared at him, gaping stupidly. He was absolutely, incredibly, almost impossibly handsome.

A string of inane ba-ba-ba sounds came from her mouth.

The blue-garbed figure gave her a smile that was somehow both obnoxious and charming. "I trust your *sleep* was refreshing," he said, blinking innocently. He sat down opposite her on a matching brocaded chair.

A dazed nod was the best Willow could manage. She was mesmerized by his eyes, which glittered and shimmered like an exotic turquoise sea.

His thick dark brows contrasted startlingly against his peach-coloured skin and long silvery blaze of hair. He sprawled one leg over the armrest and leaned back comfortably, regarding Willow with a confident grin.

"I'm not quite what you were expecting, am I?"

This time Willow found her voice. "Are *you* Nezeral?" Even as she asked it, she knew it couldn't be true. He looked no more than seventeen! Just a kid like her.

He rose from the chair. "At your service," he declared,

sweeping her a low, graceful bow. His blue tunic glimmered like deep water at midnight. A smell of cool ocean breezes washed over Willow. She shook her head, fighting off the hypnotic effect he seemed to have over her.

"But you're just ... How old are you, anyway?" She folded her arms protectively. He was staring at her again, making her feel vulnerable.

A mystified look crossed his face. "Is this of importance to you?" he asked. He resumed his casual position on the chair. "My age?"

"Yeah," said Willow. "You don't look any older than me."

Nezeral appeared to think about this. "Well, I suppose on Clarion we would be considered the same age. But in this dimension, I am closer to about five hundred years of age."

Willow blinked at him. She knew that being immortal meant that you lived forever. But somehow her brain still couldn't fathom how this gorgeous-looking teenage boy was a five-hundred-year-old being.

Trying to regain her equilibrium, she peeled back one of her sleeves, showing the irons bands attached to her wrists. "What are these for?"

Nezeral smiled again. But this time there was no charm in it.

"Those bands are warding irons. They neutralize magic."

Dropping her banded wrist, Willow paled, reminded suddenly of just who she was dealing with here. She folded her arms again, trying not to look afraid.

I'm immune to iron, she reminded herself. *These bands won't ward a thing.*

Nezeral's confident demeanour, though, poked holes in her composure. What if Queen Cyrraena's magic *couldn't* cloak her thoughts? Or what if the iron were some special type of magic iron, and he really *had* warded her powers?

Willow peeked down at one of the exposed bands, trying to see its energy aura. The aura was there. She could still see it. But did that mean she could manipulate it?

She looked back at Nezeral. He was still staring at her, but with a new curiosity in his eyes. God! What had she almost done? Now that would've been real bright. Making one dissolve right in front of him.

"I wouldn't advise you to try it," Nezeral remarked dryly. "The burns can be quite nasty."

For one heartbeat-skipping second, Willow thought he'd read her mind. But then she realized he'd just been reading her body language. She'd been staring at the bands cross-eyed. Anyone would have been able to figure out what she'd been trying to do. She let out a deep breath. Besides, if he really *could* read her mind, the bands wouldn't be an issue.

"So I guess this makes me your prisoner, then," she said, deciding to pretend acceptance. If she *could* use her powers, she certainly didn't want Nezeral to know about it.

Nezeral's smile was wide and friendly. "*Prisoner* is a bit heavy-handed, don't you think? Would you not prefer something less harsh, like shall we say ... *guest?*" He suddenly rose to his feet. "I know! Let us dine together and become better acquainted."

Barbecue smells of woodsmoke and roast chicken wafted through the room. Willow turned her head. Behind her in the large fireplace a spitted chicken was dripping savoury juices into a fire, and two chairs and a food-laden table had appeared. She gaped. He'd done in an instant what would have taken her at least a couple of minutes to do! She felt her blood rush from her face.

Nezeral gripped her hand, pulling her to her feet. Willow gasped as a sharp pain knifed through her head. She stepped back from him and snatched her hand away. "Thank you, but I think I can manage," she said, moving stiffly past Nezeral and straight to the table. She felt her pocket for Brand's comforting outline. She was hungry. That's why she was so light-headed.

Nezeral followed in her wake, gallantly pulling out a chair for her. "I really must apologize, my dear Princess, for that lump on your head. My magic is so powerful on this pitiful realm that I often overdo my spells. You're not too queasy to eat, I do hope?"

Willow said nothing. If he was so sorry, then how come the lump was still there? She reached for a soft pear slice, ignoring his patronizing smile. She shoved it into her mouth, chewing gustily just to prove to him exactly how *un*queasy and *un*fazed she was by his powers and hyperactive spells.

Sitting across from her, Nezeral speared himself a wedge of pungent cheese and leaned back, regarding her quizzically. "So, tell me, in which of the realms did Cyrraena manage to age you so quickly? Truthfully, I never felt a hint of her spell. The realm must have been distant."

Would knowing about Earth alert Nezeral to her iron immunity? But what else could she say? She didn't know the names of any other dimensions. "I was brought up on Earth," she finally answered, figuring it was better to look gutsy than afraid.

For the first time Nezeral seemed disconcerted. "But ... but that is a corporeal realm. You would have had no powers whatsoever there." His white face registered shock and something else. Willow thought it might be fear.

Nezeral sat up straighter in his chair, studying Willow with new eyes. She could almost hear his thoughts whirling and spinning, wondering how this new development would affect his plans.

"So, how was it that Cyrraena trained you, then?" he asked casually, offering her a warm bun. "Without any magic, it would have been much like training a knight without a sword."

Willow accepted one of the buns and smiled. Nezeral was totally spooked about the no-magic thing. She decided to shock him a little more. "She didn't train me. I hadn't learned one thing about magic till yesterday."

"*Yesterday* ... " He blinked at her in disbelief. "No. You are lying," he growled, clenching his fist. He stood up and banged it on the table. "I do not believe you. This is Cyrraena's doing. Another attempt to mock me!" He shoved back his chair and roared into the ceiling. "You will pay for this, Cyrraena! Do you hear me?" And with that, a dark cloud of smoke poofed up around him.

Shaken, Willow stared at the now dissipating smoke. Nezeral *and* his chicken dinner had vanished from the room. She cleared her throat and swallowed hard. Maybe egging him on like that hadn't been such a good idea. Ways to make Queen Cyrraena pay, after all, probably revolved around Willow herself or the Game. She dropped the bun that was still in her hand onto the table and stood up. Maybe she should find Nezeral and see if she could calm him down.

She spun around, looking for the doorway, but there were only tapestry-covered stone walls or window casements. She marched over to a heavy tapestry and lifted it to check underneath. Nothing but grey stone. She checked beneath the bed and the carpet. No trapdoors either. She leaned out over one of the tower windows, staring down at the fifty-foot drop. And, apparently, no Rapunzel ladder of hair.

She sank to the floor beneath the sill, her courage sinking with her. What was she going to do when Nezeral came back? A vast emptiness yawned in her mind. "*Come on,*" she whispered. "*Think. Think.*" But nothing came to her. No thoughts. No theories. No plans. Dropping her head to her knees, Willow closed her eyes.

CHAPTER 26

*A*FTER A FEW DEJECTED moments, Willow lifted her head. She'd suddenly remembered the bands. The warding irons that had supposedly neutralized her magic hadn't yet been put to the test. She held out her arms, shaking and afraid.

A horrible thought had just occurred to her. What if Nezeral could sense what she was doing the way Queen Morwenna could sense what Varian and Terrill had done? If she made the bands come off, he'd know, and that'd be the end of any surprise tactics she might think of. She chewed her bottom lip. But on the other hand, if she couldn't do it, then the surprise would be hers.

Willow soft-focused her eyes until light blinded them. The band joggled between her fingers but held on. She concentrated harder, staring at the dense molecules till they writhed and squirmed like an insect swarm. The band was moving now, sliding ...

A tangy wind suddenly whipped her hair into her face. Startled, Willow blinked back her magic, folding her hands quickly into her lap. Nezeral was back, but he wasn't alone. He was grinning wolfishly and had his fingers pressed over the eyes of a young woman as if he had a big surprise for her.

"Are you ready?" he said, bending low to her ear.

Willow stared apprehensively at him as she climbed to her feet. She didn't like the trigger-happy edge to his voice or the way the woman's mouth trembled. No surprise was a good surprise if Nezeral was behind it.

What was he up to? Willow squinted hard at the woman. And why wouldn't Willow be a good surprise?

As his hand was pulled away, Willow realized the cruel trick he was playing. Red hair. Wide brown eyes. Thin gold circlet on her head. The woman was her mother — the princess Diantha. Who was about to meet her only child, only she didn't know it yet. Nezeral was pushing her forward, explaining just what he was up to.

"I told you that an infant was merely a bother," he said. "Look, see what Cyrraena has done. She has saved you ever so much trouble. She has ... "

Willow panicked, bolting forward. "Don't! Please don't!" Willow wasn't ready for this. She'd been so sure that her mother was lost to her forever. And now Diantha was standing here with that growing look of horror on her face. It was some type of trick. He was trying to make Willow snap.

Nezeral released the woman's arm. "Princess Diantha, meet your daughter," his smile was victorious as he spat out, "the princess *Willow.*"

Complete silence ruled. Nezeral stepped back to take a ringside seat on one of the brocaded chairs, while Willow and Diantha stared at each other like statues.

She wasn't as tall as Willow had imagined. Only about chin level. But she was definitely beautiful, the portrait Willow had seen only a faint intimation.

A tight knot twisted inside her. It wasn't a trick. It couldn't be.

Tears stung Willow's eyes. Her mother was so young. It wasn't fair. No one should have to face what she was facing:

her own three-month old baby standing in front of her all grown up. Willow winced. Must be like having your kid snatched and then finding her years later, a tall anonymous stranger.

"I'm sorry." There didn't seem anything else Willow could say.

"*No.*"

The word was low and harsh and didn't sound like it could possibly have come from Diantha's gentle mouth. But the young woman drew herself up and glared at Willow. "You shall not say that to me," she continued in the same caustic whisper. "Only *he* shall I allow to say it." She faced Nezeral. "When my beloved's blade slices through your coward's heart, you *will* say it. You will *choke* on it!"

"Come now, your scathing words do wound me. Even my great patience has its ... *boundaries.*" The last word Nezeral sharpened into a threat. Diantha went pale. When he saw that his words had had the proper effect, he smiled and rose from the chair.

"By your leave, miladies," he said, bowing deeply. "I shall allow your reunion to continue in private." He stared hard at Diantha, then vanished from the room.

Willow turned to Diantha's sigh. Whatever had given her that furious courage had now left her. She was worn and defeated, a sad rag doll with its stuffing knocked out. She sank down on the sofa, sobbing into her elbow.

Pulling uncomfortably at a loose cuff thread, Willow looked away. She knew it wasn't her fault she'd grown up, but that didn't seem to keep her from feeling guilty about it.

Diantha must have sensed her thoughts, because she slowly lifted her head and turned around. "Please forgive me," her voice rasped. Her hard-eyed anger was gone. She wiped at her tears. "I swore he would not make me cry again, and here I am weepy as a waterfall." A shy smile wobbled onto her face as she held her hand out to Willow. "Come, sit beside me. Let me look at you."

Nervous, Willow sat on the couch edge, staring at her big booted feet, which, of course, looked embarrassingly gigantic next to her mother's tiny slippered ones. She tucked them beneath the couch. Why did all the females in her family have to be so darn little?

A soft touch pulled her chin up and tentatively caressed her cheek. Diantha was studying her like a newborn, lifting her hands and checking to make sure she had all her fingers; tracing her nose and the shape of her face; feeling her hair and eyebrows; and even making her stand and twirl. "You are as tall almost as Alaric," she laughed. "I should never have expected that. You were such a tiny thing."

Humour glinted in her brown eyes. "I assume you've met my father? He must have been heartened to see your Somerell blood so evident."

Willow laughed. Now that was an understatement. King Tarrant had all but renamed her Diantha. "On my first night," she told her mother, "he announced to everyone that I was his new heir and that he wasn't going to allow me to be queened."

"Oh dear, that would not have gone over very well with the court." Diantha's lips pursed into a tight smile as she reached for Willow's hand. "Is there any word," she whispered, her eyes suddenly earnest, "of your father ... my Alaric?"

Willow swallowed, her hand drifting to the slight bump in her tunic pocket. Didn't her mother know about the Capture? She drew one of the White Knights from her pocket, peering at the hard white eyes and long aquiline nose. Yes. This was the right one. Then she placed the little figure in her mother's quavering hand. Diantha's hope visibly sank. "It happened just after your ... " Willow had been about to say *death* " ... after your disappearance. He was going with his mother to tell your family ... and was ... and was ambushed by your father's men. They all, umm ... thought you were ... you know, umm ... dead."

Diantha nodded. "Nezeral told me this," she admitted. "He himself took me out of the Game. He made it appear as if a White Player had Captured me by killing me with a knife. 'Twas all a ploy, though, to anger my father into playing the Game. But I thought mayhap ... mayhap he had lied about Alaric." She set the chess piece on a small side table, her fingertips lingering over the tiny helmeted head. When she turned back, ashen and limp, her eyes were so full of sorrow that Willow couldn't bear to look at them.

Something had to be done. Willow felt her throat tighten with fury. The whole Game thing was just so senseless. So stupid! She jumped to her feet and began pacing the room. Beating Nezeral was taking on a new meaning. She just couldn't let him win. Couldn't let him get away with what he'd done.

"Does he ever sleep?" she asked, whirling to face Diantha. "Is there ever a time when he's vulnerable? When he could be attacked?" She sat back down beside her mother with her onslaught of adrenaline-driven questions. "And guards? Does he use guards?"

Diantha shook her head. "Stop," she pleaded. "You must not ask me such questions. He is sure to be listening." Suddenly, she cried out. She threw herself away from Willow and soundlessly began to writhe on the couch.

Willow climbed instantly to her feet. "Coward! Do you hear me, Nezeral? You're nothing but a stinking coward!" Her fist slammed air. "Leave my mother alone! Or are you too afraid to come back? To fight me face to face!"

Diantha was suddenly freed. She sat up, staring fearfully around the room. "Oh Willow," she whispered, "what have you done?"

"I ... " Willow began. But her mother was rapidly fading away until Willow was left staring at an empty couch.

The smell of dank seaweed alerted her to Nezeral's presence — and his anger. She closed her eyes, hoping that some miraculous idea would suddenly spring fully formed into her head.

Nothing, of course, came to mind.

CHAPTER 27

"SO, PRINCESS, YOU ARE READY, I presume, to do battle with me now, are you?" Nezeral stood before her, emanating his supremacy.

Willow stepped back. What was he going to do? Magic or no magic, Nezeral could beat her — and beat her bad. She was nothing more than a bug to him, an annoying fly waiting to be swatted. It was just a matter of when.

A strange harsh growl suddenly came from Nezeral. His arm shot into the air. Willow flinched, expecting to be consumed in flames or devoured by mad dogs or something equally horrible.

Nezeral snorted. "Don't worry," he said, dropping his arm. "I do not intend to destroy you — not just yet. I have something I wish to show you first." He pointed past her, deliberately jerking his hand at her face to make her flinch again.

Creep! Willow glared at him. She stiffly turned to follow his gesturing hand.

The Game prototype stood before them. It was even more ornate and fantastical-looking than the ones King Ulor and King Tarrant had used. The board itself, which stood on a tree-trunk-thick pedestal and was crafted from onyx and ivory-coloured marble, was as big as a rec-room pool table, with Players the size of dolls. As always, Willow was struck by how real they seemed.

Nezeral brushed past her and casually scrutinized the board. "Well, well, it would seem that I may not have to destroy you after all. Your uncle is very close to accomplishing it for me."

Willow felt the downward slide of any hopes she had for living past her teens. From the looks of the Game, Varian was at the back rank now, only two jumps behind King Ulor. She probably had one, maybe two days tops, before he could catch up with him and pull off a checkmate. And it was clear from what Nezeral had just said that a checkmate meant that all losing Players, including herself, would be turned to marble.

"So," said Nezeral softly, "I guess that just leaves it up to me to choose." There was no mockery or laughter in his voice. He was deadly serious, his eyes concentrating on her with reptilian focus. "Ah, choices, Willow. We all make our choice. I think I must make mine."

Willow felt it first as a faint probe, as if someone had gently caressed her throat. It was a pleasant feeling, nothing to be afraid of. Nezeral's eyes were reflecting stars at her, shimmering so tantalizingly close she could almost touch them. The pressure grew firmer, like a massage. She relaxed into the starry green pools, imagining she was floating.

Then something squeezed — and it squeezed hard.

Willow flailed, choking for breath. Too late, she realized what he meant to do. The "choice" he had made. He was strangling her magically. He had decided that it was better to kill her himself than wait for Varian to Capture her.

She tried to speak, to scream, to beg, anything to make him stop, but the crushing force on her windpipe was too strong. She couldn't see properly; Nezeral was outlined in a murky brown haze. He was smiling, a thin feral grin that sickened her.

"No ... " she finally managed to gag out. She didn't want to die, not like this, not so ignobly. Nezeral's smile widened. The pressure grew worse. Willow was seeing light everywhere, white, dazzling light. It hurt her eyes because they couldn't blink. Suddenly the light began to change, to break into smaller particles of itself.

No, not light, she realized, but auras!

Willow twisted her head frantically, trying to escape the squeezing pressure. She clawed at her neck, but there was nothing there. Blackness was beginning to edge in around her vision. Panicked, she thrust her banded wrists in front of her, fighting to stay conscious. The auras; she had to manipulate the auras. With her last strength, her last will, she tried. There. Whatever strength was left her, she'd used it up. Her eyes still couldn't close, but it didn't matter. The bands weren't on her wrists, they were on Nezeral's. She could see the bands in her mind with long chains attached to them, imprisoning him to the wall.

And suddenly the pressure was gone. Willow dropped to her knees, choking and gasping. Her throat was raw, hurting so badly that just swallowing was torture. She collapsed on the floor, mercifully passing out on the way.

&

Cold air blew around Willow, making her shiver. She was confused and disoriented. Something was burning her throat. Her eyes flew open. *Nezeral!* He'd tried to strangle her. To kill her!

Heart racing, she lifted her head, wincing at the pain it cost to move. Right across from her was Nezeral. He was sitting on the floor in stony silence, watching her, long chains dangling above him that attached to his iron wrist bands.

Willow sat up, keeping her eyes glued to Nezeral's face. This could be a trick. Some kind of psychological cat-and-mouse game. But he didn't move or speak and the bands didn't suddenly pop off his wrists.

That's when Willow noticed that, except for the gigantic chess set, the room had not one stitch of furniture in it. She shivered again. Why was it so cold? An icy breeze against her back answered her. She turned around and saw that the breeze had come from a window, the one she'd opened earlier.

Still dazed, she struggled to stand, fighting the blackness that spotted her vision. Her throat ached terribly. She held her numb fingers against it, making her way to the window.

Outside, the winter snow she'd left behind in Keldoran was doing its best to make up for lost time. It battered against the trees like a relentless army, obliterating the green under a shroud of heavy white. Down below, where the gardens had been, there was only a smooth, colourless sea punctuated by an island of bushes or a patch of long-stemmed flowers.

Willow closed the window. What did it all mean? Had she won? Was the Game over?

She spun around to Nezeral to ask him if it was true about the Game, but only a raspy croak would come out of her mouth. Gingerly, she touched her swollen neck. If pain was any indicator, it was definitely bruised. She might even need a doctor. No! She could fix this herself. She remembered how Queen Morwenna had healed Gemma.

Willow took a deep breath and placed both her hands

around her neck. No one had actually taught her a healing spell, but she supposed it probably worked along the same principles as the others. She unfocused her gaze, waiting for the aura lights to wink into existence. When they did, she closed her eyes, imagining her throat pain-free and healthy.

Her neck grew warm, then began to tingle. A thick wave of heat swept over her, and when she opened her eyes, her throat felt perfectly normal again.

When she spun around to face Nezeral this time, she was smiling confidently. "Well, Nezeral," she whispered, testing her voice. It worked. She spoke a little louder. "I guess there's just one thing I want to say to you. And that is ... checkmate!"

Nezeral regarded her contemptuously, although there was something that looked very much like amusement glittering in his eyes. "Check, perhaps, dear Princess," he said. "But hardly *checkmate*. Look in your pocket."

Willow narrowed her eyes, expecting some kind of trick. She still couldn't quite believe that those thin little bands had neutralized his powers.

"Go on," he said, "look."

Keeping her stare locked on his face, Willow slid her hand into her pocket. She knew what was in there. Her fingers wrapped around Brand and pulled him into the light. He hadn't changed any. He was still a hunk of white marble.

"The other one's over there," said Nezeral, gazing at Alaric's Knight, which lay on the floor beside the board. "Your father, I believe."

Willow blinked at him, not answering. What was he getting at? Was he trying to say that the Game spell was still functioning? She looked down at Brand again. Why hadn't he changed yet? Both he *and* her father should have changed back by now.

"That's right," drawled Nezeral. "The Game's still on. And your time is running out. Varian will soon be succeeding where I have failed."

A queasy, stomach-sinking feeling swept through Willow. She remembered the lecture about intrinsic and extrinsic magic that Malvin had given her once, about how magic either became a part of the object or stayed controlled by the mage. She sighed. It didn't matter that she'd trapped Nezeral's powers. The Game was intrinsic. It would just keep going until it was over.

"So what happens now?" she asked, setting Brand on the window sill and stepping toward Nezeral. "Sending you back to Clarion won't solve my problems. Is there some sort of deal you want to make?"

"I don't need to make any deal. I just need to wait."

Willow stood looking down at him, frowning. "What do you mean? If I get changed to marble, you'll freeze to death up here."

Nezeral shook his head. "This castle has gold hidden all through it. I have servants, one of whom, I am sure, for the right price, will rid me of *these*." He jangled the chains and grinned.

"Not if I send you back to Clarion first." Willow didn't know if she could actually do that, but she'd say just about anything to wipe that smirk off his face.

"Can't do it," he said. "Not unless I agree, which, I assure you, I won't."

Anger slammed into Willow like a fist. He was going to win. This selfish, rotten pig, who'd ripped apart her family — who'd tried to *murder* her — was going to win! God! The fury clenched her teeth together. She had to do something. Something to make him pay!

Her focus narrowed along his exposed throat. She saw his aura, dense and muddy as a stagnant swamp. It repulsed her the way touching something icky would, but she ignored it, concentrating instead on the constriction of Nezeral's throat muscles and the shocked surprise in his goggled-out eyes.

There! her mind cried. *How do you like* that! *And that!* She compressed his neck in a series of tight squeezes, watching as he gasped and wheezed, twisting his head in helpless desperation. He couldn't speak. His face was dark red and his eyes rolled wildly in their bulging sockets. Maybe immortals could die after all. Like vampires. You just needed to get them when they were powerless. They certainly could suffer.

Willow felt something warm and wet running down the sides of her face. She wiped at it savagely. *No!* Those weren't tears. They couldn't be. No way she'd be crying for that rotten scumbag.

The phantom tears, though, were streaming down her neck and into her shirt collar. They were blurring her vision and making her nose run. A sob burst from her lips.

She couldn't do it. She couldn't murder someone.

Even if that someone was Nezeral.

She sank to her knees, crying in quick, shuddery breaths and trying to block out the choking gasps that were coming from a few feet away.

Oh God, what was she going to do? Two whole countries had been counting on her, and she'd blown it. She'd let everyone down. Brand, her family, Queen Cyrraena — everyone.

She sat back on the floor and buried her head in her knees. "I — I'm sorry," she whispered. "I tried. I really tried."

Pain welled up inside her. It wasn't fair. She didn't want to die or be a chess piece. She just wanted to be a kid. A normal kid.

She sighed, bouncing her head into her knees. Was that too much to ask? Just to be normal?

Suddenly she stopped in mid-bounce.

Hey, wait a minute. That was the one thing she'd forgotten. She *was* normal. In fact, she was the only freakin' normal person in this whole realm.

Willow lifted her head. She'd been going about this all wrong, trying to play the Game by Nezeral's rules. She had to look at things the way Queen Cyrraena had told her to — from her own unmagical perspective.

Making a soft choking sound to clear his throat, Nezeral broke into her thoughts. "See, Cyrraena? See what happens when you send infants to do a hero's job?"

His words mesmerized Willow. He didn't know it yet, but maybe, just maybe he had solved one of her problems.

CHAPTER 28

WILLOW LOOKED CLOSELY at Nezeral. She'd been too busy trying to stay alive to notice much about him. For all his composure, she figured that while she'd been unconscious he must have been whaling pretty hard on those chains to make his wrists bleed like that. And his hair was hanging in loose strands as if he'd been whipping his head around too. So maybe he wasn't quite so cool and collected. Maybe he was just as scared as she was.

"What is *wrong* with you?" she asked suddenly. "Why are you doing this?" She'd heard Queen Cyrraena's side of things; now she wanted to hear his.

A flicker of anger sparked in Nezeral's eyes. "I am an upper realm immortal," he said, his voice cold and arrogant. "Nothing is wrong with *me*." He ran his fingers through his hair, casually lifting the loose strands away from his face. "I will answer your other question, however, because it suits me to do so."

Wind suddenly howled outside the windows, sending icy shivers through Willow. Without taking her gaze from Nezeral, she made a blazing fire spring to life in the large hearth behind her. She leaned forward on her knees to listen, despite the hostility in his glittering eyes.

"Can you imagine," he said softly, "what it is like to live forever?"

Willow shook her head.

"It is wondrous and marvellous and ... boring."

Boring? Willow gave Nezeral a skeptical frown. How could life as an all-powerful immortal being be *boring?*

"In my world," Nezeral continued, "every person is beautiful and perfect. No one grows old. There are no illnesses or deformities. Everyone has the self-same magical powers. Everyone *is* the same."

"I don't know," said Willow, adjusting her long legs so that they curled beneath her. "Sounds pretty good to me."

Nezeral flashed her a look of contempt that changed to a dry smile. "What do you think we do on Clarion to pass away the eons?"

Willow shrugged. Elves were a mystery to her. She imagined, though, remembering Queen Cyrraena's beautiful Timorell, that they probably did aesthetic stuff like creating great works of art or composing brilliant symphonies or something.

"We play games," said Nezeral matter-of-factly.

"Play games? You mean like chess and Monopoly kind of games?" This was hardly the soul-stirring answer she'd been expecting.

"No, I mean games of life."

"Games of life?"

"Yes. On Clarion, we turn every aspect of our lives into games. All the different elf kingdoms create elaborate magical games and compete against each other. I am of the House of Jarlath, the reigning game house of Clarion." Nezeral leaned against the stone wall and casually crossed his legs at the ankles.

Willow didn't get it. What did any of this have to do with

turning her and her family into chess pieces? She studied Nezeral. His handsome face was all angles, high-sculpted cheekbones and strong chin. He looked like a teen model or a movie star. Not some unfeeling monster. "Would you just get to the point and tell me why you're doing this."

"Do you not comprehend? This is a new game. If I succeed in getting the humans to play it to its conclusion, the elf council, which banned interaction with other dimensions, must lift the ban. New games. New rules. New players. Don't you see? This will keep us as the reigning game house for eons to come."

What Queen Cyrraena had said about the prejudice against humans was frighteningly clear from Nezeral's words. He didn't care that his games had disrupted lives and torn families apart. Humans were expendable. Nothing more than toys for him to play with. Willow frowned. But still, Queen Cyrraena had said that not all elves felt this way. So why would they lift the dimension-travelling ban and create such havoc? "I still don't get it. If you make us play the Game to the end, why does that mean your council has to lift the ban?"

Nezeral cocked his head at her, strands of silver hair falling into his eyes. "When council makes rules, it usually adds clauses to amend them." His greenish-blue eyes twinkled with amusement. "Rule One: Elves are not allowed to dimension travel. *Clause* One: Unless called to that dimension by a being who lives there. Rule Two: Once called to another dimension, an elf may choose to cast game spells on the beings that live there. *Clause* Two: If beings play a game to its conclusion, the elf ban of dimension travelling to that dimension will be lifted. However ... " he nodded at Willow, "*Clause Two(a)*: If the beings find a way to thwart the game, the elf must return back to his or her own dimension. See, there are even clauses for you humans."

"But that's not fair!" cried Willow, anger flaring through her. "You elves are, like, *ten* times more powerful than us! You can't just come here and use us like we're your little toy soldiers or something. Where's the fun in *that?!* Where's the sports-manship?"

"Fun?" said Nezeral, looking at her blankly. "Sportsmanship? These are human concepts, not elvish ones. We play games for one reason and one reason only: *power.*" His face grew arrogant. "I am from the blood of the Ancients, the old gods who used to rule your Earthworld, and I will set things as they once were."

Willow gaped. So here it was, the *real* reason for his com-ing to Mistolear.

"Many of us wish to return to the old ways when ruling the lower realms was our birthright. Of course, Earthworld and the other material realms are forever closed to us. But you Mistolearians have finally opened the way to the lower magi-cal realms."

Sickened by his malice, Willow stood up. This whole game scheme was about nothing more than gigantic egos and ignorance.

She focused on Nezeral's dirty brown aura. She supposed that what she was about to do was, in a way, creating a new type of game. A game that would promote knowledge and tol-erance instead of ignorance and hatred.

The elf prince paled. He could see she was readying her magic. "Wait. I answered your question. I believe you owe me the same courtesy."

Willow blinked at him, scattering his aura light. "I don't

owe you anything," she said sharply. "You should be glad just to be alive, and that *I'm* not the kind of person who can hurt someone who can't fight back."

Was that a sheepish look on his face? Willow squinted at him, not sure whether he was just putting on an act for her. "That was an unfortunate mistake. I let my anger get the better of me. For what it is worth, though," he said, gazing at the floor, "I would not have killed you."

"Yeah, right," Willow muttered. He must have thought she was pretty stupid to buy into that one. She crossed her arms. "Okay, go ahead, ask your question."

"In fact, I have two questions. The first one is how is it that you were able to magic these?" He held up his wrists, indicating the iron bands. "No one can magic iron. So how is it that a lower realm mortal, who grew up in an altogether non-magical world, can have such power?" He studied her carefully, his face greedy for the answer.

Willow knew what was going on inside his head. Ruler-of-the-Universe dreams were shining all through his turquoise eyes. He still thought he was going to get out of this. And, if he could somehow acquire her iron immunity, so much the better.

"Honestly?" she lied. "I don't really know. No one does. Next question."

Nezeral hesitated, his cool demeanour suddenly switching into scared-and-vulnerable mode. "What do you mean to do with me?" he asked quietly. He was a shy teenage boy to her then, uncertain about his future and looking to her for mercy.

A soft smile spread over Willow's face. "I mean to give you a second chance," she replied, beginning to unfocus again.

Triumph broke through the vulnerable act, and Nezeral

let out a happy whoop. He held the wrist bands up so she could see them better. "You shall not regret this, Princess," he said, grinning broadly. "I may decide to remove you from the Game spell permanently. We shall join forces. With our powers united, we shall see no barriers."

Willow didn't contradict or believe him. She just nodded and watched the way his aura leapt with excitement. Already her mind was concentrating on the change, imagining him into his second-chance form. She observed how his aura brightened from dark shades of brown to deepest crimson to red and finally to a sweet, innocent pink.

When she blinked her eyes back into focus, the Nezeral that had once been was not to be found. His chains and iron bands lay empty on the floor. In his place, gurgling among his pile of clothing, was a kicking, squirming baby boy with a silky fine dusting of silver hair and eyes the carefree greeny-blue of a tropical bay.

Willow leaned over him, smiling, bringing his sweet pink aura into view again. She wasn't the one who needed Nana's wish for a second chance. She was proud of the person Nana had helped her to become. She didn't need to go backwards. But this boy, if *he* had another chance ... maybe things would be different.

She had to laugh as he rammed his tiny fist into his mouth, gumming it for all it was worth. With her magic, she diapered him and dressed him in snuggly pajamas, then changed his old clothing into a thick warm blanket. The baby squealed happily and waved his hands in the air.

Gently, Willow touched his plump cheek. "I still have to do something about that nasty old Game spell." She tucked his blankets tighter around his chin and stood up, staring at his round little head. At least he wouldn't be able to hurt anybody else — even if her Game spell idea didn't work out. And now she had the peace of mind to focus on the spell.

As she turned to face it, the chess set looked eerie. A storm outside had darkened the room and the Game's tall, thin pieces were casting weird firelit shadows that seemed to flicker into life. She took a deep breath and peered at the Game. She knew that Nezeral's spell was too strong for her to break. No chance of that. But maybe she could alter it just a little.

Thinking about second chances had made her think about her computer. About how you could save a game and replay the same one over and over again till you got it right. And that had made her wonder whether the spell could be made to do the same thing.

White light glowed around the edges of the chess set. She could see the molecules, the way the magic had woven them into an impenetrable pattern. If she attempted to destroy them, they would have resisted. Instead, she was only going to rearrange them a bit. The spell would be exactly the same, with one slight difference. Her eyes narrowed, focused, unfocused again. She knew exactly what she had to imagine.

There. Willow shook away her blurry vision and stared at what she'd done. The humongous chess set was gone and in its place was her grey Toshiba laptop. Her monitor was on showing a chess game in play mode with the pieces set up in the exact same positions as on the other set.

She crossed her fingers, breathing a short prayer that her plan would work. Her heart seemed to pound in her ears as she touched a shaky hand to the keyboard. She mouse-clicked the Game button and then pressed Close. The computer prompt asked if she wanted to save the game. Willow clicked on Yes, clearing the screen back to a grey blank, then she quickly exited out of the chess program and shut off the computer.

Instantly, fire engulfed her body, but this time, instead of burning in, it was burning out. She gasped, crumpling to the floor, feeling as though some huge machine was siphoning the life out of her. Her body curled into a fetal position and her hands crossed protectively over her chest. It seemed to take forever for the magic's volcanic heat to drain from her, but finally it was over. It had only been a few seconds.

Quivering from head to foot, Willow slowly unclenched her body. She was wet and clammy and her eyes burned, but she was alive. *It worked! I'm just plain ordinary me again.* She closed her eyes in relief, panting in rapid shallow breaths.

"Willow?"

That voice. Willow's eyes popped open. She knew that voice. "Brand," she said weakly. He was beside her in an instant.

"You did it! By the gods, Princess, you did it!" He laughed, eyes glistening, as he hugged her tight. Willow noticed that neither of them had the Game-glow anymore.

Another voice, a happy woman's voice, echoed throughout the empty room. "Alaric!"

Willow sat up to see her mother standing in a newly materialized doorway. Diantha raced across the room and flung herself into the arms of a tall fur-cloaked man with dark hair and a bewildered expression on his face. "Diantha," he said, blinking at her in surprise, "you are alive? The Game is ended, then? We are free?"

Diantha could only nod as she nestled in his arms. Alaric smiled down at her and then looked over her head at Brand

and Willow. "The explanation shall have to fall on you, Brand. My wife appears to be welded into my chest."

A playful backhand swatted his head as Diantha threw her arms up around his neck and drew him down for a kiss.

Willow blushed in embarrassment. Those were her parents over there, and they were kissing! Not that it was gross or anything. It just felt weird. She teetered, still a bit light-headed from the magic drain, as Brand helped her to her feet.

Diantha, she could see, was now whispering something into Alaric's ear that made him look at Diantha in shocked surprise. His arm slid bonelessly from her shoulder as he turned to stare at Willow, anger and disbelief warring across his face.

"This is ... our *child?*" he whispered, looking back to Diantha for reassurance. "But ... but how? Who did this to her?"

Diantha shushed away his questions, leading him toward Willow. "Willow," she said, beaming, "this — this is your father."

Shy smiles passed between them as Willow gazed into the clear blue of her father's eyes; clear, icicle-blue like King Ulor's. The similarities between father and son ended there, though. Prince Alaric's chiselled features and tall muscular body had no traces of King Ulor's heaviness.

His hand reached out to touch her face. "Is it to you, then, Daughter, that we all owe our lives?"

Willow nodded, feeling the strength of his fingers against her cheek. She couldn't speak. Her voice was caught somewhere in her throat and her eyes were blinking rapidly. This was her father. She *had* a father!

"Well met," he said, drawing her into his arms. "The

bards will have another Farrandale to sing of." The cool, smooth leather of his tunic pressed against Willow's skin. She felt him lean in close, encompassing her in his horse and leather-musk scent, to kiss the top of her head.

Tears suddenly squeezed from her eyes, and she clung to him like a small child. It was over. Everything she'd been through in the past couple of weeks was finally over! Her mother's arm slipped around her back and, for the first time, the three of them embraced as a family — one big teary-eyed happy family.

A loud howl, however, shattered their peaceful silence. Every head turned to the small bundle on the floor, its cries punctuated by a tiny swinging fist. Diantha's hand rose to her mouth as she gave Willow an astonished stare. No words passed between them, but Willow knew her mother had figured out what she had done.

Speechless, and with her hand still pressed to her mouth, Diantha knelt beside the wailing baby, staring down at him in misery. She did not, however, touch him.

Willow stood behind her and squeezed her shoulder. "If *we* bring him up," she said softly, "he won't be evil. We can teach him about what humans are like and ... caring about people and stuff. But, you know, if you don't want to, maybe we could find somebody else."

Diantha didn't say anything. She stared at the baby and her hand slid up to her shoulder to press on Willow's. "Are you sure?" she asked, turning to look into her daughter's face. "Are you sure this is what you want — for us to raise him?"

Willow smiled and nodded. She'd never been more sure of anything in her whole life.

"Alaric?" Diantha's voice trembled with uncertainty. "Do

you wish it as well?"

Alaric came to stand by them, staring down at the squalling infant, his face thoughtful and sad. Finally, he spoke. "Aye, I do wish it." He picked up the baby, rocking him against his chest. The baby quickly settled, his eyes closing. Alaric handed him to Diantha, who rocked him in her arms.

Willow smiled. They looked like a family. She clasped Brand's fingers and moved to join them. To join her family.

CHAPTER 29

S OON AFTER THE BABY fell asleep, Queen Cyrraena appeared in a blaze of golden light. She wore sun-coloured robes, and her long chestnut hair spilled over her shoulders like a silken cloak. She went instantly to Willow, resting her hand on Willow's cheek, her eyes shimmering like green stars. "My netherchild, you chose wisely."

Willow felt a rush of pure elation. She *had* chosen wisely. She glanced at Nezeral snuggled securely in Diantha's arms. No one had battled. No one had had to die. Her decision had actually worked out so that everyone had gained something. Gallandra and Keldoran had their magic back. Prince Alaric and Princess Diantha had a baby, albeit not their own. And Nezeral would now grow up with a new understanding of humans. Everyone had benefited. No one was a loser.

Nana's proud, time-worn face surfaced in her mind. No one, that is, she amended with a bitter pang, except maybe Nana and that poor boy Pawn, Terrill Longbottom. They hadn't come out of the Game winners. They hadn't come out of it at all.

"I am no mage," said Brand, interrupting Willow's thoughts, "but is that spell truly strong enough to keep Nezeral an infant?" He frowned at the small bundle in Diantha's arms. "Is it not possible that he might break the spell?"

Queen Cyrraena shook her head. "No, Squire Lackwulf.

The princess' spell was cast with the magic of a whole kingdom inside her. It will not break."

"But the Game's over," Willow said. Brand's question had raised doubts in her as well. "Shouldn't my spell end too?"

"Intrinsic spells do not end with a loss of a mage's magic. You cast the spell intrinsically, so it will stay an intrinsic part of Nezeral whether you possess the power or not." A radiant smile filled Queen Cyrraena's face. "Come now," she said, wrapping an exuberant arm around each of them, "let us make ready for your return to Tulaan."

In the blink of an eye, she had magicked everyone into rich fur-trimmed costumes that sparkled with jewels and the eye-catching golds and purples of the House of Farrandale. Elaborate golden crowns encircled the heads of Willow and her parents, and a squire's jaunty feathered cap rested dashingly low on Brand's forehead.

Thanks to Queen Cyrraena's magic, their trek to Tulaan was sun-warmed, short and comfortable. When they reached the city, the celebration was overwhelming. Willow's reception was surpassed only by Diantha's — no one had expected ever to see her again. When they reached the castle, the entire Farrandale and Somerell courts were waiting.

There was one family member, though, who stood back from it all, tall and regal, waiting for the commotion to die down. She had bright, orangey-red hair pulled severely into two tight braids and rolled at the sides. Her skin seemed whiter than the courtyard snow and her eyelashes and eyebrows were completely colourless. But her aqua eyes made up for the lack of colour. They were so bright and intense that they seemed to glow like clear blue lights.

Willow pulled away from her Keldorian grandparents and

stared at the woman, who gave her a small, subdued smile and held out a gloved hand. Prince Alaric touched Willow's elbow and whispered in her ear. "Come, I'll introduce you to your Farrandale grandmother." The others moved aside as Willow and her father walked the short distance across the courtyard.

"Madam," he said, smiling at his mother and drawing Willow to stand in front of him, "your granddaughter, the princess Willow."

Queen Aleria's composure wobbled a bit but then she steadied herself, reaching out her hand to take hold of Willow's. "My dear, to have a granddaughter such as you — is a great honour."

Tears brightened Willow's eyes as she clasped Queen Aleria's outstretched hand. She couldn't say anything. She was too lost in their similarities. In how she and her grandmother stood eye to eye and how their long-limbed figures were almost identical. For the first time ever, Willow didn't feel like a clumsy giant.

"She takes after you, don't you think, Aleria?" said King Ulor, who'd had his long journey to Tulaan magically short-ened by Queen Cyrraena and was now hugging his wife's shoulders with youthful exuberance. "When she first came here, we had her wearing your shoes!"

Queen Aleria smiled and held Willow's hand palm to palm with her own. "'Twould seem, my lord, that you are cor-rect."

Willow saw that their long fingertips stretched to meet each other. It was like holding her hand up to a mirror.

A loud cry ended their careful study. Willow dropped her hand, turning to search out Diantha and Alaric. The crowd had grown quiet again. Confused faces strained to catch a glimpse of the bundle in the prince's arms. Murmurs rose. *An infant? What was the prince doing with a new infant?*

"This child," announced Prince Alaric, "is the elf prince Nezeral." More murmurs. Alaric raised a hand for quiet. "My daughter has saved our world from tyranny. It was her choice to gift Nezeral with a second chance. And now it is our duty to make sure that her gift is not in vain." He searched the crowd with earnest eyes then said solemnly, "Princess Diantha and I have agreed to raise Nezeral as our own son."

For a moment, Willow thought the crowd's silence would turn to dissent, but a cheer broke out instead and then another one. Pretty soon everyone was congratulating her again and clapping her back. She made her way, along with her family and Brand, to the foyer of the castle. Willow found Gemma and Malvin loitering on the front steps, waiting for their chance to greet her. They gathered around her and Brand.

"Now that's a neat trick ye did there with Nezeral," said Gemma, beaming up at Willow. "Who'd have thought he'd make such a sweet babe?"

"Aye," agreed Malvin, "'twas a most fitting defeat."

Gemma smiled and gave Brand a playful punch. "Master Brand, nice to see ye're all loosened up again. Mayhap we should have a nice game of chess sometime."

A loud groan came from Brand. "Not funny, Gemma. Not funny in the least."

Willow filled them in on how she had defeated Nezeral.

"So your Earth mechanism was able to reverse the spell," said Malvin, eyes narrowed in scholarly contemplation. "Most amazing. Who would have thought an intrinsic construct of such magical magnitude could be altered? I suppose, though, if the spell was not interfered with, it could be done."

"Well, I'd say that's plain," said Gemma, grinning. "If it couldn't be done, we wouldn't have Her Highness and Master Brand back now, would we?"

"I still say you should have blasted him," muttered Brand. He was having a hard time dealing with the fact that a heroic quest had ended with the villain being turned into a baby. "What if he grows up wicked again? Who's going to defeat him then? 'Tis like taking home a baby dragon. All's well till he starts burning down your manor and eating all your livestock!"

Willow laughed but refused to be drawn into the argument. She linked arms with her friends and led them inside. "No more fights, because tonight we're gonna party!"

The banquet that night was magical. Really magical. The chefs and musicians and entertainers had all had their magical powers restored, so it was unlike anything Willow had ever seen before. First came a floating Castle of Cookery that drifted to the centre of the great banquet hall, hovered a moment in the air and then settled gracefully to the floor. Each corner had a tower, and each tower was lit from within with sparkling lights.

A fire-breathing boar's head was in the first tower; a great pike in three sections, each cooked differently, was in the second; a fire-breathing roast suckling pig in the third; and, in the fourth and final tower, a beautiful redressed swan, who was also breathing flames, sat on a nest of golden twigs.

Willow thought nothing could be better, but the desserts were even more magical. Marzipan sugar spun into brightly coloured birds flew to the plates, and tiny unicorn ice sculptures melted into strawberry sorbets.

The music that was played was magically transformed

into each guest's favourite song. Willow listened to Pachelbel's "Canon" and Ben E. King's "Stand By Me" over and over. And when the jugglers, acrobats and dancers performed, the entire banquet hall was dimly lit with fairy lights. Real fairy lights — hundreds of little fairies flew over the room, sprinkling silvery dust on the performers.

When the dancing started, Brand was the first to claim Willow, holding her close and spinning her around the room. Her father was her next partner, then Malvin. Toward midnight, when she was tired and flushed with fun, Queen Cyrraena tapped her on the shoulder.

"Might I steal a moment with you?" she said, linking arms with Willow. "I have something to speak with you about."

Willow followed her out a side door into the snow-covered garden. It was quiet and peaceful but very cold. Willow shivered, rubbing her arms for warmth. "Do you want me to get us some cloaks?" she offered, about to turn back inside.

Queen Cyrraena stopped her. "That won't be necessary," she said, passing her hand in front of them. Willow's face broke into a huge smile as the entire courtyard was suddenly encased in a giant bubble of summer.

"Come," said the queen, taking her arm. "This won't take long." She led Willow down a warm, moonlit path to a secluded bench.

"Have you given any thought to your nurse's gift?"

Willow sat on the bench and looked up at the moon. "I know what Nana was trying to do. But I don't think I need to grow up again. I think I'm happy just the way I am." She looked at Queen Cyrraena to judge her reaction. The elf queen, her beauty breathtaking in the moonlight, was smiling at her.

"Again you do your nurse a great honour. I think she will be very proud of your decision." Queen Cyrraena reached for Willow's hand. "Walk with me. I have something else to offer you." They began walking along the path again.

"The council was much pleased with your dealings with Nezeral. They have decided that they wish for the first time ever to ask a lower realm mortal to sit on a council seat."

Willow blinked at her. "Really? But isn't it a council of Magic? Won't they care that I don't have my powers anymore?"

It was Queen Cyrraena's turn to blink. "But, my dear, you *do* have your powers. In fact, you actually have a potent double-dose of spell-casting talent, as both your mother and your grandmother Aleria are master spell-casters."

"Really? But the magic ... I felt it drain out of me." It had never even occurred to Willow that there might be some left.

"No. You felt everyone else's magic drain from you. Not your own."

Willow stopped walking and let her gaze unfocus. Bright electric aura lights rose around some tightly closed crocus buds that bordered her feet. It was true! She *was* a spell-caster. A spell-caster *and* a princess! She laughed out loud. *If only Melissa Morrison could see me now.* And behind her, as she started walking along the narrow path, the crocuses bloomed in the moonlight.

EPILOGUE

WILLOW ADJUSTED THE THIN GOLD CROWN on her head, lifting it to a more comfortable angle. She pushed back long hair and nervously smoothed out imaginary wrinkles in her elegant brown velvet court gown. Her parents and her Gallandrian grandparents stood beside her, also dressed elaborately and wearing their crowns, Sir Baldemar flanking her father and King Ulor.

An excited quiver ran through Willow. She watched the huge golden door at the end of the throne room, willing it to open. A whole week had gone by since the breaking of the Game spell, and Willow and the rest of her Farrandale family were back in Gallandra, staying at their main palace in Carrus. Brand, Malvin and Gemma had come along too and, unbeknownst to them, were about to be honoured for their parts in helping Willow make it safely to Tulaan.

Finally, the golden door opened. Willow tried to contain her smile as her mystified friends drifted toward the throne podium. Brand searched out her face, his dark questioning eyes locking onto hers. She nodded, giving nothing away, and let her gaze slide over to Malvin and Gemma. They, too, gave her quizzical looks. Her lips twitched. The sappy smile she'd been trying to hide burst onto her face.

Murmurs rose in the throne room. Only a couple of courtiers who lined the tapestried walls knew what was taking place. Willow spied Brand's proud father, Lord Cedric, and Malvin's teacher, Headmaster Ewert, standing near the front, ready to come forward when called.

Gemma reached the podium first and sank into the required curtsy. Her deep scarlet gown contrasted startlingly with the creamy paleness of her skin. Willow grinned at her reassuringly and then winked at the boys as they rose from their bows.

"I have called this assembly," announced King Ulor, stepping forward in a flourish of purple silk, "to honour these three young people: Brand Lackwulf, Malvin Weddellwynd and Gemma Fletcher." Polite clapping came from the audience. King Ulor waited for silence then asked Brand to mount the podium.

Brand climbed the three steps and stood hesitantly beside the king. Prince Alaric and Sir Baldemar motioned for Brand's father to come up, too, and the four of them, the king, the prince, Sir Baldemar and Lord Cedric, made a proud line in front of Brand.

Prince Alaric spoke next, his deep voice echoing around the throne room. "Brand Lackwulf, in helping my daughter, the princess Willow, in her journey to reach Tulaan, you have shown great bravery and loyalty in the face of danger. By putting your own life at risk, you saved the princess from certain Capture and enabled her to complete her quest." He placed a firm hand on Brand's shoulder and said solemnly, "Kneel Brand Lackwulf, as you are to become a knight this day."

The look on Brand's face made all of Willow's secret plotting worthwhile. She clasped her hands, trying to hold back another huge grin. Knightings, her father had said, were grave and dignified matters. No giggling or grinning allowed. She focused on Brand's bowed head, the glossy sheen of his brown hair. She had touched that hair. Yesterday, out in the snow, she'd brushed cold snowflakes from it, and he had kissed her. Willow flushed. She blinked and quickly looked back to her father. Being dignified didn't work when your face was three shades of red.

Brand had made his vows, and now Prince Alaric touched each shoulder with a shining sword. "Arise, Sir Knight, and accept these gifts of your knighthood." King Ulor came forward with a silver shield emblazoned with a black wolf and a white swan, Lord Cedric had a matching silver cuirass, and Sir Baldemar a helmet. They adorned Brand in their gifts, then Prince Alaric came forward again, holding a sword in a beautiful jewelled scabbard. He held it out to Brand and said, "This sword has two sharp edges. It is a knight's constant reminder that justice and loyalty must go together. Do you accept this responsibility?"

"I do." Brand clasped the sword and tied it around his waist. The crowd cheered until Prince Alaric signalled for quiet. "I understand that you have already given your knight's pledge to my daughter. Do you wish to give it again?" he asked, smiling. "In public this time?"

Brand turned to Willow. She could feel the weight of his dark stare. He nodded and came to stand before her. He got down on one knee and pulled his sword from its scabbard. Instead of bowing his head, he gazed directly into Willow's eyes. "I, Brand Lackwulf, son of Cedric Lackwulf, lord of Rueggan, do solemnly swear to serve and protect thee, Princess Willow, heir to the throne of Gallandra, for all thy days." He paused. Willow stood drowning in his deep gaze. Finally in a husky voice, he finished the oath. "I pledge thee my loyalty, my sword, my life."

This time Willow did not hesitate. "Arise, Sir Brand. I accept thy oath of fealty."

The crowd cheered again as Brand stood to his feet, placing his new sword in its scabbard. Queen Aleria quieted the room this time. She set her aqua eyes on Malvin and smiled at him. "Malvin Weddellwynd, come forth."

Malvin, his hair its usual shock of frizzy blond, bobbed his head and came forward. He wore his long blue mage robe belted at the waist with a gold sash. Pointed red shoes poked from beneath his hem. Willow felt a rush of warmth at his shy smile, at the nervous way he crossed his arms.

"In assisting my granddaughter to reach Tulaan, you, too, have shown great bravery and loyalty that must be rewarded." Queen Aleria turned to Headmaster Ewert, who had followed Malvin onto the stage, and asked him to come forward. The spindly headmaster, in his billowing black scarecrow robes, came forward and handed the queen a square of folded purple silk.

"This mage robe," she proclaimed, "is the sacred purple of a master mage's apprentice. You, Malvin Weddellwynd, are to become apprentice to Headmaster Ewert. At such time when you become a master mage yourself, you shall have the opportunity to pledge your services to my granddaughter, the princess Willow."

Malvin gaped, his blue eyes wide. A purple robe hadn't seemed like much of a gift to Willow, but clearly Queen Aleria had been right about how much it would all mean to Malvin. He was lit up like a kid on Christmas morning.

"Thank you. Oh, thank you," he said bowing to Queen Aleria. He accepted his apprentice robe and held it up for the cheering audience.

Willow's heartbeat began to quicken. Almost time for her turn. She rubbed damp palms along her velvet dress, hoping she'd practised enough.

"Gemma Fletcher," boomed out King Ulor's voice, "come forth."

Gemma climbed the three steps to the throne podium, gripping tight to the folds in her dress, nervous awe making a small "o" of her mouth.

King Ulor smiled at her gently. "You put yourself at great personal risk to help my granddaughter, and for this you, too, shall be rewarded." He took Gemma's hand and turned her toward the expectant audience. "Gemma Fletcher, from this day forward, you are a free citizen of Gallandra. I, King Ulor, regent of Gallandra, bestow upon you lands, a castle and the peerage title of Lady."

Clapping resounded throughout the room. Willow came to stand beside Gemma. She waited for quiet, then spoke in a firm, clear voice. "I have another gift for the lady Gemma." With sure hands, she undid the top buttons of Gemma's high-necked dress. She folded back the collar. The brand mark stood stark against white flesh. For a moment, Willow's confidence faltered. Her fingers trembled.

Gemma nodded at her. "Ye can do it," she whispered. "I know ye can."

Willow inhaled deeply and touched the terrible scar. She unfocused her gaze and imagined Gemma's skin lapping against the burn like a pale ocean, slowly covering the mark in its white, healing waves. When she blinked and looked down, the brand was gone.

Tears glistened in Gemma's blue eyes. "Thank ye, Yer

Highness. Thank ye."

As they embraced, the cheers of the assembly echoed up into the vaulted ceiling. Willow turned to Brand and Malvin, drawing them closer. "I can't tell you how much you three mean to me," she said in a whisper meant only for them. "All I can say is thank you. For being my friends." Friends, family, belonging. She had it all now. All the things that Nana had wished for her.

In a corner, beyond the people on the stage, Willow saw the aura lights dance. It was only for a second. But that second was long enough to glimpse Nana and know she was pleased.

THE END

🙞